A Life Came Calling

by

Ann Howard Creel

Cover Art by *Teddi Black*

The Wild Rose Press, Inc.
PO Box 708
Adams Basin, NY 14410-0708
Visit us at www.thewildrosepress.com

Publishing History
First Edition, 2025
Trade Paperback ISBN 978-1-5092-6262-5
Digital ISBN 978-1-5092-6263-2

Published in the United States of America

Acknowledgments

Many people helped me bring this book to life, including my editor, Nan Swanson; railroad expert Jeff Wilson; research librarian Brennan Cooney LeQuire; and historian Carroll McMahan.

As always, the support of my family makes everything possible. In *A Life Came Calling*, I've tried to stay as true to history as possible but made a few small adjustments for story purposes.

To learn more about me, please visit: AnnHowardCreel.com.

Prologue

"I Had the Craziest Dream" - Harry James and Vera Lynn, 1943

It happened because of the dancing. In the dream, she's on the street in a one-main-street type of town surrounded by mountains crossed by long, drifting clouds. Music and revelry float in the air. *Blue-Smoke Mountains*, a place she has never heard of, whispers in her ear.

How is she here? Around her, people she doesn't know are on the streets celebrating in a frenzy, almost recklessly, as if the world has suddenly been set free of something.

And there's a man. She's never seen him before either, but something about him feels familiar, as though she should know him. His face joyful, his body slides through dance moves with abandon, as if no one's looking and even if they were, he wouldn't care that this was no dance floor. The man spins her around till she's dizzy, and his hands on her are solid and warm and feel like they are meant to be there—she doesn't want him to let go. They dance on, and it's as if life is wrapped up in this one moment, and the moment is all about wonder.

The night sprays millions of diamonds onto the darker-than-black satin sky. Later she doesn't remember the beginning or the end of the dream. She will not even remember if it really happened, but somewhere in the dream time, she and the lovely man are kissing, kissing deeply, exploring each other's mouths as if exploring their minds.

Chapter One

"I'm Nobody's Baby" - Benny Goodman, 1940
Philadelphia, PA, Sunday, April 29, 1945

Janey Nichol jumped into her suit, stepped into high heels, fixed her face and hair, and fed her cat, thinking, *This will be the best day of my life*. Then she was off to the corner bus stop. Luckily finding a seat on the crowded bus, she gazed beyond the window, where patriotism streamed by.

Victory felt so close these days. American flags, war posters, and banners hung in row house windows—a blue star meant a child in uniform, a gold one meant a loved one lost. Thousands poured in to work in machine shops and factories, even on the weekends. Women streamed in from farms and towns for the prospect of making a dollar an hour in one of the plants. The Americans and the Allies sat perched and anticipating the good news of an Armistice in Europe, waiting tense and ready, like birds just set free and about to fly.

But Janey was waiting for something else, too, something more personal.

The bus churned into the nucleus of the city past stores and diners with clean windows reflecting the bright sunlight like mirrors. Lining the streets were street salesmen and shoeshine boys, and in a parking lot, a group of older men conducted a tire drive. Women wearing their city smarts were out collecting for the Red Cross and setting up tables to sell war bonds.

Janey wore her best suit, charcoal gray with wide lapels on the jacket, and black pumps on her feet. A dark-banded maroon hat she'd swiveled until she found its most stylish tilt, and a smart clutch bag tucked under her right upper arm completed the look. She'd slept on curlers overnight so her bangs curled under and her hair moved in waves just touching her padded shoulders. She'd patted her face with makeup and glazed on ruby red lipstick. Nothing needed adding to her eyes, which were dark and huge and wide-set, giving her an inquisitive kitty-cat look.

She walked to her favorite downtown diner to meet Todd for a treat. Pausing just as she reached the door, she took a glance around outside. She wanted to remember everything about this day; she'd save these memories in her mind the way she'd once saved mementos in a scrapbook.

It had to be the day—she felt it coming.

The day was warm and sunny, the sunlight blinding as it caught on pollen that floated in the air like fragments of some delicate fabric. It reminded her of wedding lace so fine it floated and hovered, not falling, as if weightless and suspended in time.

She released a few strands of hair caught under the hat brim.

Would he propose with a ring? She'd rather choose her own, but Todd was a man who liked making decisions. *Would he bring flowers, get down on one knee?*

After sitting at the large U-shaped counter, she ordered a baked apple with vanilla sauce and waited for her order to come clacking out on a conveyor belt. Every minute seemed interminably long—she kept checking her watch and caught herself tapping her fingers on the countertop.

Finally her sweetheart of the past year sat down on the stool next to hers. When he turned her way, his face opened up like the moon coming out from beneath clouds. She had become accustomed to the adulation in his eyes and the little satisfied smile that said he wanted to kiss her.

He gave her a warm peck on the lips. "Hello, gorgeous."

She smiled. "Hello to you, too. But now I have to clean you up." Janey reached inside her handbag and retrieved a handkerchief.

"Am I sporting Victory Red?" he asked with a grin.

"You always know this will happen. And still you do it. Not that I'm complaining, mind you."

"For one of your kisses, it's worth it."

Janey said, "Thank you kindly," while she dabbed the color off gently, also peering into the eyes and face she'd fallen for quite easily. In love for only the second time in her life, although she was twenty-seven, she knew Todd Dempsey was quite a catch.

Of average height and build, Todd had a privileged upbringing that he didn't flaunt. Lately he'd been wearing his hair closely cropped, matching the military style of the times. Always well-dressed in conservative attire, today he wore his requisite black suit and white shirt, looking dapper as usual. He'd gone to college majoring in English literature and was employed at J.B. Lippincott. Only twenty-nine, he'd already risen to Associate Editor.

"One of these days I'm going to kiss all that red off," he said.

"But it's a sign of rebellion. It's well known that Hitler hates red lipstick."

Finished dabbing, she sat back, perused his face, and whispered, "Now, you're all spic and span, good as new."

"Thanks for taking care of me." He leaned closer. "You look beautiful, by the way."

She positioned herself for the big question—facing him straight on, sitting up tall, her hands resting demurely in her lap. "I wanted to go all out for the important conversation you've lured me here for. I've been waiting on pins and needles."

"All in good time, my love," Todd said as he signaled for the waitress, a black-and-white-uniformed, middle-aged woman wearing a matching peaked cap atop a curly tangerine nest of hair—and also wearing the requisite red lipstick of the day.

Janey said, "I've ordered already, by the way."

"Of course you have," he quipped and smiled, then ordered coconut cream pie and coffee for himself. He turned her way and winked. "My gorgeous independent girl."

"Such flattery."

"Which will never stop, by the way."

"Ah, promises, promises."

Janey sat patiently as Todd drummed his knuckles a few times on the countertop. In some ways, they were so alike. He was a bit nervous about this, too; it was a huge step. He sat still for another long moment before his face softened. "I've asked you to meet me here for a very important reason." The serious look on his face made

Janey momentarily doubt his purpose.

She said, "Our anniversary, of course."

"Patience, please," Todd said, then sighed, and touched the tip of her nose. "You're interrupting my train of thought."

Janey made herself remain silent, patient.

"Of course it has to do with our meeting here a year ago. I read up, you see," he said, tapping his temple. "The one-year mark is a good time for something special. But it goes beyond that obvious reason for celebration."

"I'm waiting."

"Geesh, you really are impatient."

"And you've always known that."

"Hush now."

"Yes, sir."

He smoothed the front of his suit, pulled in a deep breath, and letting it out, said, "Perhaps you've guessed what it is."

"I have a hunch. You know, you're no longer much of a mystery to me."

Todd smiled wryly. "I'm not sure that's a good thing."

In truth, Todd had never been much of a mystery. He'd followed all the expected rules—starting slowly with just once-weekly dates, then increasing the frequency over time, until now, when they managed to squeeze in a walk or a date about four days a week. It had been a smooth step-by-step march to arrive here. His intentions had been clear from the start.

"It's a good thing," Janey said with surety. "We know each other well."

He smiled and appeared a bit more relaxed, then took her hands in both of his and peered clear-blue-ly into her eyes. "Well, this might not be the most romantic place for such a thing, but since we met here, I chose it as the place where…"

Not knowing why, Janey's mouth went dry.

"…where I ask you to be my wife."

Janey smiled and touched his freshly shaven cheek with her right fingertips. "And you're expecting an answer?"

Adopting a patient grin, he shook his head. "Always joking. Even during the most meaningful of moments."

"I'm sorry."

"Well? Of course, I'm expecting an answer."

"And of course, you know what the answer is."

"I'd like to hear you say it."

Janey put her right hand back in his. "I love you dearly, Todd Dempsey. And I do want to marry you and be your wife."

He kissed her on the lips again. "That's a relief," he whispered in her ear.

She feigned wiping her brow. "You can say that again."

"Janey Dempsey. Has a nice ring to it, doesn't it? Now and forever," he said, then asked, "Were you worried?"

She shrugged. "Not really. It made sense. I could tell you'd been planning something long before you mentioned rendezvousing here today."

"How did you know?"

"Well, let me guess. You never fail to mention things you want to do in the future, plans you've made for us. That sort of thing."

"I guess I have been pretty transparent." The waitress delivered their desserts and coffee. "I told my parents, and of course they're thrilled. I decided against asking your father for his daughter's hand in marriage—decided that was a bit too provincial. Do you wish I had?"

Janey shook her head. Todd came from old Philadelphia money on his father's side and grew up in the Old City. But he always seemed unaffected by her diner-owning, middle-class family. Except for the obviously expensive clothing he wore and some pretty hilarious "hand-me-down" furniture in his apartment, he didn't scream well-off. He also didn't judge others by their financial status. He seemed to disdain any flamboyant displays of wealth.

He snapped open a napkin and placed it across his knee. "I have the wedding all planned. Nothing fancy. Just our parents and some close friends at the courthouse. You can buy a new dress, and I'll buy a new tie. I want this to happen as soon as possible."

Janey's fork paused on the way to dig into her dessert. "When?"

"Maybe next weekend or the one after that."

Janey's hand froze. And the strangest thing happened—it was as if all sounds disappeared from the room, and a tiny sense of foreboding struck her in the throat. Long engagements were rare during a world war. But she and Todd had no reason to rush. And she'd expected to feel elated; instead, an unknown pressure lay down on her chest, something she couldn't describe and hadn't felt before. Glancing around, she heard herself ask, "Why such a hurry?"

He laughed. "Will you stop joking around? Now that I've made the decision, I don't want to wait another second. Besides, you've let it be known you don't like big fancy weddings. Have you changed your mind?"

Janey took in his face—honest, handsome, confident. But something about the light in the room had changed, as well as the way it landed on his features. She felt as though suddenly she was looking at the world through a new lens.

She shook her head. "No. I think a big wedding is frivolous during these times. A simple courthouse wedding is perfectly fine. It's just that…it suddenly feels so…sudden."

His face fell. "You're not kidding."

A flood of memories and sadness, the last thing she'd expected to feel. "No."

His eyes looked a touch wounded. "I don't understand. Is there a problem?"

Was there a problem? She had to ask herself. In a rush, the past year came back. That first afternoon she and Todd were together, sitting in this very place, learning they'd attended rival high schools, endured the depression during their formative years, and that they shared the same determination to build independent futures. After high school, they furthered their education, his in college and hers in secretarial school.

Janey gathered herself. "Everything has been perfect since the day we met. We seemed destined to be together."

In this very place, they'd ended up sitting at the counter side by side and he'd asked her for a first date. He had taken her to the library after they'd grabbed hot dogs on the street, and in the faraway book stacks, they had to whisper and lean in closer in order to hear each other. Later she realized the library date was by design, to get closer to her.

Soon they were dating regularly, and Todd, who appeared only a little bit bookish, opened up a world of fine literature for her. Although J.B. Lippincott primarily published textbooks, Todd was a voracious reader of fiction. A reader too, Janey had favored nonfiction, especially history. For her, truth was more fascinating than fiction.

She had scarcely believed her luck. Todd had all the fine qualities she'd waited for, and he felt the same way about her. Their future together had opened up like a clear morning.

But today, it was turning into a confusing tangle. A flash of memory. Cole's smile. His face by candlelight. The warmth. A sense of magic. Holding hands in an Italian restaurant, sharing ice creams later. Vivid memories rushing back.

She pulled her hands away. "There's something I need to tell you."

"Would you stop clowning around? You look so serious."

She gazed down at her hands.

When she glanced briefly back up, his face had fallen. "I guess you're not—"

Finally she met his gaze steadily again. "No, not clowning around." Todd didn't like surprises, and it dawned on her then—she should've told him the story long ago. Waiting until today made it seem more important than it was.

He leaned back. "So, out with it."

She lifted her hands in the air, then let them fall in her lap. Exasperated, almost laughing at herself. "It's really kind of an ordinary story. Girl meets soldier passing through. You know…"

11

"What? When?"

"Long before we met. In forty-three. May fourteenth."

"You remember the *date*?"

"It had never happened to me before. Even with all the soldiers coming through Philly, I was working so hard at Walker Scott, trying to climb out of the typing pool—and...it had never happened *to me*."

He turned away, faced forward, and clasped his hands together on the counter. "You're stalling now."

"No. You keep interrupting me."

"A soldier. Of course it had to have been a soldier."

It was hard on the men who weren't serving. Often they were looked upon as cowards. Todd had been born with a club foot, and although surgery had corrected it to the point that he walked with only a barely discernable limp, he couldn't pass the physical.

"What happened?"

She shrugged and tried to look comfortable, casual. "What you might expect. A little whirlwind romance. Only three days."

"Well...there has to be more, or we wouldn't be talking about it now."

She fidgeted. "He sort of proposed."

"Sort of? Did he do it or not? Come on, Janey, this is beneath you."

"He did propose."

He reared back. "After three days?"

"Yes."

"Don't tell me you accepted."

"I accepted."

His entire demeanor had changed, his tone, his expression. She'd never seen him this way. They'd never once argued or even disagreed other than on a minor detail here and there. A twitch tugged at the corner of his mouth. "And you never thought it was important to tell me before now?"

"He died. A Navy man. He was on his way overseas. He sent letters when he was in port. Then they stopped. He had sent my address to his parents in Tennessee. They wrote just after they found out his ship had been hit by Japanese torpedoes. In a battle called Kolombangara. The ship had to be scuttled, but another Navy ship took off most of the crew. But sixty-one men perished, one of them their son."

Todd's face showed some sympathy, then relief. "I'm sorry he died, but you didn't know him well enough after just three days." He sat back and perused her. "I've never known you to be so impulsive. You've always been a no-nonsense girl. I can't believe you fell for a guy in three days."

She shook her head. She *had* been described as practical and no-nonsense before. But not by those who knew her well. Had she ever shown her other side to Todd? Did he know or sense that part of her?

"Those times..." she tried explaining. But she couldn't stop the rush of memories. Meeting Cole for breakfast, then not being able to eat. Her hand in his as they took the ferry across the Delaware and back just for the ride. In the brisk air, he'd kissed the back of her neck, the inside of her wrist. "It was different. It was almost two years ago." She searched for something to say that might reassure Todd in some way. "And I've grown up since then."

He sat silently for a moment, as if letting it sink in. With more kindness in his voice now, he said, "Well, I wish you'd told me this earlier, but you've told me now. I admit to some jealousy that you fell for the guy, especially so darn fast, but he's gone. I don't see how this makes any difference to us."

"It doesn't. Not really. But...I have a feeling of..."

"Go ahead. You really are stalling."

"Just a moment ago, your told me to be patient. I'm trying to explain."

He waited.

"I guess you could say, I have a feeling of unfinished business. It took months for his body to be retrieved from overseas, and by then I'd just been moved upstairs to secretary on the manager's floor. I couldn't take time off to go to the funeral and meet his parents in person. Or maybe I lacked the courage to go and endure the suffering. I don't know. But the point is, I didn't go. And I should've." She stopped.

"What are you saying?"

She'd had no idea this was coming, but now the plan was formulating as it came out of her mouth. "Now I need to close the chapter. Put a dot at the end of the sentence."

He reared back again, as if she'd said something contagious. "*What?*"

She hadn't known she was going to say this, but now it appeared before her so clearly. "I never realized it before, but I need to go to Tennessee and say a final goodbye."

He shook his head and chuckled with a bit of bitterness in his tone. "Thinking of another man on the day I'm proposing..."

"I'm sorry. I didn't think this would occur to me, but it has. And all of a sudden, it feels very important. I have to do this."

"No, you don't." He took her hands again. "Listen, I get it. You're soft-hearted. You're a sweet person, and all these deaths have been difficult, tragic for everyone. But how serious could this have been after just three days?"

You have no idea.

The sun streamed in through the windows, hot. The first really warm day of the season. The concrete outside steamed.

"I need to go. Before we get married."

His tone rather harsh again, he said, "If I wasn't witnessing this in person, seeing your face at this moment, I'd think this was one of your elaborate practical jokes. Something you'd pull on Tessa."

"I have a strong feeling...and it...it just now happened. Now I'm certain I must do this."

"Or what?"

"I'm not issuing any kind of ultimatum."

"But you don't want to get married until you've traipsed off somewhere."

Slowly, she nodded. "I'm sorry."

Todd pushed back from the counter, lifted the napkin from his lap, and tossed it on the counter. "On second thought, maybe you're not ready to get married after all." He stood and fished out a dollar bill, dropping it on the counter where their desserts remained untouched. "I need some fresh air." He left without another word.

Janey batted her eyes; they were beginning to tear. So much for having a good day. Earlier they'd made plans to go strolling about in favorite areas of the city, maybe later taking a short drive.

Feeling watched, she glanced up at the redheaded waitress, who stood solemnly a few feet away, a hand on her hip. "Well, that went well."

Janey rolled her eyes before a tear could fall. "You can say that again."

Chapter Two

"Into Each Life Some Rain Must Fall" - Ella
Fitzgerald & Ink Spots, 1944
Philadelphia, Monday, April 30, 1945

About 6:30 the next evening, she walked into the
diner her parents had owned for two decades. The dinner
hour was one of their busiest times, and often Janey came
over after work and helped out by bussing tables or
serving food.

Nichol's Diner was a no-frills place with a regular
clientele where patrons could get breakfast, lunch, or
dinner made to order at a reasonable price. The servings
were generous and the service fast, and Janey's parents
had found a way to stay in business even during the
depression by serving three meals a day plus the late-
night crowd, doing most of the work themselves. Janey
remembered only one vacation taken during her entire
youth, to the Poconos.

After donning an apron to protect her suit, she piled
up plates in the backroom sink and ran the water. Her
mother paused on the way to the dining room. "We
haven't seen you in a while."

Janey plunged her hands into the soapy water. "I'll
tell you about it when the rush is over."

Her mother seemed taken aback, but she slipped into
a pleased smile. "That sure sounds interesting." Then she

swept away, as she had orders to deliver.

Janey turned so she could glimpse through the doorway as her mother looped about the dining area, a square room with linoleum floors. The tabletops were Formica, and the wallpaper flowery, window curtains pushed open.

Bertie made work into an art form, so smooth it seemed a choreographed dance. And her father, Reuben, was equally adept in the kitchen. He did most of the cooking and had found a way to make every repetitive plate of food into something special.

During the lull between dinner and the late-night crowd, Janey and her mother sat down at one of the empty booths. "Mom, you and Dad are working too much, way too much. Business is booming everywhere. Can't you hire some more help?"

Janey's mother, Bertha, whom everyone called Bertie, smoothed back her hair on both sides and tucked it behind her ears. Nearly fifty, she appeared older, her forehead lined from years of worry but creases at the corners of her eyes from years of smiling, too.

"We're working on that," she answered. Bertie rarely took a break; she also never complained. She went from the diner to the family home in a modest area of Wynnefield and barely drew a tired breath. Her brown hair had turned steel gray, and she wore it cut short and blunt for ease of care. She never troubled to curl it.

Bertie said, "We're going to take on a third cook and some more waitresses. But we can't even get people to come by and talk to us. They say they're coming and then don't show up. Do you know of any girls who might be interested?"

Janey shook her head. She couldn't imagine any of

the women at Walker Scott waitressing in a diner. Even the factory women were making better money than what Janey's parents could pay.

Sadly, the life of a restauranteur was not for Janey or her sister, either, for that matter. The hot kitchen and daily scrubbing and mopping held no appeal. Bertie and Rueben hadn't been able to afford college, so Janey had worked another job throughout high school as a babysitter in order to save for her secretarial course.

Forging a way out of the family diner had driven her to heights previously unknown in her family, and her success gave her pride but also pangs of guilt. She now worked for one of the most powerful men in Philadelphia, on the penthouse level; she had moved on while her sweet parents would probably work in this place until the day they died.

Bertie's eyes swam with a knowing look, and then she glanced down for a moment. "I guess you wouldn't..."

Janey plastered on a hopeful face, despite the fact that women were driving cabs and trolleys and doing such unfeminine things as welding and riveting. They were making more money than they'd ever dreamed and jamming into department stores looking for clothing and accessories to give themselves a glamorous look. No one she knew would want to work like the devil in a diner these days, but she didn't have the heart to say it. "I'll ask around. Have you tried an ad in the paper?"

"We might. The sign in the window isn't bringing anyone in. I guess we're going to have to do something else or keel over here one day from working so hard."

"That's not funny."

Bertie snorted, then gazed over Janey and adopted

her curious, concerned stance—head tilted just slightly to one side, like a mother bear monitoring her cub—a look so familiar it made Janey's heart sad. "So...what's up?"

Janey knotted her hands together on the tabletop. "You'll be surprised."

Bertie took a sip of steaming coffee. "So, surprise me."

Janey opened her mouth but then became suddenly mute. She couldn't believe all that had happened the day before. Ever since the meeting at the diner, Todd's angry words kept coming back....*maybe you're not ready to get married after all.* The depth of his reaction had stunned her. She kept circling through a cycle of regret, wishing she'd never mentioned Cole at all, to feelings of determination that this was something important, something she needed to do for herself, but also for Todd and their future.

The night before, she'd lain awake, focused on the ceiling, remembering Cole but also wondering why this determination to find closure in Tennessee had only hit her now. Of course it would be much more difficult after the wedding—Todd would probably have forbidden her to go, if he dared. But she hadn't seen this side of Todd, not even in a year of spending time together. Now, it seemed they were facing their first disagreement, and it hadn't gone well.

Finally Janey said, "Todd proposed."

Bertie set down her mug, pushed it away, and threw up her hands. "Well, hallelujah!"

"Mom, I'm not done. Would you just listen?"

Not listening at all, Bertie said, "And it doesn't surprise me at all."

"Mom," Janey said. Pleasing her mother was one thing, but even at her age, Janey also didn't want to disappoint. "It just happened yesterday…" Then she couldn't quite finish.

"It's about time." Then, with excitement flashing in her eyes, Bertie insisted, "So tell me. How did he do it?"

"At the same place we met, another diner."

"I want to know all the details."

"Would you just hold your horses? I'm trying to tell you that everything didn't go as planned." Saying those words nearly choked her. It was still difficult to believe just how badly things had gone. How to describe it without worrying them too much?

"Oh, you worrywart, you," Bertie scoffed and then beamed again. "It was probably nothing. But tell me about it anyway."

While Janey was still searching for words, her father nudged her over and slid onto the bench seat beside her. He wiped his hands with a small towel and set it on the table, then put his arm around Janey and hugged her, once, firmly against him. Her father was as humble and hard-working as her mother was. Reuben and Bertie— quite a pair, a perfect match. One made in Heaven, her father always said sarcastically, although he really meant it.

"How's my old girl?" he asked. A ridiculous saint, he'd called Janey *old girl* ever since her sister was born.

"I'm fine."

"You still not married yet?"

He always said this, too. She shoved him. "Daddy!"

"We're still waiting to go broke on a lavish wedding and get some grandchildren. I'd like four, two boys and two girls, please."

The pressure was on. And Janey was unlikely to forget it. Her younger sister, Tessa, was a diabetic and unlikely to have children, putting the burden of bearing progeny on Janey's shoulders. "I'll get right on that."

"Progress has been made," Bertie inserted. "Todd finally proposed."

"Well," Reuben said, long and drawn-out, as he leaned back and peered at Janey sideways. "Good for you. You didn't scare him off."

"Apparently things aren't settled yet," said Bertie.

"Thanks, Mom."

From her father, "Better drag him to the altar before he gets cold feet."

"Let's hope she's working on that," said Bertie.

"Now I know why I don't talk much," Janey said through a heavy sigh. "I never got a word in edgewise."

Reuben looked at Bertie. "Cut back, my dear. Behave yourself."

"Do you remember Cole?" Janey suddenly spurted out.

A moment of silence. Then her mother sighed. "Poor man."

"I'd never told Todd."

"That doesn't surprise me, either," said Bertie. "Why would you?"

"I had to, and…he didn't take it very well."

"Why did you tell him? Wait a minute. Don't tell me you mentioned this on the day he proposed?"

"I did."

Bertie exclaimed, "Lordy!"

Janey sighed again. "I knew I shouldn't have told you. I can't tell you anything."

"How many times you been a bridesmaid, old girl?"

Reuben asked.

She sighed. She always had to go through all their teasing before they could get down to business. "You tell me. You paid for all the dresses."

"Well, they're so old now, they smell of mothballs. Everyone's out-married you by now."

"How many times have you said that to me?"

"You wait too long and I'm going to spend your dowry on a vacation."

"You *should* take a vacation *and* spend my dowry. That word makes me think of noblemen who had too many daughters and bribed men to take them off their hands."

"Is that an option? I'll do whatever I can."

"Besides, if I do get married, I'll pay for everything. I'll even pay *both* of you to behave yourselves."

"No kidding? How much?"

"Hush, Reub. She's trying to tell us something," interjected her mother, finally.

"What are you waiting for, girl?" from her father.

Her eyes came close to tearing up. How lucky she was to have them. She hugged Reuben. "I'm waiting for a man just like you."

"We don't have forever," her mother said.

Janey released her hold on her father and sat up straight, prepared for the onslaught of outrage. "I told him I needed to visit Cole's hometown and his grave before I get married."

Her father threw his hands in the air. "There go my grandbabies!"

Then silence.

Her mother leaned forward. "Honey, it was a sad chapter in your life. I understand that. But it's over.

Please don't risk what you have."

"We like Todd. A lot," said her father.

Janey turned to face him. "What do you like about him?"

"He's steadfast." Nodding. "He'll make a good husband."

"He's a nice man," her mother added.

A family walked into the diner and both of her parents took notice. Reuben began to get up. "No more time for all this flam-doodle." He patted her shoulder before he left her sitting there. "Forget the past. You better get a move on with that man."

"Roger that, Dad."

Her mother wrung her hands on the tabletop. She really did. "Did you tell Todd you wanted to visit Cole's grave? Is that what went wrong?"

"Yes. He was angry at first, but he ended up telling me to do what I had to do. If this is meant to be, he'll wait until I'm ready. I think…"

Bertie harrumphed. "Good men don't wait forever. When are you going to do this?"

"At work tomorrow or the next day, I'll ask for a week off as soon as they can spare me." Janey's stomach did a funny little fall when she thought of it. "I want to get it over with too."

Bertie shook her head in a way that showed her disbelief. "How's the new job, by the way? Didn't you just start the best position—?"

"It's great," Janey answered. "I like it, and I'm pretty sure they're satisfied with me." She filled her mother in on her new duties and responsibilities. Out of the typing pool for only three years, she'd already gone from secretary to lower-level managers and had climbed to the pinnacle of success for women within the company. Her mother listened as if consumed by a faraway tale, even though Janey often downplayed the significance of her position. She gave her mother the short version.

Bertie placed her hands flat on the tabletop and rose. "I'm impressed, and I want to know all of it later."

"I don't think you've listened to me, Mom. Really listened. Todd isn't happy with me right now."

Bertie sobered and said gently, "It'll be all right. You'll make it right. And remember, we just want you to be happy." She studied Janey's face for a long moment. "We can talk more later."

Reuben tapped the tabletop as he rushed past. Bertie sighed. "But for now…time to get back to work."

Chapter Three

"It's a Blue World" - Tony Martin, 1940
Philadelphia, Tuesday, May 1, 1945

For the rest of the evening and after work the next day, Janey filled the hours listening to news. She hadn't heard from Todd since Sunday. They often skipped talking on the phone on their busiest days, but this felt like a void, perhaps purposeful in design. Maybe he wanted her to have some time alone, hoping she'd change her mind. But her compulsion to go had only become stronger. She tried not to dwell on it.

On that day, the world had learned of Hitler's death in Germany, further raising American hope that the war in Europe would soon come to an end. She tuned in to hear from President Truman and Lowell Thomas, then quickly collected newspapers for the neighborhood paper drive, one of those wartime activities citizens were asked to do, and finally bleached some cotton hose since she couldn't find nylons.

After she'd made supervisor in the typing pool, she'd managed to purchase her own row house in the Strawberry Mansion part of the city, where she could walk or take a bus or trolley and get almost everywhere. It was a very rare thing for a woman to own a home. It was almost unheard of for a *single* woman, unless she was a widow on a pension.

"Fixer-upper" was an understatement to describe her place. It had been lost by its previous owners for non-payment of property taxes and had fallen into disrepair. Located in a close-knit community she found charming, it was a perfect place to dig in and work. For six months, she spent her weekends scraping, sanding, and painting walls and baseboards and even the ceiling. She scrubbed windows and waxed floors. One by one, she replaced the furnace, the kitchen sink, and the claw-footed bathtub. She bought a new white stove and checkered draperies.

Looking around her place gave her a feeling of pride she expressed to no one, not even Tessa. She had accomplished a lot but rarely told people about it. There were some spells of time, before Todd, during which she wondered if this would be her home forever. Would she never marry? Always forge through life alone, except for her family?

She didn't like that prospect, but it didn't terrify her, either. She'd make do no matter what. But lacking a clear direction had given her pause. She'd learned she was better off planning than waiting.

When Todd dropped by on Wednesday evening, a surge of hope lifted her chest. Seeing his face brought back many memories of the last year, almost all of them bright and hopeful. Funny, she mused again, that they'd never disagreed before Sunday. It seemed almost impossible, but it was true. Their politics and religious beliefs weren't exactly in line, but they'd just avoided those topics.

Today, Todd wore another of his black suits, but he'd removed his tie and unbuttoned the top two buttons of his white shirt, indicating he might be planning to settle in, relax, and stay for a while.

Maybe he'd changed his mind and would support her decision to go to Tennessee. Maybe they'd have a much-needed long conversation and work it all through together.

But as she invited him in, she found his face solemn and unreadable.

It was warm enough to sit outside on her small back porch, which was more like a stoop, where they could barely fit side by side on the steps. They'd been out here before. The propriety of the day indicated they probably shouldn't spend a lot of time closed up indoors, which might have sent tongues wagging. Janey had the feeling gossip would've bothered Todd more than it did her. She doubted her neighbors would pay all that much attention.

In the garden at the back of the house, she had endured thorns and blisters to make it beautiful again. In the middle of the yard she'd placed a wooden mock-up of a wishing well given to her by her parents.

He said, "We need to talk," as soon as she'd opened the front door. She led him through the house and the back door. There, she sat on the stoop and waited, sending her gaze into the yard, where the moths were beginning to come out against the oncoming dusk.

Before Todd, she'd spent many nights out here alone, the stars as her ceiling and the night air as her blanket, her only company a yellow tabby cat named Cheese. Too ambitious for her own good, according to her father, she'd concentrated on career over matters of the heart. Now Todd had spoiled her with his company.

Todd seemed to look at her with hesitation, but thankfully he didn't beat around the bush. "I've been giving this a great deal of thought," he started. She could see the sincerity in his eyes.

And there was no doubt what "this" was.

He plucked his shirt off his chest, scratched his neck. "It ruined my editing time. My pen was off. Doing what I do well takes intense concentration."

She smiled sadly. "I'm sorry."

"I shouldn't have let it do that to me."

"I'm sorry."

"You've already said that, and I'm sorry too. But the question is, what now?" He paused. "Now that you've had a chance to think about this for another day or so, how do you feel?"

Janey longed for a good answer, something he might understand. Her feelings ran deeply like a river within, but when she dipped her hands in, she came up with only small beads of water too small to hold. Nothing she could form into easy words. It took her another moment before she could gather her thoughts together.

"Janey," he said. "I asked you how you feel now."

"I know. I'm trying to think of a way that'll help you understand."

"Forget that. Just say something, anything."

She pulled in a ragged breath. "Maybe I don't want him to be forgotten so easily," she said, when in truth, she'd never truly forgotten. Despite her feelings for Todd, Cole's face had never left her completely. Often she saw it when she first awakened after a dream state. Other times it filled her head and led her into a deep well full of sweet water as she fell asleep. Unconsciously and inadvertently, she'd kept him alive.

Janey said in her softest voice, "You dismiss it as a three-day affair that couldn't have meant very much, but he *was* planning to come back to me, Todd. He *was* planning a life with me, and I never really acknowledged that by going to meet his family and facing his death in person. If I go there, I think I can finally do that and then let it go."

He stood and walked a few steps, turned around. "Geez, J. I came here hoping to leave feeling better. I'm beginning to think it'll be just the opposite."

"I'm trying to explain, to make it clear for you."

"What's becoming clear is that you value that fling more than us. You're risking what we have."

It was tough to swallow that. Since Todd, her life had become much more complete. She had a great career and also a beau. They'd dined out and occasionally lived it up. She'd bought new dresses and used her ration book to buy new heels. Life had moved swiftly, a blurry ride of talk and dances and dinners. She remembered the quieter moments, too. Strolling through Fairmont Park, walking the Strawberry Mansion Bridge across the Schuylkill, and perusing the small shops on York Street.

"If what we have is worthy, it can survive my taking a few days to…rid my head of him."

"That must have been some three days, J."

She felt herself getting closer to exasperation. "Look what's happened to us in just the past two days. A few days can change everything."

"That's a pretty darn negative outlook. Thanks for the confidence."

"That didn't come out right."

"Sure it did," he said. "But the worst of it is that you waited until now to tell me." He paused. "Did he give you a ring?"

"No, there wasn't time for that."

"Yes, as I recall, he just *happened* to be passing through, *happened* to meet you on his way overseas to face an uncertain future, and he just *happened* to meet the woman he wanted to marry."

"I understand you're hurt, but please don't mock me. You know I'm no fool. I wasn't deceived, if that's what you're getting at."

"How do you know? He died before you had a chance to see if he came back to you."

Janey quipped, "You don't say."

Slumping, she had to admit that what he'd said was true, and it occurred to her that maybe one of the reasons she wanted to go to Tennessee was to find out if he would've indeed come back to her. His letters after he left were loving, but it was obvious that the effect of being in a war theater was taking its toll. He wasn't expressing himself very well, or maybe he simply wasn't a good writer.

What had he told his family about her? They'd never tried to get in touch with her until they learned of his death. And when they wrote her about his death, they never mentioned the engagement. The letter was direct and to the point. But they were also probably in the throes of grief. Maybe they weren't in any state to care about others' feelings. Maybe she needed to go to Tennessee for some answers, too.

A clench in his jaw, Todd stuffed his hands into his pockets and glanced down before he met her gaze and said, "I'm beginning to dislike the sound of this more and more. You've changed overnight, Janey. And I'm not sure if I like what I'm seeing now. Yes, of course, do what you feel you must, but in the meantime, I feel I must withdraw my proposal."

The air froze. Stunned, she'd never imagined she had derailed things with Todd to such an extent.

Nevertheless she nodded.

"See me out?"

Instead of standing, she probed his eyes. "Isn't this a bit of an overreaction? We've had a year together, and we were planning to go forward as a couple. How can a few days away pose such a risk to all of that? I feel that you're the one risking what we have."

"What did you expect?"

She shook her head. "Perhaps a bit of kindness, maybe some understanding."

"Don't you get it? I could find kindness in any other situation. But this is about another man."

"Who happens to be dead."

"Well," he finally said. "He's not dead to you, is he?"

Janey couldn't answer, just stared at him. He must see the plea in her eyes, she thought.

But he said, "This is exactly what I was worried about. Something that happened two years ago and you didn't think was important enough to mention to me before, is now suddenly the most important thing in your life. Silly me, but I want to be the most important thing in your life."

"You are."

"You know that old saying, 'Actions speak louder than words'? That's what I think about ever since you told me you wanted to go there. No matter what I say or do, you're going anyway. Putting priority on that rather than us. Your behavior tells the truth."

"My *behavior*?"

"Yes, it's odd, to say the least."

Janey shook her head in dismay.

They remained in silence for long moments. Finally

Todd took a step toward the back door. She glanced up at him and saw him in a selfish light for the first time. He did seem self-centered at that moment, and worse...a tad bit cold.

She rose to walk him through her house to the front door, but with each step, the ground in the yard, the concrete steps, and the floors in the house seemed to vaporize beneath her feet. Everything felt different, forever altered in just a breath of time. She had never imagined it, but their faith in each other had vanished suddenly, as with the death of two fallen stars.

Chapter Four

"Time Waits for No One" - Helen Forrest, 1944
Philadelphia, Thursday, May 3, 1945

Although still in her first month on the new job,
Janey had to do it. After Lorraine arrived, the time had
come. She waited until Lorraine had checked her face in
her compact, stowed her handbag in a drawer, and
arranged her scarf into its perfect position.

Just two weeks prior, Janey had formally assumed
her position as Executive Secretary to the vice president
of Walker Scott Electric, one of the biggest of its sort of
companies in the country. Lorraine, executive secretary
to Mr. Scott, the company president, had been training
her. Awash in Chanel No. 5, Lorraine was a slim, almost-
platinum blonde about forty years old who reminded
Janey of a swan poised to take flight—always graceful,
quick, and efficient. Lorraine wore a beige suit with a
pale blue blouse and an expensive-looking, multi-
colored scarf looped about her neck. Janey had already
learned that Lorraine had a fabulous wardrobe.

"By the way," Janey began. "I know this is bad
timing, but I'm afraid I already have to ask for a
favor…in fact, some time off."

Lorraine was looking at her in a queer, inquiring
way now. Her usual playful pitch vanished. Lorraine
slipped up to a partial sitting position on the edge of her

desk and crossed her legs one on top of the other. "Time off now?"

"Yes, I know it's awkward and the last thing I should be doing. But I have been with the company for five years, and in the past I was almost forced to take my vacation time."

"What's this about?" She nodded toward the inner offices, where the president and vice president ran the show. As of yet, they hadn't arrived for the day. "They'll want to know."

Janey's eyebrows furrowed. "Of course." She didn't know whom to trust, but she was going to have to start putting her faith in Lorraine.

Despite being beautiful and married to an attorney, Lorraine chose to have a career of her own. It was known she had no children, and Janey would never ask why. Her co-worker was well liked and pleasant, something Janey had considered before accepting the new position. Nothing was worse than working with people who didn't like their jobs and quarreled.

But even if Lorraine hadn't been a joy to work with, Janey would've been hard-pressed to turn down her new salary of $1,800 a year.

She pulled in a shaky breath. "Two years ago, I met a navy officer passing through. We had three sublime days together, and then he shipped out, only to die in a torpedo attack. I didn't go to the funeral because I'd just been promoted to secretary to one of the executives on Fourteen. I never met his family or visited the grave."

"So…?"

Janey wasn't used to opening up so much, but it had to be said. "I've been dating another man for a year, and he asked me to marry him." She didn't mention that he'd retracted the offer.

"Congratulations."

"But I realize now that I can't go forward until I close that old chapter in my life. I have to go to Tennessee to do that."

Lorraine examined her fingernails. "Well, the timing isn't good." She lifted her gaze and set it back on Janey. "But let me handle it. I'll talk to Mr. Walker when he comes in. Then he'll probably want to talk to you."

"Great. Our first real personal encounter since my interview, and I'll be asking for time off."

"I'll make it right," Lorraine said with a wink and then lifted herself and sashayed to her desk.

Exactly twenty minutes later, Janey sat in a leather armchair facing the man she worked for, the vice president of the company, Mr. Walker. Pressed into a nicely tailored black suit with a white shirt and gray tie, he was a fiftyish man—a bit portly, with a balding head that shone under the lights, and he wore horn-rimmed glasses. Two deeply curved grooves ran from the edges of his nose to the corners of his mouth. He reminded her of a school principal. But was that some softness, some kindness in his eyes? She forced herself to think so.

As she tried not to fidget, her gaze swept about the private office of Mr. Vice President. Carpet so thick she had felt it give under her steps every time she entered. Dark paneled walls, and bookcases filled with leather volumes all illuminated by more gleaming windows, it was as solemn and quiet as a library.

Mr. Scott, Mr. President, entered, closed the door behind him, took the chair next to her, pulled it back a bit, and angled it to face her before he sat down.

Her breath halted. She'd had no idea that Mr. Scott

would join the conversation.

He was a little thinner and younger than Mr. Walker, maybe forty-five, but he was dressed almost identically to Mr. Walker and wore similar glasses. They could've passed for brothers, except that Mr. Scott still had a full head of steel-ribboned, dark-brown hair.

He greeted her, and Janey's voice cracked when she said, "Good morning."

"No need to be nervous, Miss Nichol," said Mr. Scott, who had a kind look about him and was soft-spoken despite being the president of one of the largest electric companies in the nation. For a moment, Janey wished she were his secretary instead of Mr. Walker's, but that would never happen. Lorraine was smart enough to probably never leave her post.

"Let's get on with it," snapped Mr. Walker, who had already struck Janey as impatient—a disagreeable blowhard, indeed—although she'd rarely talked with him during the past two weeks. But so far, his reputation had been spot on; she was to work for a man known to be allergic to smiling. Indeed, now his lips were pressed into a thin, hard line.

He said, "We understand you need some time off to attend to some…personal matters."

Janey nodded.

"I'm not used to you yet," said Mr. Walker. "So go ahead and take care of this business before you get acclimated up here."

She fought the urge to bite her nails, an old habit she'd almost cast away. "Yes, sir."

Mr. Scott added, "After that, we expect any time off scheduled far in advance, so we can bring up a temporary replacement."

"I understand."

"Everything that goes on up here is vital, confidential. It must be taken very seriously."

A slight sweat was breaking out on her forehead under her bangs. She already knew the company had undergone a tremendous wartime conversion, now making radios, radar, and other electronic and communications equipment needed by the military. There were no longer any washing machines, refrigerators, or radios in stores. A bit overwhelmed and surprised, she couldn't help screwing her hands together in her lap.

"I do, sir. I do take it seriously."

Mr. Scott leaned closer and held his hands together down in between his knees. "Let me spell it out for you," he said. "Up here, we manage every aspect of the company. We direct our executives and teams and make all major decisions. We meet with government officials and wealthy investors. Our secretaries are like our right hands, and when you're absent, we're limited in some ways. But we understand your request has to do with a deceased soldier, and we're going to allow you to take the time."

Mr. Walker nodded. "Take all the time you need, but be back on Monday."

Janey found it difficult to swallow. "I have to travel all the way to a remote part of Tennessee. I imagine it's going to take several days just to get there."

Mr. Walked sighed. "Take all the time you need, but be back *a week* from Monday."

"You want me to go now? I was going to plan—"

"Now is better. Before I get too reliant on you."

"Yes, sir. I appreciate the kindness. I'll be back, and

I won't let you down."

"We're counting on that," said Mr. Walker, then he smoothed the sides of his head as if the absence of hair was still a surprise to him.

Back at her desk, Janey sat back and calmed herself. She felt winded, as if she'd been running.

"It went that well?" Lorraine asked.

"They told me to go now. Before they get used to me."

Lorraine blinked hard. "That makes sense."

"Should I finish the day?"

"My guess would be yes."

Therefore she went through the hours and performed her duties as if sleepwalking. For the first time, she missed the energy of the typing pool—full of smart girls in skirts and cardigan sweaters, alive with the clacking of typewriter keys and the scent of expensive perfume.

Down there, they worked for managers who didn't have their own secretaries. Often multiple copies were needed, and even with carbon paper, only about three good copies could be made with one pass. Sometimes they had to type the same document over and over. But here she had only to prepare Mr. Walker's personal and business correspondence. There was even an idle half hour or so in the afternoon, which today wasn't all that welcome.

The next morning, Janey withdrew money from her bank account and headed to the Broad Street Station at Broad & Market streets, where the passenger trains of the Pennsylvania Railroad departed. Located just west of City Hall in an aging building, it featured gothic spires and arched windows. The lower levels of the structure were very old and rusticated, having been built in the previous decade, while the upper stories emphasized the height of the building.

Cole must have come into the city and left it via this station, and he must have admired the old architecture, too.

But thoughts of Todd were plaguing her that morning. She needed to speak with him, but Todd was one of the only people she knew who didn't have a telephone at home. Once he'd told her in a joking manner that he didn't want his reading time interrupted, but Janey figured he was serious about that. Often he called her in the evenings from a pay phone booth near his place to talk a bit and plan their meetings, but she'd heard nothing from him since he'd left her two nights before.

At the ticket office, she learned that she'd be able to travel by rail to Knoxville, but no train service extended beyond that. Personal travel had been discouraged since the beginning of the war in order to conserve resources for the military, but it hadn't been altogether banned. Still, all the trains across the country would be filled with migrating troops. The rails were extremely busy, so her travels couldn't begin until the next evening, Saturday. Her journey would take her through many stops and stations, and she wouldn't arrive in Knoxville until the early afternoon on Sunday.

After purchasing the train tickets, the agent advised her to go to Rosenbluth Travel, where, although the agency was barely operating since the war, she could probably make further transportation arrangements and book a hotel. The train fare had cost more than she expected, so Janey had to return to the bank for more money on the way to Rosenbluth's.

The travel agent said she wouldn't have any

problem finding a room for one night in Knoxville before heading into the mountains there. But a nagging sense of doubt about what she was doing wouldn't completely go away, especially as she was spending almost all her savings, every dollar she had worked for and put away for a vacation or a rainy day.

But the drive to go was more powerful, so at Rosenbluth Travel she was able to book a room at a large hotel in Gatlinburg that would also send a driver to pick her up in Knoxville on Monday morning. The only thing left unplanned was her accommodation in Knoxville Sunday night, but the agent told her she wouldn't have any problem finding a place to stay there.

That evening she sat on her back stoop, staring into the night as if it could give her some answers. A thunderstorm had passed over quickly, leaving air so still she could hear neighbor women clanking dishes and running water in sinks, snippets of distant conversations that floated out of open windows, children's laughter as they slammed out of a door, and the building song of crickets and grasshoppers. None of it troubled her. She welcomed those sounds of ordinary domestic life. They were her friends for the evening, keeping her company, and leaving her less alone.

Janey picked herself up and went to the diner at the last moment, after loneliness got the better of her. She broke the news of her travel plans to her parents as they were closing for the night.

Both looked exhausted. They listened quietly and even stayed quiet for a few more minutes, studying her. Finally Bertie sighed heavily and said, "I just hope you're not taking off on a wild goose chase."

"I promise not to bring home a wild goose."

Reuben's face was riddled with worry, but he said pleasantly, "You better bring home a husband. The one you almost had hooked might not be waiting when you come back."

Janey gazed off. "If it's true love, he'll wait."

Her father glanced up to the heavens, his hands upturned, then he focused on her again. "Famous last words, I'd say."

They continued to jest with her for a few more minutes, then softened, hugged her, and said that even though they didn't understand what she was doing, they had her back no matter what.

Chapter Five

"It All Comes Back to Me Now" - Gene Krupa, 1941

Philadelphia, Friday, June 4, 1943, the day that changed everything

At the time, Janey had no idea it would change everything. After an ordinary day working for several middle managers on Fourteen, she found an empty bench seat on the bus about halfway down the center aisle. Leaving later than usual on a Friday, the end of her second week out of the typing pool, she sat and slid in close to the window.

As she gazed out at the gathering dusk, she relived the week. The manager she worked for had told her she was "working out well," big praise coming from him. Down with a cold, another secretary had called in sick one day during the week, and Janey had taken care of two of the company's middle managers with finesse. She had kept up with the work for both of them, and another good review of her was added to her file.

Another day she'd changed the wording in one of a manager's dictated letters to improve the transition between paragraphs, and when he read the final piece, he said, "Nice work." He then told her she could improve his letters any time.

Her confidence, infused with a feeling of

belongingness and purpose, was soaring. Janey had always lived in Philadelphia, but her rise within Walker Scott had bolstered her sense of city-love to be even stronger. Philadelphia pulsed in her blood—a force of life that kept her striding forward.

Someone sat beside her.

"Hello."

She turned to face the voice and saw it was a naval officer, uniformed, dressed to the T. Two other naval officers stood in the aisle.

Speechless for a moment, she'd never seen anyone like them on the bus before. As officers, they had to make enough money to take a taxi.

"Hello," she asked. "May I help you?"

"I hope so. I've been following you," the man next to her said in a husky voice with a southern accent. He was a big man, and had he not been in uniform, she might have thought him a dockworker or a lumberjack. His face was too broad and his brow too dominant for him to be considered classically handsome, but he was ruggedly lovely on the eye with his square jaw and an intensity in his eyes that struck her. Backlit by sun streaming in the bus windows behind him on the opposite side, his ultra-blond hair had a sheer quality that seemed to float.

"I beg your pardon?"

"I followed you."

Janey shook her head once. "Since when?"

"Ever since you walked out of that building back there."

He stared as if he were stroking her with his eyes.

She asked, "Whatever for?"

"To meet you, of course."

Trying to fathom his tactics, she gave another little

shake of her head. It seemed he had no game. "To meet me."

"And spend the evening with you."

He came across as strangely guileless. Was he a boy in a man's wrappings, or was he simply mature enough not to play coy?

"I'm not sure whether I should feel flattered or terrified."

He smiled—the first time she'd seen him smile, and it softened and opened his face. A killer-diller smile could do that; it could transform a person. A spicy scent—his aftershave—wafted over. "I give you my word I mean only to flatter, never to terrify."

She let out a long sigh. "That's *somewhat* reassuring."

"I'm Cole Huxley. Lieutenant Cole Huxley. And you are…?"

She inhaled sharply. "Jane, but everyone calls me Janey."

"Pleased to meet you, Jane, whom everyone calls Janey."

His stare was becoming unnerving. She took her eyes away and aimed her gaze out the window, not really seeing what passed by, instead wishing her instincts would kick in and tell her what to say to this dynamite-looking but oddly behaving navy officer. She'd been pursued before, but never this way. He emanated a strong sense of manliness that rattled her. It was one of the only times she could remember having no response, no idea what to say.

She turned back, and with her eyes drinking in his face, she blatantly studied him as he studied her, and she found interesting things—he was a mix of a boxer, with that burly body, and a fairy prince, with his angelic hair. Nothing on his face should've worked, but all the pieces came together in an appealing way. Odd building blocks stacked up to make a structure that drew her inside the open doors of his insistent eyes.

Everything within her tripped and came to a stop, and in that tiny wink of time, nothing existed but the two of them. He held her gaze with that stare, as if he was absolutely certain of her and what he was doing.

Finally she managed to turn her head and gaze straight ahead into the back of another passenger's head—that of a girl with strawberry-blonde hair escaping from under a slumped hat, Janey would remember later.

"Come have a drink with me," he said.

Night was settling over the city, and something baffling was drifting down over Janey against her will. Her rational mind was betraying her.

Still not facing him, she said, "I don't know what to think of this."

"Why think?"

She shook her head once. "I'm always thinking."

She kept her face turned slightly away from his, more questions falling into her mind, and a sense of something unknown tilting her off guard.

At the next stop, he grabbed her hand and guided her off the bus, leaving the other naval officers on board. "There's a bar around here somewhere," he said.

She let him steer her down the street into an area she wasn't familiar with. They made a few turns she scarcely remembered, walked past the blurred faces of businessmen and women. Total darkness came on quickly due to the blackout, and the sky was brighter than the ground.

She didn't even know if she'd be able to find her way back to the bus stop. The air raid wardens—mostly 4-Fs and 3-As who volunteered to patrol the streets and make sure all the lights were out and people weren't wandering around with no place to go—were out on the streets already. Surely one of them would help her.

They entered a private club. One glance at Cole's uniform and the attendants ushered them inside. Inside it was all bubbling champagne, pianos set up for duets, and the scents of perfume and aftershave. They took seats at the bar that stretched all the way to the back of the room lined with candles sputtering a soft glow like lights on distant ships at sea. The place hadn't filled up yet—there were only a few couples at tables, and a group of young people, full of banter and play, were gathered around the piano waiting for the music to begin. Twinkling prisms of light glinted from small overhead chandeliers, and curls and puffs of cigarette smoke drifted.

Cole had not let go of her hand, and she was shocked that she wanted it to stay there.

This was foolishness, and it was time to stop. She wasn't sure how to get back home from here. As she was planning how to end this, he lifted the hair off her shoulder and draped it back with a touch as light as breath.

For long moments, she couldn't move or speak. Again. Groping for something to say, desperate to say something, she asked, "Where are you from, Lieutenant?"

"A place you've probably never heard of. Outside Gatlinburg, Tennessee. Do you know of the new national park, the Great Smoky Mountains?"

"Yes."

She steadied herself and focused on making conversation, regular conversation, but found her body slanting closer into the candlelight that illuminated his face and made his ever-so-fine-and-wispy hair glow.

He said, "It's a beautiful place."

"Like Philadelphia?"

He bumped out a cigarette from a pack of non-filtered Luckys and offered the open pack to her. She shook her head, and he lit up with a match and inhaled deeply. "Well, I love Philly, but it's not the same. I assume you're from the city?"

"Native."

"I've been here several times. They say even us country boys have a *city*. A city that fits us. Where we could be happy living. Mine's Philadelphia."

"Thank you. On behalf of the city."

A waitress appeared, and Cole asked, "May I order for you?"

He ordered red wine for himself and a rose-colored one for her. "It's best to begin your wine experience with a sweet one," he said.

"How do you know I have no experience with wine?"

"Do you?"

"No."

"Just as I thought. Most Americans don't drink it, but my grandmother was from Italy." He looked askance for a moment when he said "Italy." After all, the US was in a war with the Axis, which included Italy. But the hard feelings aimed at those of Italian descent did not rise to those aimed at people of German or Japanese descent. Acceptance was more common in Philadelphia anyway—it was a city of immigrants and the children and grandchildren of immigrants.

"You don't look Italian."

"You've been fooled by pigeon-holing. The myth that all Italians have dark hair and are somewhat swarthy."

Normally she would have taken offense at being told she was brainwashed, but she instantly felt that Cole just said what came into his mind.

"Maybe," she finally said.

The wine came, and he let go of her hand.

"My grandmother Agnese made wine just like her grandmother had taught her as a teenager back in the 'old country,' near Florence. Man, could she make wine. I've been a fan since I was a kid."

He taught her how to swirl and smell the wine before tasting. At first the sip tasted of sweetness—albeit a prickly sour sweetness—but the aftertaste landed bitterly on her palate and she couldn't claim to enjoy it.

"What do you think?" he asked. He rested his hand on the back of her barstool.

"This is a sweet one?" she asked with a smile. The pink fluid in her wine glass glowed like a mirror reflecting the candle nearby.

He chuckled. "Yes."

"I don't think it's for me."

"I'll teach you to like it."

As if they were going to see each other again. Janey pulled her hands into her lap and stared ahead into liquor bottles set up on glass shelving against the back of the bar. How could he assume they would be spending time together? Then again, she had let him lead her off a bus and into a bar with few questions asked.

They sipped the wine for a moment in silence.

"I assume you work in that building where you emerged, looking like a movie star."

"Yes."

"And?"

"It's a great job." She could've elaborated, but she wanted to know more about *him*. "What did you do before the Navy?"

"My family owns a farm."

"No kidding. I wouldn't have pegged you for a farmer." More like some kind of Greek god, she now thought.

"Pegs don't easily fit me."

"I see," she responded and had to look away.

"I've found some great spots here."

Her mind spilled the words, *Take me with you.*

He seemed to read her, paid for the drinks, and again led her away. The sound of her heels on the pavement was lost in the hum and shuffle of the streets, or was she floating?

He took her to a place that reminded Janey of musical clubs that had brought a bit of Times Square to previously quiet neighborhoods. Inside, the place was demure with muted lighting, dark paneled walls, and a low ceiling. They moved as close to the stage as they could, though many of the front tables were taken. Sitting side by side, they faced the stage, where a skilled jazz-piano player moved his fingers over the keys like birds and, even alone on the stage, his was a commanding presence.

Cole kept one arm around her, but with his other hand he tapped on his thigh, and his eyes fluttered to a close for moments at a time as though savoring the music, playing it in his mind. Instead of awkward, now he appeared to be one of those people who felt completely free to express himself anytime, anywhere.

The waitress wore a form-fitting black dress, and she had either found some hosiery or had drawn a perfectly straight black line down the back of her legs. Janey wasn't dressed right; she still wore her work suit. She slipped off the jacket and Cole helped her, then hung the jacket on the back of her chair.

They ordered drinks. The air translucent with cigarette smoke and sweet with the scents of aftershave and cologne, the place was an underground escape from the city above to a different world of low lights and music. Some people danced, but most of the patrons simply sat, listened, and conversed in hushed tones. Several groups of girls sat together—single young men had become rare unless soldiers were in town. And yet there was a feeling of sweet energy in the air. It was a place for sipping on a good drink and listening to music so velvety, yet alive, she wished she could take it home with her.

They danced on the tiny dance floor to a slow song, and when he slid his arms around her, she heard him draw in a breath and hold it. He wrapped his arms all the way around her as they swayed together like the sea.

She had almost forgotten what this felt like. She hadn't dated anyone in a long time and had buried the need for this so deeply under work and family duty that she'd thought only an act of God could unearth it.

They kept dancing, listening to the music, and later talking.

Maybe it was the alcohol or his anticipatory stare or his obvious desire—she didn't know—but she found herself letting down her guard, talking about herself: her parents' diner and how much she wanted to get away from it, the boring years in the typing pool, and her family's odd hobby of mushroom hunting. She confessed she often joined her parents in the woods west of the city, and she had become the expert at determining if the species were edible.

Cole looked bewildered and impressed at the same time. "What do you do with them? I'm afraid to eat mushrooms I find in the forest."

Janey replied, "There's a saying, 'Every mushroom is edible *once*.' "

He threw his head back and laughed.

"My father makes a special soup for his customers with the best of them. It's so much better than the stuff that comes from a can. Some people turn their noses up at mushroom soup, until they taste it."

He listened to her raptly, and his face and lips made it clear he wanted to taste *her*.

"I'd rather do just about anything over eating a mushroom. Funny what different people like. I like caves. I'm fond of spelunking."

"I love that word, *spelunking*. But it sounds like an awkward gait."

He laughed. "And people who do it are often awkward, too."

But not you, Janey thought. "So you like small and dark places, like this club?"

He smiled. "I hadn't figured it that way. But I can see what you mean. This is kind of a man-made cave."

"Of sorts, yes."

"Beauty and brains," he said with an admiring look. "That's an intoxicating combination."

Her mouth went dry. Could this gorgeous, suave guy really be interested in her? Despite being from a farm, he came across as much more worldly than she was. "So what is it about caves?"

He shrugged. "I don't know. They feel safe to me. Tucked away, you know. I hadn't thought of this before either, but I'm to be in the bowels of a ship leading a supply team. Guess it's a good thing I like caves, man-made or not."

"Let's hope it keeps you safe." Just as the words left her mouth, she stifled a gasp. With the risk of bombings and torpedoes, the bowels of a ship were probably the worst place to be.

He saw her all the way to her door, late that night.

After capturing her hand, he held it close to his heart and whispered near her ear, "I've longed for something like this."

When she turned to face him and say goodnight, he lifted her quivering chin with his forefinger, and leaned in as if to kiss her.

Janey whispered, "You must be shipping out soon."

The city was full of them, desperate lonely young men looking for last-minute love before going to war. She'd spent several evenings out with girlfriends, fending off uniformed, nineteen-year-old boys from Fort Dix and McGuire Air Force Base and being asked why she wasn't married. She had done it a few times when she was still in the typing pool; there were occasions when she couldn't talk her way out of it. But that phase had ended quickly.

He abandoned the kiss quest and said, "Yes, I'm leaving in three days, and I want to spend them all with you."

"This is a strange beginning."

"But strange can be good. Would you prefer common? You've been waiting for this, too."

She had no response.

"May I see you tomorrow?"

"I usually visit my parents at the diner on Saturday."

"They'll understand."

She couldn't deny that. Her parents would be thrilled she had a date. But this was happening way too fast. Cole was happening way too fast. Seeing him again wasn't a good idea—she had to act sensibly.

As she pondered how to answer him, he said, "You must say yes." His eyes showed no guile, just adoration.

She'd never imagined being the recipient of such a thing. He moved faster than any man she'd ever known, but then again, he was running out of time. And yet, he was streaming now in her blood and seeping into all parts of her, even though she knew he probably just wanted a last hurrah before leaving for a war zone.

"We have tonight and the weekend. I don't leave until Monday evening."

Over the next two days, Janey spent all of her spare time with Cole. They took a roundabout tour of Philadelphia by bus. The war had awakened a sleeping beast of a city, and now streets were clogged with traffic and smelled of gasoline and factory exhaust. Lines snaked outside restaurants, and nightclubs were packed even on weekdays. Retail establishments were bustling, people buying despite increased rationing, and there was an air of gaiety in contrast to the realities of air raid drills, blackouts, and warnings of espionage. "Loose lips might sink ships" and other signs cautioned the nation to always keep American interests close to the vest.

They went to lunch at the seventh-floor restaurant of the biggest department store in the city, and as the afternoon went on, they became a "we" instead of a pair of two "I"s. Cole would say, "Hey I have an idea for what *we* can do next," "When I come back, *we* will go to Tennessee together," and "I think *we* should order." They were rarely not touching.

He told her about the family business, a large farm and ranch outside Gatlinburg. Despite it having been a great way to grow up, he'd always wanted something different. He went to college and obtained an architectural degree. He wanted to design and build extraordinary buildings, the taller the better. He pointed out architectural features on Philadelphia's old city structures that Janey had never noticed before. Then came Officer Training Command and a commission in the Navy as a junior lieutenant in the Supply Corps. He'd never doubted he would do his duty to country, but after the war, he would resign his commission to pursue other goals. She told him about secretarial school and her rise from typing pool to secretary to executive secretary within Walker Scott.

Cole was well-travelled and had even been to Europe before the war started. In the summers while in college, he and two other buddies had traversed the country, hitting its high points, and then had ventured overseas. His parents must have been much better off than hers were.

He didn't brag about his travels, almost shy about his worldliness, instead waiting until she asked. It was obvious he didn't want her to feel "less than." When he did finally speak of it, his eyes danced. He said he hadn't made it over the pond until five years before. Though most of his time was spent in Italy, he'd also visited France, Portugal, and Spain. He confessed to loving it, and after the war he wanted to travel more, especially to see England and Ireland.

It wasn't until their last night together that she could ask. Eyes on his skin and his eyelashes, which she had discovered were as soft as mink, she asked Cole, "Where are you going?"

"You know I can't tell you the destination. I can say only that I'll be heading to San Diego and then to Hawaii."

So he would be in the Pacific Theater. She looked down. "I'm sorry I asked."

"No need to be sorry," he said ever so softly. "I want no regrets to come between us."

"I can't bear to think of you leaving."

"Then marry me, Jane."

Didn't he know that no one called her Jane, her legal name? She'd never liked it, but the way it came out of Cole's mouth was like pure truth.

He touched her face and studied her with such care it made Janey want to weep. This was the way everyone wanted to be loved, with abandon, diving in, despite it all. This was wanton love and lust, kind and merciless, satisfied and still hungry.

"We can go to the courthouse tomorrow morning."

Her lungs in the grip of a vise, she finally managed to say in a solid voice, "I have to work tomorrow."

"Call in sick."

For a moment she considered it. "I don't want to hurt you or disappoint you." She muscled herself together. "But I can't take time off, especially with no notice. I've just been moved up from the typing pool to work for the high-level managers. They depend on me."

"If you explain the situation, they'll understand."

"It's not like that at Walker Scott. Personal interests be damned. Everything about what we do feels dire. Gossip has it that we're working on a top-secret military project, something about torpedoes, something that can help us win this war, something that might end up to help...keep you alive. Even expectant mothers come to work. Every day."

But it was more than that. Her parents were hard-working, sensible people, and she had been raised to be that way too. Avoid rush decisions, be careful, take your time—those were messages drilled into her.

She found flecks of gold in his eyes she'd never seen before.

Maybe she was ready to stop being so cautious. Maybe it was her time to drink in what it was to live on the edge. *Just love me*, her mind pleaded.

As if reading her mind, he said, "You know I love you."

And because she did know it, she had to close her eyes and find her voice. "I love you too."

Searching his elated face, she looked for even a hint of deceit in his eyes, a guilty glance aside, a curve in his lips that appeared smug, anything that might indicate he was pulling off an amazing acting job. But no matter how hard she searched and how seriously she studied him, she saw nothing but love. He was genuine. His feelings were genuine. There was no doubt in her mind.

But her parents and life in general had taught her there were always consequences to our actions, especially those that hadn't been thought through. Hasty love matches, engagements, and even marriages were taking place daily during this time of war.

From the quiet chambers of her mind, a calming voice told her to stop, don't do it, it's not what your mother taught you to do. But something else, a commanding voice, one that came from a more instinctual place, said *We both want this. We both need this. This is what people live for.*

She might have done anything he asked at that moment, but he surprised her by stopping at kissing, not asking for more. She could feel him swallowing back desire. Then he simply held her entwined. Over the past few days, they'd done everything together, including going to Chinatown and roller skating, picnics and nice dinners, but he was treading carefully with her heart.

His idea was lovely to think of, but she couldn't quite hold up her end.

"Cole," she began. "I accept your offer of marriage…for when you come back."

He pulled back and put a hand on his chest, feigning pain. But he donned a smile. "You're the boss." He glanced away for a moment, and his eyes looked as if he'd flown somewhere else.

He turned back and kept his voice steady and pleasant, but Janey recognized an edge, like something he could fall from. It struck her then. Cole was afraid of what lay ahead. Of heading out into the unknown, alone as an open sea. And why wouldn't he be?

She asked, "What are you thinking about right now?"

He brushed his eyes gently over her and then said with certainty and tenderness, "Moments like this when I'm so happy I think it will burst me."

Men like Cole would never admit to fear, probably

not even to themselves. And they'd rarely if ever talk about it. She was frightened, too. Often she'd wondered about how all of the boys and men she'd seen passing through were holding up. Some of them, especially the eighteen-year-olds, acted as though they were heading out on a grand adventure. But the officers and older soldiers were more somber. Perhaps having experienced more of life, they were wiser. They also might have had homes, good jobs they gave up temporarily, and families. More to lose.

Janey couldn't bring herself to speak, only to kiss him again. Her fears fled, for the moment. She couldn't show fear while Cole was being so brave.

After they came up for air, he said, "You're a beautiful girl. Life at its best moments is filled with beauty. Don't worry, Janey. These moments will sustain me."

His eyes leveled only on her, and his pitch was certain. "Leave it to me. When I get back, I'll find us a hideaway for a honeymoon, maybe a place few people know about."

His acceptance of her decision made it all more difficult. He was putting her first, despite all that lay ahead for him. If the heavens could be reached, she'd be there surrounded by silver light, weightless and floating. "That sounds...wonderful, Cole."

He touched her cheek, softly like a kitten brushing by.

He continued, "It will be. After the war, I want everything we do together to be different. We'll go places no one else visits, we'll eat out at exotic restaurants, and go dancing at underground bars."

Janey shrugged with a smile on her face. "I'll follow

you anywhere."

"But we'll start with my hometown and the Smokies. I know places few people have ever seen. Some buddies of mine found a crack in the ground, the entrance to a huge cave, and they're going to develop it for tourism after the war. We'll get there first."

"Don't tell me you went inside an unexplored cave."

He nodded. "We had to sliver down a hole."

She laughed. "I take it back. I probably won't follow you there."

He smiled hugely. "That's okay. The other places I'm thinking of don't require that much of an adventurous spirit."

"Or foolishness. You could've gotten trapped."

"We tied a rope to a tree up on the ground, so we knew we could always get out."

"Smart kids."

"My best friend—everyone calls him Junior—and I explored every chance we got. I know of an old moss-covered stone bridge, on the road coming from old Elkmont. It looks like it belongs in a fairy tale. In fact, there's a charming old cellar built into a hill that some locals call the Fairy House. I can find hidden waterfalls and brooks. I also know where thousands of fireflies flash on and off in unison for a few weeks every summer. Better than a fireworks display."

"That sounds much better than the cave."

"My father's family is from Elkmont, a town from way back, but they had to sell their land and move to start over when the park came to be. Now Elkmont is mostly quiet with a cemetery that still gets used. Junior and I combed through all of it."

"It sounds like you never worked or went to school."

"We did both, but we always made time to play games. Traded marbles, mischief at night, those kinds of things. I had a great childhood, but I want the rest of my life to be even better, with you."

Listening to him was like getting swept up in a flood. It was hard to believe that love had simply walked into her life on a bus and sat down beside her. For the moment, all her skies cleared.

After she had to say goodbye and Cole left, she collapsed on the divan and held her head down to keep from fainting. Cheese the cat licked her face, which made her cry harder. She couldn't shake the feeling of having wronged the first man she'd ever loved.

When she wandered out to the wishing well in her garden, she sent imaginary gold coins into the well and heard them plop when they landed in the imaginary water below. Each wish was for Cole's safety. She didn't know if she could live through it if he died, and regret washed through her so fiercely she had to sit down and hug herself.

Her self-indulgence didn't last long, however. She wrenched herself up. Her routine took over, a clockwork that kept her going despite it all, the way soldiers who'd seen too much death must in some horrific way get used to it. The dedicated worker she'd turned into kept running automatically, just like the war had to.

****

Within two weeks, she received a letter from Cole from Hawaii. In it, he was full of loving words. He adored the islands as well and said he would take her back here someday, and on that trip, he'd buy her every beautiful tropical flower they could find. She wrote back to his APO address, having no idea when it would reach him or where, added letters she'd already penned, and sent the bundle.

Weeks later, she received a packet of six letters. In each one he described life aboard the ship, his role as leader of a supply team, and how much he already missed her and home.

By the most recent letter he'd written, his tone had changed. She felt touches of anxiety and fear, surmising that he was most likely in the Pacific theater by then and his ship had perhaps already seen some action. She could tell he was downplaying it, but there was a sense of loneliness between the lines. He talked a great deal about what he missed about home, and he admitted that the close quarters on the ship had been harder on him than he'd realized they would be. But he always ended with an upbeat tone that sometimes didn't sound altogether genuine.

Janey found herself worrying way too much, so she started volunteering at the USO, because she wanted to serve in some way, but also she hoped to meet other women who were in the same situation. But by then all of America had been warned about Hitler's horde of spies, saboteurs, and couriers who were sweeping the nation in search of wartime secrets and plans. Many German spies had been captured, tried, and imprisoned. Some had come from Germany, but others had been American citizens. No one was to be completely trusted. Even soldiers at the USO were not to be questioned about their shipping-out dates, or where they were going. Defense workers were not to talk about their jobs in public. A war was on, and everything out of the ordinary must be suspect.

****

Cole's next batch of letters lifted her spirits. The last one contained a hint. He'd written: *No news of where we've landed for a while, but it does remind me of that Saturday night at Dock Street. Remember when we sampled some delicacies, some little tasty things that came in a jar? I can't remember the name.*

Janey put the letter down for a moment. What was Cole trying to tell her? She thought she could recall every moment from that night, so she filed through her memories. At the Dock Street Market, they'd looked at a huge array of knick-knacks and salvaged items, but Cole had written little *tasty things that came in a jar*, so it had to be food. She remembered corn cakes, almost-black rye bread, up-country pepper sausage, and pickled eggs. Wait a minute—she stopped herself. Those pickled eggs were guinea eggs. She had it. Cole was telling her he was in New Guinea.

After leaving the diner on the following Friday, she hurried to the library before they closed and pulled out an atlas of the Pacific, then found New Guinea, a huge island off the coast of Australia. Janey sat in silence and placed her hand softly on the island, then just sat there for almost half an hour.

A librarian passed and stopped once. She glanced down at the map. "Miss, are you all right?"

Janey had been lost in memories. She shook herself out of it and smiled weakly. "Yes, thank you for asking. But I'm fine."

"We're closing in about five minutes. If I can help you find anything, let me know."

Janey nodded. "Thank you."

But she couldn't move just yet. She felt closer to Cole with her fingers placed on New Guinea. She was probably the only person in America who knew where he was.

When the letter arrived on October first, postmarked from Gatlinburg, Tennessee, Janey's first reaction was joy and curiosity. His parents had finally written her. But the letter was direct and short.

Cole was gone.

The world went silent, and Janey's flesh chilled as if she'd been plunged into a faraway, icy sea. It choked in her chest, and she barely remembered breathing while the sickest feeling overcame her. Lost in a stark world suddenly swept clean of brightness, she saw herself as a bird with a broken wing, struggling on the hard ground, never to fly again. In one swift blow she'd lost the love of her life.

She called and asked her parents to meet her at their home, and somehow they closed the diner early and did just that. When she passed the letter from Cole's mother to them, she maintained an amazing calm. She didn't even cry. Perhaps she'd cried every tear she was capable of producing from her body already.

They consoled her as well as they could. But they hadn't known Cole. It wasn't a personal loss to them. And still, her mother's eyes swam with worry, and her father kept shooting her inquiring glances as if he were trying to figure out what lay behind the façade and what the future held for her, looking for answers in her blank, brave face. And there was none of the typical, good-natured taunting.

She had to make them believe she would get over it. At this point in their lives, they didn't need to be frightened for their grown daughter. They worked endless hours in the diner, but family was paramount.

Community came next. They had managed to put aside food for those less fortunate during the depression. The diner was a reflection of their lives—sometimes hectic and overwhelming, sometimes quiet and calm, but always suffused with smiles and goodwill, which they carried back to their home. Janey hoped that God had something wonderful waiting in the afterlife for people like her parents.

They would've sat with her for hours, even if she said nothing. But Janey was ready to go home and face the demons she knew would surface in the middle of the night. She went upstairs to use the bathroom first, and as she was about to head back down, she took a glance inside her old room.

As a girl, she and her sister had been fortunate to have their own rooms. Janey's had remained much the same—floral wallpaper somewhat yellowed, twin bed with a worn pink chenille bedspread, white-painted wood furniture chipped by books, dolls, and play. Nicked by life. Tessa's bedroom, however, had been updated as she'd grown older and stayed at home. Completely transformed into an adult place.

It was almost as if her parents had kept Janey's room the same way in case she had to return some day. As if they knew to keep it for her. Had this room, frozen in time, portended her precarious journey? Did it foretell bad luck? Was it an invitation or a reassurance that no matter what, she always had a home here?

She was exhausted. Suddenly so overcome. Janey crept slowly into the room and then lowered herself on the bed, lifted her legs, and lay down on her side, hugging her old pillow. She gazed out beyond the window, where the sun was sinking and sparrows flitted in the branches just outside. It brought back memories of Tessa's and her pigtail years—climbing trees to keep up with the boys, playing make-believe, and practice-dancing with each other while listening to their parents' radios. And now...*Cole*. Janey kept herself from reliving what had happened; she'd already done it too many times, and no peace was to be found.

She should have married him. He might have died a happier man, but she'd denied him that. He was more than worthy of her giving herself to him. Instead, she blinked and wished for the impossible. If only she could go back in time, way back in time, to those days of her youth that had seemed complicated, only now they looked simple. Those days when all good things seemed likely, spread out before her like a shining river she had only to step into and flow onward to happiness.

Instead, this dense flood of regret. In the quiet of this old room, she remembered the boys she had refused while a teenager. She had been a picky person and had probably hurt many an innocent boy's feelings. Maybe she had even been a prickly person. She had turned away several suitors because she wanted a bigger life before settling down into a marriage. It had felt sensible to wait, but now looking back, it seemed as if younger people simply met, dated, fell in love, and got married. Easily, effortlessly. Lived happily ever after? She didn't know about all of them, but at least they had taken a shot at happiness back at a more innocent age. But not her. She had let the opportunity for a simple courtship, romance, and marriage simply float on by. Now she was faced with the most tragic love, the loss of the most complex person, the most pain in her life.

She supposed she had been like Cole, desirous of a

life outside the ordinary. She had held out, only to be crushed by this horrible sinking and drowning. So much pain she thought her body couldn't hold up. As if it would surrender.

If only she could go back in time. But then she wouldn't have met Cole. If only they had met when they were younger and more innocent, before the war.

A light footstep. Her mother.

Bertie gently sat on the edge of the bed behind Janey and placed her hand on Janey's back. "You don't have to say anything," she murmured. "You don't have to say anything at all."

Janey closed her eyes and just relished being there with her mother, surrounded by stillness and the sense of peace and empathy Bertie brought with her.

Her mother's silken voice eased out every word. "It's obvious that you're suffering, and I want to tell you something." She paused, her voice even softer and more heartfelt, if that were possible. She rubbed Janey's back once, up and down, slowly.

"I've had a happy and successful life with your father. We love each other, but that love has been tested. You have no idea how close we came to losing this house and losing the diner, too. My grandpa used to say that when poverty comes in one window, love flies out the other. We never stopped loving each other, but it was tough there for a time."

Janey could hear her mother's deep, easy breathing. In and out like a heartbeat.

"It might not be the death of someone. It could be something else, but I know this: You have a foundation as strong as a cliff wall; nothing will ever beat it down. So...you will get better. You don't believe it now, and that's okay."

Janey didn't move, just listened.

"You don't think this was your last chance at love, do you?"

Janey shook her head slightly but enough for her mother to receive an answer. Not an honest answer, but the only one she was willing to give.

"Don't be afraid to feel sad for a long time, and then let him go. You'll have another chance. Even if you feel now that Cole was the only one, it's not true. Each love in your life is different. I have a feeling that it'll be that way for you."

Janey couldn't imagine it. She would never love this way again; she would never find this again. But how could she speak of it?

Suddenly she didn't want comfort any longer. Wanting only to keep hearing Bertie's soothing voice, feeling her loving touch. Trying to block those swells of regret that she'd never be able to wash away.

Bertie said in little more than a whisper, "My grandpa also used to tell me that although there's no rhyme or reason to it, some people go through life as if they're walking straight down a long hallway, always steady, never stumbling, never hitting the walls. Just a sure, gliding path. And others go through that same hallway like a zigzag, bouncing off one wall and then the other. They eventually make progress, but not without suffering bruises along the way. No one person is deserving of the smooth path more so than the other. It just happens."

With her fingers, Bertie combed Janey's hair off her shoulder and left her hand there.

"Tessa got the bumpy journey growing up, and you

got the smoother path. I don't know why—as my grandpa said, there's no accounting for it—but there it is. Now you're suffering the bumps, but it doesn't mean you aren't going to end up at the same place, a place of peace, of joy. Your path is just a bit more cluttered and interrupted right now; it'll take some time to get through. But you will get through, my sweet Jane. You will get through it."

Chapter Six

"Solo Flight" - Benny Goodman, 1941
Philadelphia, Saturday, May 5, 1945

Barely dawn. Janey listened to the morning news on the radio. The Germans had begun negotiations with the Allies just a few days before. A series of partial surrenders took place—but in the east, the fighting was continuing. Janey sighed as she listened. Each day brought them closer to an armistice in Europe, but the war in the South Pacific held no such promise.

A knock sounded on her door as she was packing.

"Hello!" It was her sister's voice. She'd let herself in just after knocking and rounded the corner into Janey's room. "Wow, you're really going."

Janey's younger sister, Tessa, with her flaming red hair and tawny freckled face, looked like some sort of Irish Dalmatian, small as a sprite. Her wild hair could only be tamed by a ponytail. Tessa wore stylish clothes she bought secondhand but which were nonetheless quite modern and sophisticated and were great on her petite but voluptuous frame. Tessa had always been different— first she was a diabetic, she had flaming red hair, and she dressed in her own unique way. Kids used to tease her about it. Janey was older and often stood up for Tessa, who wilted under any criticism.

"Why aren't you studying?" Janey asked, looking

up from her suitcase.

"It's Saturday morning!"

"Well, I hope you didn't come over here to try to talk me out of going."

"I came so you can give me a key and show me where the cat food is."

Janey shook her head. "Oh, of course. I almost forgot about the cat."

"My, my. You must be very distracted."

"You better not have come here to try to change my mind."

Tessa plopped down on the corner of the bed. "Not me. I think it's about the most romantic thing I've ever heard of. On the other hand, Mom and Dad think you're..."

"Crazy?"

"Maybe a little." She sighed. "In truth, they're just worried about you, thinking maybe it's a delayed reaction to Cole's death, but they wouldn't be themselves if they weren't worried. We're girls, after all, and will always need guidance of some sort."

Janey glanced at her sister, feeling gratitude that they'd always had each other. Janey remembered so many things—as a kid, Tessa never had many close friends, whereas Janey had almost too many. So when a new girl moved into the neighborhood and she latched onto Janey almost immediately, Janey backed away, so the new girl could become a close friend of Tessa's. The ploy worked. During those tough years for Tessa, Janey gave her as much time as she could. They danced to the radio in their pajamas when they were supposed to be going to sleep, memorizing the lyrics, trying on makeup they'd scrounged to buy at the five-and-dime, having pillow fights, roller skating when they could afford it. Janey was older and did everything first, but Janey had always made sure she didn't leave Tessa behind.

Tessa continued: "But mind you, you have it easy. I'll always be the sick one. Try being the sick one. They're always going to treat me like an invalid."

Tessa's diabetes was under control now with daily insulin injections she gave herself, but her childhood years had been tough. Now she was working her way toward a teaching degree. Still living at home and waitressing at the diner, she could take all of her tip money and use it for tuition and books.

"By the way, when are you coming back?" Tess asked.

"I don't know yet. I'll play it by ear, but I don't have much time. I have to return to work a week from Monday."

"What will you do once you get there?"

"I don't know that, either. I'm still debating whether or not to go see Cole's parents. On one hand, I want them to know how much I cared about Cole, but I don't want to bring back their grief. I'm hoping a clear decision will come to me once I get there."

"How will you locate the grave without help?"

"I don't know that, either."

"Geez Louise, Janey. What *do* you know?"

Janey streamed her gaze around as if hoping that a convincing answer would come to her from out of the air. "Only that I have to do this."

"What are you hoping for?"

Janey shot her sister a feigned indignant look. "Again, I have to say it, because *you*, as usual, aren't listening. I don't know. How many times do I have to say it?"

"Because I want answers."

"Forget it."

Tessa rolled over on her stomach and propped herself up with her elbows on the mattress, hands under her chin. "As I said, even though it's sad, I find it terribly romantic. You know, when he was still alive and you were writing and planning his return, you were the happiest I'd ever seen you."

That stilled Janey, making her even more confused. Suitcase full, she finally closed it and latched it tight. "You've never said that before."

"Back then…" She gazed off into the air as if conjuring dreamy images. "You were radiant." Then she shrugged. "Once he died, I figured it didn't make any difference. It was all over. But now I see, maybe it isn't over."

Janey stared at her sister. "Haven't I seemed happy since I've been with Todd?"

Tessa shrugged again. "Somewhat, sure. But you don't act madly in love like you were with Cole." She tapped her temple. "I can read these things, you know."

"If you can read my feelings, you'd know…" Janey picked up a pillow and tossed it toward Tessa. "…that I'm sick of all these questions."

Tessa smiled a sad smile. "You know if it weren't for my finals around the corner, I'd go with you. That's the only thing worrying me. That you'll be alone. It could hit you hard again."

Janey was still stuck on Tessa's previous words. "I haven't acted madly in love with Todd?"

"No."

"But I've been happy."

"Not the madly-in-love kind of happy."

"Watch it, or I'm going to throw another pillow at you."

"You asked me the question. Don't ask me a question unless you can take an honest answer."

"Yes, ma'am. You'd think you were the older sister, and I'm the inexperienced baby of the family instead of you."

"Don't call me a baby."

"With your pixie looks, it's always going to happen. Get used to it."

After a pause, Tessa asked, "I have time to go with you to the train station. See you off?"

"Sure."

****

Janey wore her charcoal gray suit with a pale blue shirt underneath and a smaller black hat that coordinated with her black pumps. She'd tucked her hair into Victory rolls and left only a few tendrils hanging. As she dressed, her hands trembled a few times, giving her pause but only a few moments of doubt or regret.

Sure she asked herself why she was doing this, something rather out of character, especially since she had no specific goal in mind. And yet, that goal was there, blurry as it was. Like a song that gets stuck in your head, Janey couldn't let it go. That whirlwind weekend with Cole still haunted her. Her refusal to marry him before he shipped out shamed her. But there was something else, wasn't there? Something needed to be discovered in Cole's dearly beloved mountains, in that place he called home, that place he so dearly loved, but she'd know it only when she came across it.

Why did her time with him still feel mysterious?

Why hadn't she heard from Cole's parents after Cole left, until they sent only a short note after he died? What was she missing? Going in person was the only way—now, she was even more convinced. She couldn't just let the questions about Cole lie unanswered for all time. She'd found that even a vague compulsion could be all-consuming, and nothing was going to stop her now.

That evening at the station, it hit Janey that she'd never traveled alone. She'd barely traveled at all. But Cole had promised to go away with her a great deal. He'd be pleased that she was doing this.

"Aren't you the least bit afraid?" Tessa asked as they struggled to say goodbye at the station, which swarmed with uniformed servicemen and civilians, the scents of train exhaust, smoke from cigarettes, and aftershave in the air. People rushed about everywhere, tense as a wire strung tight. Every day, they awaited news of Germany's surrender.

Janey glanced around. Because of the war, the US Office of Defense Transportation had banned all express buses, leaving only trains for long distance travel. Regardless of the "Is your trip necessary?" series of posters that served as a reminder of the national travel crisis, some other civilians were there not only to see servicemen off but were traveling too.

"I'm a little nervous," she said to Tessa, "but I know I have to do this."

"My, my, but you're brave. I hope someday I'll be as brave as you are."

"You're giving me much too much credit. Last night I kept waking up, checking that my tickets and hotel information were still where I put them."

Tessa's eyes looked glossy. "I should be flying off

the handle, you know. You're leaving me the only one to help in the diner for two weekends in a row."

"I might be back before next weekend."

Tessa cocked her head, then peered into Janey's face as if searching for something.

"What?" Janey demanded.

Tessa shrugged. "I don't know exactly, but I have a feeling you're going to have to tear yourself away. Don't you dare abandon me here."

"Never."

Fighting tears, Tessa threw her hands in the air. "Just get out of here, will you?"

Janey watched her sister disappear into the throng of people—servicemen, women, and children—waiting to board the hissing train.

She had a spare moment and quickly located a pay phone booth. After stepping inside, she slipped in a dime and waited for a dial tone. She dialed Todd's work number. He often worked on weekends, so she hoped he'd pick up. Not knowing if he wanted to hear from her, she still thought it best to let him know she would be gone for a few days or more.

She checked her watch. A few minutes before 7:00—Todd could still be in the office.

The woman who worked for the editors answered the phone, "Lippincott."

"Is Mr. Dempsey in?"

"Yes I think so. Who's calling?"

"Janey Nichol."

"Just a moment, please."

Janey held on for what felt like an eternity.

Finally the woman came back. "I'm sorry, but he's heading into a meeting right now."

Janey already knew meetings were rarely held on Saturday, especially Saturday evenings, when only a few die-hards like Todd came in. But she thanked the woman for her time and hung up.

So it seemed that Todd didn't want to speak to her. Did this mean they were over? For good? That idea put a clamp on her stomach and brought on the sickest feeling. She had one last moment before getting on the train. She could change her mind and go to Todd. She could wait for him outside the Lippincott building and then spend the rest of the weekend with him, apologizing and making it up to him. She could stop taking risks and marry a good man, just like her parents wanted her to do. She could stay comfortable in Philly and not take off for God-knows-where.

But she boarded with the other women, children, a slew of soldiers in uniform, some older men, and the conductor, a stocky man with white hair. Another middle-aged man too old for military service, too young for retirement.

Janey fidgeted as she took a seat in the dining car and watched from the window as the city slipped away. Tessa's words kept echoing in her head....*You don't act madly in love like you were with Cole*. She tried to examine the way she felt about Todd in that moment, and many warm feelings rained over her. She already missed his company.

But remembering Cole had opened an old wound that now felt like an empty space. Before Todd's proposal, he had filled that hole, or so she'd thought.

Chapter Seven

"Comin' In on a Wing and a Prayer"- Willie Kelly and His Orchestra, 1943
Knoxville, Tennessee, Sunday, May 6, 1945

After an uncomfortable night on a lower berth all night, Janey crossed the line into the state of Tennessee, which was prettier than she'd expected. Most of the trees were fully leafed out here, and the land looked rich and green, mostly farmlands spread out in all directions until they ran up against hills and heavy forested areas. The train crossed many a small stream bubbling and skipping, and she glimpsed the occasional utterly still lake before the train approached the outlying areas of the city ahead.

On the last leg of the journey to Knoxville, Janey met a group of three married women travelling to join their husbands employed by the government to work on a military project in Oak Ridge, Tennessee. Oak Ridge was only "spitting distance" from Knoxville, but the women were planning to stay the night in Knoxville and then move on in the morning to start their new lives in government-provided trailers for housing. The ladies advised her to follow them to the hotel they had booked and get a room there.

It was mid-afternoon by the time they debarked at the two-and-a-half-story Southern Terminal Station building. The first level housed the dining rooms, baggage check, and mail rooms, and the second level contained ticket offices and waiting rooms. A bridge connected the upper level with Depot Avenue. Outside, Janey admired the corbel-stepped, gabled roofs and imagined Cole here looking up at the very same sights on the way to and from his travels.

The station's location at the north end of Knoxville's downtown area made it an easy walk to Market Square and the nine-story hotel there. Beyond the warehouse district, the buildings were primarily two- and three-story brick Victorian-era buildings with tall windows. It was charming and full of old architecture, but some of the buildings needed repair. Much of that kind of work had been postponed because of the war.

Getting a room was easy. The lady at Reception said, "Sure, I'll find you a room, honey. First time in Tennessee?" she asked with a wink.

Janey nodded. "How did you know?"

"Look at you," said the woman whose hair was tall, swirled up like a cupcake, and whose name pin read Connie Sue—really, what a name! She winked, too. "You're all dressed up like a firecracker on the Fourth of July. Love those shoes, by the way."

Janey couldn't help but smile. "Why thank you very much! Oh, I just remembered. Can you help me arrange a ride to Gatlinburg in the morning?"

"Sure can, sweetheart."

The ladies had dinner together at the recommended restaurant on Gay Street. Her companions heading to Oak Ridge were in their early twenties, two married to engineers and the third married to a mechanic. All from northeastern states, they exuded excitement about beginning new chapters in their lives.

While they waited for the waitress, who was at least as cheery and gregarious as Connie Sue, maybe even more, they relayed tales of food shortages and air-raid drills as well as scares that had taken place along the eastern seaboard.

"What's going on in Oak Ridge?" Janey asked a moment later.

The one from Connecticut answered, "We aren't sure. All we know is that it's a big project for the military."

The youngest, from New Jersey, leaned forward wearing a conspiratorial smile. "It's top secret. Our husbands can't even tell us what it is."

"If they even know," added Connecticut.

"A friend of mine is there," the third girl, from Maryland, piped in. "She got hired to help make some small parts. She doesn't know what the parts are for. Even some of the people who work there know nothing."

Janey frowned and said, "That seems to be the way of things now. I work for Walker Scott Electric, and we know we're doing some top-secret work, too. It's all very mysterious, isn't it?"

"Yes," answered New Jersey. "But I'll be asking lots of questions. I won't be able to stop myself."

"In our company, we've been warned not to do that," Janey added. "People might think you're spying. It's kind of outlandish, the lengths they're going to."

Connecticut asked, "What about you? You've never said what has brought you to Tennessee."

Janey paused. She had dreaded these kinds of inquiries. "Hmmm, i-it's a long story."

"A secret?" asked New Jersey.

"Not really, just a sad story." She shrugged. "Not all that extraordinary but sure to bring you down. You girls are happy and looking forward to being here. No need to rain on your parade."

Janey glanced down at her hands, and around these married ladies, the absence of a wedding band on her left ring finger seemed like glaring evidence of failure. Had her plans not changed so abruptly, she might have been well on her way to marrying Todd and be wearing his ring by now. As her mother had said, Todd was a nice man and a good catch. Just a week ago, she'd thought herself very much in love with him. Could she be making the biggest mistake of her life?

"That's okay," New Jersey said. "We're beginning to get used to secrets."

At the end of the evening, Janey exchanged addresses with the women, all of them promising to write. She might hear from them, and she might write a letter or two. But she doubted they'd become long-time pen-pals. War-time relationships were often harried and fleeting. It was naïve to think they would all be lasting.

That night during her waking and worrying hours, memories of her times with Todd, instead of those with Cole, tormented her. Over the last year, her life had felt full to the brim. She'd achieved a balance between her ambition and her personal life that was more like that of others she knew.

She and Todd had gone to the Academy to hear the Philadelphia Orchestra on Saturday nights. On Friday nights they often took in a movie or a play and had drinks afterwards at a popular hotel bar. There had been many other nights and days together, marked by laughter and adventure, all with a man who adored her.

If she were more her usual sensible self, she'd pack her bags this instant and return to Philadelphia in the morning. She'd abandon this quest.

And yet, try as she might to brush it aside, a strong sense of intuition told her something was out there in the mist of the unknown future, something she needed to reach into the hazy ether and grab hold of with both hands. Something she was supposed to find and uncover. It could be as simple as closing the book, albeit with fond memories, on the story of Cole. Or it could be more than that.

Her compulsion to go had surprised her with its intensity. Instinct told her she needed to do this, and that drive was still speaking to her day in and day out.

And as to discovering why she needed to do this, there was only one way to find out.

Chapter Eight

"A Little on the Lonely Side" - Frankie Carle, 1945
Knoxville, Tennessee, Monday, May 7, 1945

By the time Janey awakened and made her way downstairs, her friends going to Oak Ridge had already departed. Connie Sue at the front desk informed Janey that she had arranged a driver who was coming from around Gatlinburg. "It could be a while," she said, "so in the meantime, I advise you to take a stroll around our humble little city."

Janey thanked her and checked out but left her suitcase. Connie Sue had said she could walk around the city center and check back every so often instead of waiting for her driver, who might not arrive for hours. After all, Gatlinburg was fifty-eight miles away over mountainous terrain, and it could take the driver until the middle of the day to get into town, she said.

So Janey took another walk around the downtown area, visited an oriental shop, and checked out the new Remington typewriters in the store next door. She kept checking back at the hotel, and by 2:00 p.m. when no one had shown up, she asked Connie Sue to call the hotel in Gatlinburg. Janey offered to pay for the long-distance call. After Connie Sue called, she hung up and said, "He's on his way. But he works a ranching farm in the area and got a late start."

Janey had to contain her impulse to make everything happen fast, which it obviously didn't do down here. She took in a deep breath. Instead of seeing more of the city, she decided to wait, reading *The Daily Times* from front to back, even the classifieds. She didn't want to chance missing the driver when he finally turned up.

Just past four o'clock, a tall, rather gangly young man stepped in. Wearing a white shirt and ironed slacks with a vest, he didn't fit Janey's image of a "ranching farmer."

"Miss Nichol," he said and extended a hand.

She stood and shook hands. His were a bit rough and calloused, a working man's hands. "Yes."

He removed a brown felt hat, revealing light brown hair, a pleasant face, and ruddy cheeks. "I'm Luke Parker, your driver."

"Pleased to meet you," Janey said and tried to smile. She glanced at her watch. "I had hoped to get an earlier start."

"Well, I'm sure sorry about that," he said in a thick southern drawl. "That" sounded like a two-syllable word, *Tha-yat*. Luke Parker had an innocent face, his hair was a little longish, curly and unruly, and his eyes were doe-brown. A baby-faced everyman. "We're growing crops for the gover'ment and providin' meat, too. I had to fix a fence this mornin' before I could leave, or I'd be going back to half a herd."

Janey made herself slow down. His apology was genuine, and he was gazing at her as if he needed her forgiveness. The man was doing the best he could, all things considered. "I understand," Janey said. "You're here now, and I'm packed and ready to leave."

He looked a bit startled. "You don't mean you want

to leave this evenin'?"

She nodded. "I'd like to leave as soon as possible."

"I gotta go find gasoline. We farmers are 3-A, 'cuz the gover'ment wants us to farm rather than serve. No gasoline rationing for us, but it ain't"—he paused and corrected himself—"*isn't*, easy to find gasoline anyways."

"Oh, I see."

Her short answer seemed to have hurt his feelings—she didn't mean to sound curt, but she didn't have the gift of southern charm that she'd experienced so far in Tennessee. With his hat held down in front of him, he started to turn it around in a circle, by the brim. "Besides, I haven't eaten, and it's best if we start in the mornin'. We'll have time to stop along the way and take in all the sights."

"Why, thank you for the offer, but I don't think I'm going to have time to go exploring."

One eyebrow lowered. "You sure about that? Most people passin' through wanna see all they can."

"I'd love to as well, but unfortunately I'm rather short on time."

A question crossed his face. He had one of those faces that showed his thoughts rather clearly. Surely he didn't pick up many single women travelling alone. Most likely he was curious as to her circumstances.

"We'll be passin' through some of the most beautiful places in the park. It's goin' to take three hours to get there, no matter what. But it's best to take the day to enjoy it."

"Thanks again for the offer, but I was planning to take excursions operated by the hotel."

His eyes were wide open and expectant in a way that

showed he wanted to please. "If I take you into the park, it'll save you money. And we can go wherever we want, any time we want. You don't have to go along with a group."

"I'll have to think on that." She did want to see the places Cole had mentioned and didn't know what route the sightseeing trucks would take. "But for now, I do get your point about waiting and leaving tomorrow."

He nodded. "I'll go fill up and then come back to take you to supper."

He was so nice she couldn't help giving him a smile. "Thanks very much, again, but that won't be necessary."

"I insist," he said with a boyish grin. "I gotta make up for bein' tardy today."

"What about your farm, your work?"

"I arranged for some boys from town to help."

"Isn't help almost impossible to find these days?"

"I called in some favors." He nodded. "This is important."

Janey surprised herself by saying, "Okay."

As he turned away, he replaced the hat on his head, tipped it toward her, and said smilingly, "Until later then."

While he was gone, Janey checked in again and took her suitcase upstairs. Connie Sue had given her the same room, which had been cleaned. She changed into a flowery dress more appropriate for dinner in a city downtown, although she had no idea where Luke Parker would take her. She combed her hair and applied fresh lipstick.

Wearing a suit coat now, he appeared again in the lobby, holding his hat in his hands and turning it about in a circle. Something about her made him nervous, although he was trying not to show it, and she felt badly for being short with him earlier.

He led her to a cafeteria in the 500 block of Gay Street. They chose their main dishes and sides from the long line offering everything from beverages to desserts and all else in between, but waiters dressed to the T carried the trays. She decided to skip the custard pie, although she loved it, because she wanted to make sure her meal came to less than a dollar. She didn't know what Luke had expected to pay, if he was going to pay. She felt a bit lost, but he did seem familiar with the place. All the staff were dressed formally, and the ladies dining there wore hats and gloves. Janey and Luke took a table where Janey could listen to the lady piano player and admire the high ceiling and winding staircase.

Conversation with Luke Parker started out stifled. Janey had no idea what to talk to the man about, and he seemed as befuddled as she was. She knew the best thing to do in such situations was to get someone to talk about him- or herself. Reuben had taught her that.

"Tell me about your farm," she said.

He answered in between cautious bites. "It's a big family place. Three generations. My grandmother, my parents, and my mother's sister's family all own it, and we all work the place, usin' every inch of land we have to help win this war. It takes all of us to keep the place goin'."

He stopped eating and wiped his mouth with a napkin, replacing it on his knee. "We cain't hire much help right now, 'cuz all the boys we used to hire durin' brandin' time, harvest, and the like, well, they're off fightin' in the war. Even the girls—my cousins—are workin' their fingers to the bone."

She remembered that he'd had to call in some favors in order to come for her. His eagerness was humbling. "And you also drive people to and from the park?"

"Occasionally. Each of us in the family takes a few days every six months or so to get some rest, lest we turn into idiots."

Janey laughed. Her skin warmed. Luke Parker was affable, and that made him scary. He said the right breezy things that make people cast away their usual common sense and reserve. He was the kind of person you could pour out your heart to.

He continued, "Sometimes the body and mind need some leave."

"So today is one of those R & R days for you."

"Yep. Drivin' around, goin' through the park for pleasure, why these are some of my easiest days, my favorite days. But visitors to the park ain't, I mean *aren't,* what they used to be. Not nearly as many as in '40 and '41. 'Scuse me, but I'm tryin' to learn how to stop speakin' hillbilly."

He made her laugh. "You're doing just fine," she finally said.

"I've been around too many backwoodsers all these years."

Janey took a better look at her dinner companion. His wide face and rosy cheeks would make him forever look boyish. Soft soulful eyes under low brown eyebrows, and his lips that curled up a bit, said to her that he was quietly observant.

"How many years is that?" Janey asked.

"Twenty-eight. I'm almost an old man."

Older than she'd guessed. Luke had an air of earnest virtue about him, so he seemed younger. "I didn't go to college." He shoveled in some food for a few minutes. "I don't play the banjo or the fiddle. And, contrary to public opinion, I'm not plannin' to marry my sister."

Janey spurted out a laugh. "I can't believe you said that."

He must have taken her reaction as permission to go on. "On the other hand, I don't have any sisters, but if I did…sorry, I've been told I'm lackin' in the social graces."

Well, this was unexpected. She was beginning to like this guy. Maybe the hotel sent him because he sure did have a sense of humor. He could entertain people, even those who started off in a foul mood. "You're something else. Do you always speak this way to people you've just met?"

"We say pretty much anything that pops into our minds 'round here. As for you, I just had a notion you'd appreciate some joking around."

"You're right."

She glanced at his food. The usual stuff. "I might have thought you'd be eating possum and cow pies."

Now she'd done it—she'd made him smile. Eyes alight, he gestured toward *her* plate. "And instead of those vittles you're eatin' there, I figured you'd insist on caviar and a filet mignon."

Janey said, "Contrary to public opinion, not all city people have money."

"Well you gotta have some, or you wouldn't be here."

"No, I'm just a working girl."

His eyes got huge.

"Not *that* kind of working girl."

"Well, shucks, I was hopin' this country boy might

get real lucky."

She said, "You get that kind of working girl with money, not luck."

Janey sat back. She hadn't expected to enjoy herself. They'd gotten off to a rough start, but this country farmer was as charming as could be. She had the feeling that Luke Parker found something to like in everyone, and she bet everyone liked him, too. His heart seemed pure. Besides, he made her forget everything else for the moment.

He wiped his mouth with his napkin again and said, "In these parts, you also gotta have a real smart donkey to get up to her shack in them thar hills."

"Your life is flashing before my eyes." She tried to eat again. "But I warn you, I can keep this going. I'll match you tit for tat, so prepare yourself."

"Tit for tat? That sounds kinda breast-like."

Janey stared hard before breaking into an absurd smile. "Why, Mr. Farmer, you really are rather fresh, aren't you?"

He nodded. "When I think I can get away with it. But you..." He pointed. "I could see you were feisty from the get-go."

"I'll take that as a compliment."

He coughed into his fist. "By the way, I'm more Mr. Shepherd than Mr. Farmer."

"A shepherd, seriously?"

"Yeah, you know, we take care of sheep."

Janey blinked hard. "I guess I didn't think of it as a real job these days. It sounds so Biblical, real Old Testament."

"Nah, I got kicked out of Sunday School. And permanently expelled from Vacation Bible School, too."

"For...?"

"Tryin' to be funny."

She flipped a hand in the air. "Imagine that."

"Sure enough, it's a real job. Some sheep we sell. Some we keep for the wool. The gover'ment needs wool for uniforms and mutton to can for the soldiers."

Janey tried to keep a straight face. "Canned mutton?"

"Yep, it's very common."

"It sounds horrible."

He chuckled. "It's pretty near awful. I tried it. Mutton's good slow-cooked. I don't know what they're doin' to it before they can it, but it's like leather meatloaf with a weird gamey taste. I have a buddy in the army who wrote me a while back and said that after the war he's never gonna take another bite of mutton again."

It was interesting how Luke could joke and inform at the same time. "You must know everyone who lives in your town."

"Yeah, we know everybody, but like I said, we don't sleep with everybody."

"Ha!" Janey laughed. "You won't stop!"

"That keeps it simpler, only a few rolls in the hay now and then. Then nobody gets jealous when we switch up partners."

"You're tormenting me. I can't even eat."

He seemed pleased to hear that, truly pleased. "Thank you kindly. What do you do?" he then asked in a more serious tone.

"I'm an executive secretary."

He seemed curious but not overly impressed, which she liked. "Ah, typin' and shufflin' papers and fendin' off your fat-cat bosses."

"You can't control yourself."

He shrugged and said more solemnly, in a way to let her know he meant it, "I will if I'm offendin' you."

"No offense taken. You should write this all down. You could be a comedian."

"Nah, we already have Minnie Pearl from Tennessee."

She'd never heard that name. "Minnie Pearl?"

"You really should get out more. She's a right famous star."

"I work too hard. I don't have a talent, so I work all the time. I'm the right hand for the VP of a huge company."

"Well," he said and lifted the napkin to his lips. "That VP is one lucky man."

Janey took that as another compliment, but despite the laughs, she wanted to get the meal over with and return to her room as soon as possible. Luke Parker was nice enough and definitely entertaining, but the more they talked, the more likely he'd ask why she'd come—and by herself. She was going to be here for only a few days, not long enough to form any friendships, and reliving anything about Cole was too awful. People didn't know what to say.

But her brain must have temporarily cut all wiring to her mouth, because Janey found herself talking again. "I couldn't go to college, either, but my younger sister is attending now. My parents own a diner, and they've done much better during the war years. So they can help her now."

When they'd both finished eating, she said, "I guess I should get back to my room and rest up for tomorrow."

But he answered with a smile, "I'm not done with

you yet."

It seemed odd that she'd enjoyed herself so much. It surprised her. He was much too different from other men she'd known, but she found herself loath to refuse him.

After they left the restaurant, he walked her around the center city, pointing out landmarks and showing her his favorite places. At the Tennessee River bank, they watched a huge barge loaded with steel containers glide by. Then a large refrigerated barge. Luke told her that recently completed dams and work on the river by the TVA had made river transport huge business. They stopped for an ice cream and talked like old friends.

Every so often he'd lightly touch the back of her waist as if steering and protecting her. It was one of those things that gentlemen did for ladies when they were out together.

Had she misled him in some way? They were not on a date, and it never would've occurred to her to go on a date with him. He was from a hundred years ago.

But for the rest of the evening, he was a charismatic country boy, sharing stories about his exploits as a kid and then a teenager, and he asked questions about her life and then really listened when she told him more about her parents' diner, about Tessa, and Walker Scott.

She asked, "Are you this nice to everyone?"

"Nah, I saved it all for you."

She didn't believe him; something told her he was one of those rare people who liked everyone.

By the end of the evening, she had to admit she'd enjoyed herself. She hadn't been around anyone so folksy in decades, not since her grandparents sold their land and moved into the city. But although they'd left the countryside, they still had the same way with people.

Luke Parker sure did have a way with people, and he never asked why she'd come to Tennessee. She had to hand him that, too.

Chapter Nine

"Cruising Down The River" - Blue Barron/Russ Morgan/Jack Smith, 1946
Knoxville to Gatlinburg, Tennessee, Tuesday, May 8, 1945

He came for her in an older-model, rusty blue pickup truck. He made no apologies for the vehicle, instead patted it and called it his baby. The truck bed was surrounded by a wooden slat enclosure, as though it was used to carry animals. But there was no untoward scent inside.

"I cleaned out the sheep shit before I drove here."

Wearing the beginnings of a smile already, Janey shook her head. "Lordy, is this the way it's going to be all day?"

"Only if you keep reacting with a smile." Then he quickly turned back into a tour guide. "There's two ways to get to the park; one's through Maryville, one's through Sevierville. I'm gonna take you the longer, more scenic Maryville way. We'll pass through some other towns and then follow the Little River and go through the park."

Janey loved the way the Tennesseans said Maryville, like *Mare-uh-vulle*.

Luke seemed renewed and thrilled to be taking her to his neck of the woods. There was a spring to his step as he moved around to the driver's side after helping her in the passenger side.

"That sounds just fine," Janey said after he got inside and pulled out his keys.

"I'm at your command."

They left the city by the broad, concrete US Highway 441 and crossed the Tennessee River by way of Henley Bridge. Luke pointed out that Henley Bridge was the only bridge in the country flanked on both sides by stone churches. They turned toward Maryville on the hard-surfaced 129. The next sixteen miles to Maryville took them through a valley of patchworked land, barns, and more farms. Just before entering Maryville, they passed the large aluminum plant at Alcoa.

In town, Luke stopped at a grocer's and picked up food for a picnic. "I know a great spot along the river where we can watch a waterfall while we're taking our lunch."

His smile was so genuine and his enthusiasm so real it touched her, and she couldn't make herself try to speed him up. Clearly he loved his part of the state.

Beyond Maryville, she finally got her first glimpse of the Tennessee high country. A blue-gray mountain range reaching for the sky came into view and got closer and bigger and more finely etched with each new mile. Luke told her it was the Chilhowee Range part of the Smokies.

"What does that mean, Chilhowee?"

"It's the name of an old Cherokee settlement, but the meaning, well...no one knows."

"Chill-how-we? Sort of like howdy-doody?"

He grinned. "You're good at this."

The road led through a gap in the mountains, and then they were riding along the Little River, a rush of clear water with multiple small waterfalls and boulder-strewn rapids flowing down a tunnel-like, hardwood forest. The air was cool and humid on the skin, the light dappled, the scent of pine and flowers wafting in the air.

It had been a while since she'd been surrounded by nature. She'd always admired such things as sunlight landing on grass in between the shadows of leaves, the sway of trees moved by wind, the music of running streams. But it had been years since she'd been to the Poconos. How had she let so much time go by without seeing these wild places?

Luke told her that acres of old-growth forest had been cut before the creation of the park stopped it. He had a knack for turning a simple drive into something lovely, even iridescent. Just as she had in the Poconos, she grew pensive over this shimmering forest.

They stopped just past a stone bridge, and went to see The Sinks, a place in the river that had been blasted in the past to release a log jam but also ended up creating something of a crater below the falls that churned and frothed with whitewater. The morning had been chilly so far, but now Janey was able to remove her cardigan and tie it around her shoulders.

Luke pulled out a basket and the sack of food, then led her into the forest on a path. Along the way, she stopped to admire some orange-ish mushrooms growing out of a rotting log. "That's a beautiful mushroom," she said.

"You like mushrooms?"

"Yes, we pick them in Pennsylvania."

"You know the wrong one can kill you, right?"

"Right," she answered, "but this one's not poisonous. It's called a galerina."

"A mushroom that can dance?"

"Here we go again."

He seemed more self-conscious today. A little more measured. "So you know all about fungi and molds?"

"Yes. I've been known to have odd interests. Ancient history and edible mushrooms, my favorites."

"Most of the women I've known go for flowers," he said with a grin.

"Don't get me wrong. I like flowers too. But a forest is so much more than flowers and pine trees."

Luke squinted up through the treetops. "Don't I know."

Janey searched around and inhaled the scents of the forest, here a mix of vines and bushes, fresh water, and tall hardwoods. Flecks of white dogwood flower and the thrum of rushing water on its endless search for the sea. So this is what Cole had loved.

It seemed to her this land was ancient and belonged to all mankind, and she invited it to enter her fully, past her skin and bones to where it could find a familiar place. Perhaps it was primeval, as if it had always been there, even in her earliest beginnings, only she hadn't known. Had Cole felt this way too?

They arrived at a nice flat rock overlooking the tumbling falls flanked by a forest filled with maple, birch, and hickory trees. "This spot all right?" Luke asked.

She pushed aside thoughts of Cole. "It's very beautiful."

"Maybe we'll get lucky and see a bear."

She smiled doubtfully. "That's lucky?"

"You bet. These black bears won't hurt you unless you get between a mama bear and her cubs. Most of the time, you can yell at them and they turn around and skedaddle. Really. It'd be a shame to come all the way here and not see a bear."

Janey shook her head. "That's okay. I'll be fine without a bear encounter."

"Geesh, I'm not gonna let you leave here until you kiss a bear."

"Forget it. I'm serious. I've never seen a bear outside a zoo."

"And I've never seen a bear *in* a zoo. We like 'em wild here. We sleep with our animals, too."

"Oh, my gosh. You can't get started again or I'll never be able to eat. Are bear sightings common?"

"All the time."

He reached into the basket and pulled out a red-checked tablecloth. He shook it out and spread it open on the rock, then reached back in the basket and pulled out something else. An unlabeled and corked wine bottle. A wine bottle.

Janey's heart leaped into her throat. An instant adrenalin flood of thoughts and feelings. Even fear, irrational fear. The only person she'd ever known who drank wine was Cole. Now it was all back—why she came here, memories of Cole, arguing with Todd, disappointing her parents. It landed on her again as if with the thud of a falling tree.

"What's the matter?" Luke was saying. "You look like you've just seen a ghost."

Just seen a ghost? Clinging to her composure, she dug up her voice. "You drink wine?"

"Yeah, my grandmother makes it."

Hadn't Cole said the same thing? She had to sit down on the rock.

"What's wrong?"

She couldn't believe the coincidence. "I'm, I, uh…thinking."

He grinned. "I know what it is. You're getting the swoons over me."

Janey stood again and faced him. She aimed for an untroubled smile. "Sorry, that's not it."

"Car sickness from all those curves in the road?"

She shook her head. "Are you related to Cole Huxley?"

He froze and looked at her as if she'd said something awful. He had a face that showed every emotion, and this time it fell into surprise and immediately into a terrible sadness. With a lowered voice and pained eyes, he finally answered, "He's my cousin—*was* my cousin."

She couldn't believe it. But why not? Both men came from a place where lots of people were likely related and everyone knew everyone. Her heart began to ache; she was crying inside. How blind she'd been. Of course her path would cross with those who knew Cole. She couldn't decide if this was a good thing or a bad thing. But it was definitely a sad thing.

They stood through a long-suffering silence. Janey couldn't take her eyes from his face as his entire demeanor changed. She'd made him cry inside, too.

Wide eyes staring at her, as if a doorway had opened, he seemed defenseless, his voice like a wisp. "How'd you know Cole?"

He didn't know who she was. He was Cole's cousin, and obviously he'd never heard of a girl in Cole's life named Janey Nichol. "I met him when he came through Philadelphia. He'd been nearby for some training, and then he left to go overseas."

She watched Luke go through several states: confusion and more sadness and maybe a little shock. "What do you mean, you met him?"

"I met him on a Friday, and we spent that evening and the next two days together."

"You were fast friends," he stated like a fact, but his face revealed doubt.

For only a half-second she thought of not telling him. But she'd come here for some answers, and this meeting had happened by accident…or by destiny? "He asked me to marry him; we were engaged."

Luke blinked and shook his head as if letting a new awareness settle in his mind. Then his eyes filled with realization. His overall impression became muddled, and she noticed then what she should've noticed before. Beneath Luke's humorous façade hid that endless sorrow.

Janey said, "I've upset you, and I'm sorry."

"I'm stunned." He glanced off. "But it's not what you think. It's cuz no one around here even mentions his name. I don't think anybody has spoken about Cole in well over a year. The rest of the family, they cain't take it, cain't even talk about it. It's the worst thing that ever happened to us."

"I apologize. I shouldn't have said anything, but Cole taught me how to drink wine, and he mentioned that his grandmother was Italian and made it." She stopped to catch her breath. Suddenly she'd become flimsy, not even strong enough to hold air. She hated how he'd changed, how much she'd shocked him, how much she'd saddened him. "Luke, I'm so sorry. I wish I hadn't said anything."

"No. I'm glad you did. The way so many people act

around here, it's like he never *was*."

"I'm sorry to hear that, too. People have different ways of dealing with things, I suppose. I can see I've brought sorrow, however, and I feel terrible."

The way he gazed at her gave her the impression he felt terrible for *her*. But…was he holding back on something? Standing before her now, his mind in a whirlwind, probably, and feeling the loss, he was a puzzle. First impressions always revealed something, but often only a glimpse into a person. Luke had been so open and happy, she'd thought him kind of a simple country boy.

Now she saw how wrong she'd been. Sure, he'd been lighthearted and humorous the night before, entertaining her with his quick wit, but now she saw into the depths of him. His face showed pain of the most vulnerable kind.

Luke wasn't afraid of feeling things deeply and letting it show. His bafflement over others' avoidance of talking about Cole came across so clearly, as well as the agony of the loss. Here was a man who wasn't afraid of showing his feelings. He opened his other side like moving seamlessly between chapters in a book.

"But it's more than that, isn't it?" Janey asked. Because of Luke's openness, she felt free to reveal what she was going through, too. "It's written all over you. You didn't know about me, did you?"

His eyes welled, and he didn't move for some long moments, his face a map of sadness and torment. Slowly he shook his head, as if it were one of the hardest things he'd ever had to do, telling her truthfully what she didn't want to hear.

Janey asked, "There was no talk of our engagement

in his letters back home?"

He answered, without hesitation but with kindness in his voice and all over his face, "My aunt got a few letters, and sometimes she read them out loud to the rest of us. Cole wrote after OTC, then after that supply training, again from Hawaii, and I think my aunt got some letters from when he was overseas in a port."

"Was there ever *any* mention of me?"

He studied her, his eyes slightly squinted, as though seeing her through a new lens. His face quivered, and she saw shame there. He was ashamed to have to admit it. But he answered her frankly. "Not that I know of."

The weight on her chest grew so heavy she thought it might stop her heart. She gazed around for a moment, thinking the sky would surely fall. What had happened between Cole and her two years earlier was the most momentous change in her life, yet Cole apparently hadn't even mentioned it to his family.

Quickly recovering, Luke went on, "But Cole didn't write letters all that good. My aunt didn't read 'em all to us. Maybe in some other ones…"

She hated to be thinking of herself in the wake of Luke's emotions, but she'd never been one who could fake feelings. She tried reassuring both Luke and herself. "They did have my address, and they did notify me when they heard of his ship going…down."

"So, there's your answer."

It was tough to swallow, yet she said, "But beyond notifying me, there was nothing else."

His eyes glossed over again. "I've never seen my aunt so tore up. It probably just about killed her to write the words that said he'd died. She wouldn't believe it until his body got shipped home. My uncle was in shock for a long time. Cole was their only son."

"He mentioned to me that he had two sisters."

He nodded. "Louise and Sylvia. Everyone suffered. Of course we knew he was going into a war zone, but Cole had always lived under a lucky star. No one figured that would change."

Janey grasped onto her skirt on both sides. She needed something to hang onto in that moment. "I'm so sorry for all of you."

His eyes darted away briefly, then came back. "I'm sorry for you, too."

Janey's thoughts had already fractured and gone off on tangents. Maybe Cole told only his parents about her. Maybe he didn't have time to tell the others in his family. But his mother's letter to her spoke of his death but not of any funeral plans. Janey assumed they would let her know, but they never wrote again. Surely, if they'd known she was engaged to Cole, they would've invited her to Tennessee. Janey had their address, however; she could've written them and asked about it.

His brow furrowed in thought, Luke gazed off and didn't speak for a while, as though admitting there was nothing he could say. With clenched fists, he dropped all pretense and finally faced her again. His voice was different, more forceful. "I'm so stinking mad at Cole."

Janey's eyebrows lifted.

"He could've worked on the farm, and that would've saved him. He didn't have to join up. Men from farms are needed on the home front to grow food for the war. But Cole always had to do things others couldn't or didn't. In school, he was a brain, but also, when he played any sport, he was the best on the team. He took off for college and never really looked back. When he did come home, you could see it in his eyes—he was already thinking about leaving again. He could've done anything with his life, but once he started pondering the navy, there was no stopping him."

"Yes, he told me about the life he wanted to live. Travel. Doing different things. Exploring."

Despite a catch in his throat, Luke kept on talking as though in some ways it was a relief to get it out. "Cole always had big ideas. But it seemed fitting, you know, coming from him. Cole could make you feel like anything might happen. People were drawn to him ever since he was a kid. They wanted to be around him. Some of them wanted to *be* him. He was my idol."

He paused, choking up a bit, and Janey thought her heart would split in two. "After he left, did he write you?"

"Yes," she managed to say, "he was sending letters regularly. Then the letters stopped, weeks before I heard from your aunt that he had perished. But I was used to stretches of time with no letters. He sent them out when they were in a port somewhere. Often I got three or four at a time. So when they stopped, of course I worried some but just figured the ship was out at sea."

"I always pictured Cole not having any free time. But he wrote you more than he wrote us. That should make you feel…better."

She did feel better, whereas Luke was agonizingly shaken. She'd never seen a man so defenseless, so exposed. He looked at her as if seeing her but also seeing past her, through her, into a place no one else could fathom. Maybe reliving the moment when he learned of Cole's death. Maybe consoling his aunt. Maybe remembering Cole's smile or laugh. His *idol*, he'd said.

She hadn't imagined this side of Luke, either—he was a million miles away. And she had sent him there.

Chapter Ten

"Some Enchanted Evening" - Perry Como/Bing
Crosby/Jo Stafford/Frank Sinatra, 1949
Gatlinburg, Tuesday, May 8, 1945

Despite it all, Luke resumed his duties as tour guide
and took her on a walk through woods and small open
meadows, where he pointed out wildflowers, including
wild orchids and azaleas. They saw a goldfinch and a
brightly colored bluebird flit by. No longer a spring in
his step, nevertheless he named tree species and other
flowers and told her about the rhododendrons coming in
June. She liked the sound of his voice. He had a smooth
rich tone that made you want to sit back and listen, soak
it all in. He could've made it in radio.

But later, Janey would never remember all that he
said. Everything that had transpired this day had sent her
a million miles away, too. The words and the memories
that had been churned up within both Luke and her had
temporarily stolen the forest from them.

After the walk, they returned to their rock and
finally ate some, but Janey was finding it hard to
swallow… Still stunned that perhaps Cole hadn't told his
parents about their engagement. Still stumped about why
he wouldn't. And sorry she'd brought back sad
memories for Luke.

She opened her mouth to apologize again, and then

thought better of it. This place had surely doled out the heartbreaks. Traveling in Cole's tracks and knowing he'd never come back here had brought on its share of sadness. Now the knowledge that he'd essentially kept her a secret from his family was a new form of torture. And she'd certainly put a big damper on Luke's day, perhaps immersing him in sorrowful memories he had been working to get past.

On the road again, her spirits brightened. Crossing Cole's stomping grounds, she did feel his presence amidst the natural beauty. Maybe this was what she had come for—to feel him again.

Luke continued to follow the Little River, crossing bridges and veering through the gorge, stopping at various spots along the way. Janey caught him glancing over at her a couple of times, seemingly to check if she was okay.

But she was worried about him. The mention of Cole had changed everything. Luke held onto the steering wheel tightly, no longer draping a lazy arm over the top and turning her way when he talked. What had she done? Her intention had never been to talk of hurtful things or disturb anyone's peace of mind.

"I'm sorry if I upset you. Before I came I didn't figure out how easy it would be to run into one of Cole's relatives."

He seemed to have recovered somewhat. "No need to be sorry. I'm sorry for my reaction." He released his tight hold on the steering wheel and sighed heavily, his eyes on the road ahead. "Most people 'round these parts act like Cole never lived. It rankles me, but there ain't, um, isn't, anything I aim to do to change it."

Just above a whisper, she said, "I couldn't speak of

it for days. But I had to get better."

He nodded but said no more.

****

Arriving in Gatlinburg signaled an abrupt change. Still in the woodsy valley, they were met with road signs and a four-lane concrete road lined with paved sidewalks and rustic benches. Gift shops and all manner of guest cabins lined the road as well as some larger hotels, most everything made of log and stone.

Luke gestured upward and away. "The Cherokee called this valley 'the land of blue smoke.' " Blue smoke. Where had she heard that expression before?

Janey peered around. Hills and ridges hovered above the town, adorned with lower-lying clouds stretched out like long lakes of blue smoke. Now she understood how the Smoky Mountains had been named. The Smokies were green, but mists rising out of the lowlands and clouds wrapping the highlands put a tinge of cloudy blue in the air. *Blue-smoke mountains*, a voice inside her whispered.

The main street teemed with people. Luke said, "Something has happened."

Janey took a closer look. Passersby weren't walking, they were running and shouting. Laughing and holding high jars of what looked like beer. "The town's full of tourists because of a big conference going on at one of the hotels."

Luke rolled his window all the way down and stuck his head out. "What's going on?"

A man paused as he ran by. Wearing a huge smile, he shouted, "It's over! The war is over in Europe! We beat the bastards!"

Catching sight of Janey, his face changed. "Sorry,

miss."

Her heart now started to race, and she leaned over so she could say out of the window, "Calling the Germans bastards doesn't bother me in the least."

"What happened?" asked Luke.

"General Eisenhower accepted unconditional surrender. The Germans have finally laid down their arms. President Truman made the announcement."

Warmth and elation flooded Janey's chest. She shouted, "Thank you!" to the man over the sounds of the truck and the merging crowd, then waved him off.

Everything else that had happened that day fell away, and Luke's face was bright with joy. He whooped and blasted the horn. Did it again. Janey clapped like someone who has just heard the most beautiful of symphonies. Both she and Luke had their windows down now, clasping hands and smiling into exuberant faces. More tourists were coming out, joyously, pouring into the street from hotels and restaurants.

Another man popped his head into the window. "Have you heard?"

Luke asked, "Is it real?"

"Real, real!" he answered. "Truman has declared a holiday!" he yelled and skipped off.

Soon the street was so packed they couldn't move but a few feet at a time, lest they hit someone. They could see one of the large hotels a way ahead but couldn't get there in the truck.

Dozens of horns were blaring, and some people danced in the street. Others passed around unlabeled jars of dark fluid Janey assumed was moonshine.

Everyone seemed to have the same need to move. People snaked in lines and circles and in no particular pattern. The street filled with everything from a few locals wearing straw hats and smoking the compulsory corncob pipes—really!—to a finely decked-out lady dolled up for a date. Men wore everything from suits to overalls.

Sporting a terrific smile, Luke looked over at her. The sun had come back into his face. He said, "Time to get out? We're barely moving anyway."

"Of course!"

"I'll come around and get you."

Too excited to wait for him, Janey stepped out and into a stream of people, immediately getting caught up in the river of movement and elation. Young children and old men were out and dancing in a circle, holding hands. Others did the jitterbug. She quickly lost sight of Luke.

Everyone had known the armistice was coming, and the US was still at war with Japan, but still the revelry was contagious. At least the war in Europe was over; the US had freed Europe from a mad tyrant. The people could finally let the burden fall off at least one of their shoulders.

Some of the restaurants and hotels were giving out food, and beer and moonshine seemed to materialize out of the air. A group of men stood around leaning into a radio, listening to the news and hollering words of praise. Shopkeepers were abandoning their posts, and farm trucks pulled into the town, then stopped in the road, unable to go any farther. In the distance, a church bell tolled and people sat on their horns. Smiles and laughter were everywhere. Standing off the road, a couple that spoke of wealth, most likely visitors staying in one of the luxurious hotels, popped the cork on a bottle of Champagne and toasted all who surged by.

Janey slurped down a gulp of beer in a jar handed to her by a stranger and skirted a car packed to overflowing with celebrating people, some hanging on the outside as they stood on the floorboards, although the vehicle could hardly move.

It was like one huge dance of relief. Janey kicked up her heels with men, women, and children. Her face hurt from so much giggling and smiling. Several men waved American flags. Some kids had piled into the back of a pickup truck and tossed out long paper streamers. Boys chased girls. Men kissed women in passing—all restraints were off. A teenaged boy handed her a small bouquet of wildflowers.

Men lifted children onto their shoulders, the women didn't bother to touch up their lipstick and rouge, and teenagers flitted about and flirted with each other. Then she was swept up by a flow of people going in the opposite direction. Laughing, she let herself be carried off again, into the gleeful crowd and then smack-dab into Luke.

Face beaming and flushed, he took her upper arms and held her still. "I found you. I was worried. Geesh, I've never seen this many people on the street in my life."

"It's all so wonderful!" Janey exclaimed. She plucked a flower from her wildflower bouquet and put it through one of Luke's buttonholes.

"Well, thank you," he said, beaming. "Where did those come from?"

"The forest, I presume."

He laughed, then leaned closer. "I meant, who gave them to you? Probably a male of the species. I don't wanna lose track of you again."

Janey spread her arms. "What could happen?"

He whooped again and held high a jar of beer someone just put in his hand. His smile was exuberant. "It *is* wonderful. We defeated a madman. Part of this nightmare war is over, and I'm here with the prettiest girl in all of Tennessee!"

Lifting his beer into the air, Luke clinked it against the jar Janey held in her hand. Eyes sad for only a moment, he then smiled again hugely. "To Cole," he shouted over the cacophony surrounding them.

Janey yelled with jubilation, "To Cole!" then took another gulp of beer, some of it spurting out of her mouth and dribbling on her dress as she couldn't contain her laughter.

"That's my girl," Luke said and handed her a handkerchief from his chest pocket. He toasted again. "To the best damn cousin a fella could've had in all the world."

"And to an American hero!"

"To the boys coming back from Europe!"

"Hallelujah!"

Young men were kissing young women they didn't seem to know and the women didn't seem to mind one bit—it was all in good fun and glee. After he kissed a girl, one young man yelled, "Victory!"

Luke's face showed the same emotions those other young men were feeling. As he gazed at Janey, she could feel his urge to grab her and kiss her—she saw it in the slight tremble of his cheek and a movement of his lips. But he held himself back. Inside Janey, a voice whispered, "Do it!"

She took Luke's hand and twirled herself under his arm, coming about full circle. Still holding his hand, the weirdest and most wonderful sensation flooded through her like an infusion of liquid joy. She took another study of his face, his frankness open like a door, pulling her in. He was charismatic, like Cole, only in a more humble and heartwarming way.

Luke seemed puzzled, too, but only momentarily, then suddenly also happy. "Are you flirting with me?"

She guessed she was. For a few moments, her mind floated out of her body. What was it about this Luke Parker? He wasn't even all that handsome, in the classic sense, but something about his face made her want to lightly brush her hands over it. His kindness and cuteness were killing her. Her hand felt snug and warm inside his big one, and there was a softness to his touch that surprised her. But then again, it didn't. There was something inherently humane and sensitive about Luke. She'd seen that in him today.

She opened her mouth to speak, but no words emerged. Something strange was happening in her body against her will. She was overtaken by a response very like the one when she fell in love with Cole. And yet it wasn't the same.

But what was she doing? She'd come here to get over Cole so she could marry Todd. But even this week, she'd had moments when it was difficult to conjure up a good image of Cole's face in her mind. It had been two years since she'd seen him, and too many other things were competing for space. Even more baffling was the fact that Todd had barely entered her mind since she first stepped on a train in Philadelphia to come here. It was as if he was a piece of only one part of her, the city girl, the smart successful girl back in Philly, but he wasn't a part of her here on this night—this place filled with happiness and such an accepting type of human loveliness. Around

Luke was something of a circle that she just knew made everyone feel good, and that circle around him drew her to its door and allowed her to simply step through with ease.

She finally spoke so quietly she wasn't sure he could hear her. "I guess I am flirting with you."

He stared at her as if disbelieving. Then he glanced around. "You gotta be kidding. You dallying with me? I think this day is making a fool out of all of us."

"And why not?"

"I don't usually get high marks for charming the ladies."

"I find you immensely charming."

After each took another long look at the other, Luke abandoned the jar of beer to swoop Janey up in his arms. He whirled her around until she was dizzy and maybe he was too. She nuzzled her face into his neck. God, he smelled like the forest. Before she knew it, she was kissing his neck and then moving up toward his mouth.

When she got there, he put her down.

Janey landed on her feet and pulled herself together.

Luke said solemnly, "I must remind you of Cole."

A bit stung, Janey said, "No, you don't," and then let her eyes take in all of him. There was absolutely no resemblance. Luke had a baby face; Cole's had been rugged. Luke was somewhat muscled, but Cole had been huge. Luke was funnier but could also be shyer and always unassuming; Cole was seductive, sharply focused, and always confident. "You don't remind me of him at all."

He took her hand for a moment, squeezed it, then let it go before he smiled sadly again. "You're all caught up in the moment. I was just messing around about you being my girl. Not that I don't have some talents, but I'm not fool enough to think someone like you would ever be *my* girl."

She shook her head. "You're wrong about yourself." She stood on her tiptoes and kissed him on the mouth, warm and wonderful. His lips were luscious. "You're a sweetheart."

He closed his eyes, then opened them as if gazing on a new world. "You're a bit zany, but I like it. It's just that—"

She cut in, "No 'buts,' kind sir." Then kissed him again.

"Well, have it your way, then," he said, grinning. "Count me in."

****

The next hours were dreamlike. Beyond the streets, all the hotel lobbies, restaurants, and bars filled up with thrilled people, and music shook the walls. No country bumpkin, Luke could dance. Someone had taught him, or else he had a natural rhythm and instincts. Whirling around in his steady arms, she found her worries, doubts, and insecurity poured out and exited via her steady breath and dancing feet. Flickering candlelight. Smiles and big hurrahs. People spinning on the dance floor and more strangers kissing and laughing. And happy music that harkened to the crowd: move, dance, and do it with joy.

She and Luke, connected by love of country and victory, drinking in the same exalted air, flitting about on one of the prettiest little places on the planet, along with all the others, like newly hatched birds expressing the hopes and dreams of a generation. Escape and letting go, at least for now, of what might loom later. Luke's smile the most beautiful she'd ever seen, the most exultant. He pulled her close to him, carefully, as though she was something fragile and rare that he must protect with his life, then whispered, "I'll never forget this."

She would never forget it either. She didn't want it to end; she didn't want to leave. Someone must have tossed out confetti, because little pieces were floating down. Janey wanted to catch them and press them to her face and then keep them there forever.

Her hands in the air as she moved and twisted and turned, Janey had to blink and tell herself to believe it. This was the dream, really happening. Hundreds of miles crossed. A new and unusual place experienced. A perfect night underway. Then later, Luke saying, "This is the best night ever," between more luscious kisses that felt like the opening up of a new life. He kissed her again and again and pulled her into him, close. He ran his hands up and down her back, stroked her cheek with the back of his hand, and ran his fingers through her hair. Savoring every moment, she loved the way Luke's scratchy cheek felt against her smooth one, how his jaw flinched when he kissed her brow, and how sometimes he had to pull back for a moment just to breathe. On that night, the Earth and everything else fell away. It was wild and irrational and desperate and all things that shouldn't be happening, but they *were* happening. She didn't care about anything else but that moment. The release, right here, right then, and for one glorious evening, even amidst the masses, there were moments when nothing else existed except the other, on that tiny island in time.

Sure, she had just met him. Sure, they were caught up in the moment, a special moment of celebration and throwing caution to the wind. But it felt good to throw caution to the wind. Janey had always been so sensible. She hadn't married Cole after just three days, and later, instead, she had found a solid man like Todd. And she had a career so she could always take care of herself.

But deep down, something had always been missing. There was a little yearning empty place that Janey had tried to ignore, that she'd buried and believed to be just the stuff of all souls, always wanting more. But maybe Luke had been missing. Maybe she had been drawn here to meet Luke, who had pulled her into his circle of goodness and allowed her to enter with ease into his heart and soul, a patient and kind heart and soul.

****

At the end of the evening, Luke could finally move his truck to a space in front of the hotel and walk her to the door. There he lifted her hand to his mouth and kissed it, then pulled her closer until she was in that sweet spot on a person where chest and neck meet, overcome by the feel of him, pulling in the scent of him.

He tilted up her chin with the tip of a finger and touched his lips to hers in a good-night kiss, and something about it felt like beauty, promise, and as natural as living. Every one of Janey's cells were soaring high, and that horrible feeling of something missing had just up and left.

She'd never met another man like Luke and never would again.

She not only wanted to see him and see him again and again, she needed this. She had needed something to shake her up like this night had. She hadn't realized it before, but she had longed for it.

Consumed with possibility and pleasure again, yes, she wanted this, and the firm but tender way he held her in his arms, as if planning never to let go, told her he wanted this, too.

Here it was. The dream had come true.

Chapter Eleven

"High on a Windy Hill" - Jimmy Dorsey, 1941
Gatlinburg, Wednesday, May 9, 1945

In the morning, Janey opened her window and stared at the forests and mountains, breathing it in, admiring it. It was as if Luke stood beside her and she was caught up in a current—maybe more of an undertow—with a sense of drowning, of just barely keeping her head above the surface. She was back there, in last night, his arms around her, his scent, the way he kissed her—like a dying man, dying for what they had together.

She looked at the forest with new eyes, seeing it as a beautiful beast all its own, as a whole, alive and breathing. It kept pushing out of the earth in new shoots and silky pods and seeds, all of it moving and changing and catching the light—streams leading all the way to seas, trees falling that would become homes for other species until they sank lower still and then lay moldering into the ground so the cycle could begin anew. Again and again, life climbed and pushed its way out of the soil and into the sky.

She went for a walk an hour before Luke was scheduled to pick her up. She wore a button-down blouse and pedal pushers with her oxfords—good walking shoes.

Vaguely she remembered he'd said they would head

out at 10:00, but she remembered everything else vividly. Dancing, drinking, shouting, and smiling. His arms around her, his scent, the way he kissed her—solidly but ever so sweetly. How when they were close, she could feel his heart beating despite all the chaos around them. The way he had taken her wrist in his hand and drawn her closer still. His was a tender soul, and yet he emanated a quiet kind of strength.

Had the revelry put them both under a spell of sorts? No, she didn't feel that way. Had it felt dreamlike? Yes, but also like the perfect place she was supposed to be, and at the perfect time. With him. She reminded herself to think about Todd, and when she did, she was met with more questions. Had he broken up with her? It seemed so. Under the circumstances, what did she owe Todd? She wasn't sure, but she had played fair and square with both Cole and Todd. She wasn't going to lose another chance again due to some self-inflicted caution. What had happened with Luke was like magic, like everything came together into a perfect night, the beginnings of true love.

The receptionists at the hotel here were as friendly and helpful as Connie Sue had been. They told her the town housed a public library and the park's main offices, plenty of shops and places to eat. They said she could buy a fried chicken basket at one of the hotels for lunch in the park. Then, walking back toward the hotel to meet Luke, Janey's body filled with a remarkable sensation of joy, perfectly centered, surrounding her heart and emanating all the way to the rest of her. She hadn't felt anything like this since Cole, and yet it had a quality all its own.

A dark-haired, dark-eyed boy wearing trousers that

barely reached his ankles began trailing her, then said, "I know who you are." He wore a cap with a small front brim. But even beneath the brim's shadow, his eyes sparkled.

She stopped and smiled into his gleaming face. "Who am I?"

"Luke's new girlfriend."

"Oh, I see," she said, standing up straight again. "And how do you know this?"

"We saw you last night."

"Did you now?"

He grabbed her hand and led her up a street lined with craft shops and souvenir stores, all just beginning to open their doors. He took her to the front of a tiny embroidery shop, where a woman was sweeping the stoop in anticipation of customers. "And there you are again!" the woman said.

The boy introduced himself as Franky and said, "That's my mom."

"Well, I do have a name," the woman said and reached out her hand. "I'm Marilyn."

"I'm Janey, Luke's new girlfriend, according to Franky here."

"Well, are you? You must be! We were so excited to see Luke out with someone last night. And you, so beautiful and sophisticated."

Another lady from across the lane joined them. Then another. All were beaming and brimming with kind curiosity. "Where do you come from?"

She answered, "Philadelphia."

"Why are you here?"

She hesitated for only a moment. "To see the mountains, of course."

"How did you meet our Luke?" Eyes sparkling, clearly these ladies adored him.

"He came for me at the hotel in Knoxville on Monday, and we drove here yesterday."

"So you only met on Monday. Was it love at first sight?" The latest arrival, having scurried up to join the little crowd, nearly bounced as she asked the question.

Another woman wearing an apron materialized from down the street and clustered in with the others around Janey.

"We went out that first night, and he was most charming. He made me laugh so many times."

"That's our Luke!" Marilyn exclaimed.

"But it wasn't until yesterday..." She let her voice trail off. "So I suppose it was more a case of love at second sight."

The bouncy woman clapped her hands silently, rapidly in front of her chest. "We're pleased as punch for you, and for Luke. He's our favorite 'round here. Such a nice young man. He's just a gem, always helping people 'round here when they need it. He's always polite and plays with our kids, too, bless his heart. He'd give you the shirt off his back if you asked for it."

"So he's a saint," Janey said.

"I don't know about that," said Marilyn. Then with a tiny hint of mischief in her eyes, she asked, "Is he a saint?"

"I guess I don't know yet," Janey answered, then winked. "But I doubt it."

They laughed. "We want to hear all about that first date."

"Every detail."

Janey said, "I'd love to chat longer, but I have to

return to the hotel. He's picking me up…" She glanced at her wristwatch. "In just a little while."

"Then another day. You must come see us soon!"

Waving furiously as she walked away, Janey said goodbye to the women and let Franky lead her away. Before he took her back to the hotel, he walked her past other shops and restaurants, many of them looking newly built. He was obviously proud of this town.

Her short walk turned into a longer one, and as the sky darkened, Franky realized too late that he should turn back. Caught in a sudden downpour, they took shelter with other tourists and townspeople under the awning in front of a diner. Inside, the place was packed with farmers in overalls and families with children. Offered some service outside, they ordered coffee and gestured while talking about the weather as the rain continued to sheet down in slants. Others were still celebrating the victory over Germany, and still others seemed to be nursing a hangover.

Many of the men wore suits but seemed in no great hurry to get back to work or whatever they'd been doing. Others laughed at themselves for not having brought an umbrella that day. Two very young ladies used the time to flirt with the slender, dark-haired waiter who barely looked sixteen. He went out in the rain to brush away water pooling on the awning. One of the suited men offered everyone a cigarette from his pack, and Janey took one. Why not? The man smiled at her as though she'd done a nice thing for him and not the other way around, and he gave her a light.

So she smoked with strangers, yet they had already started to feel somewhat familiar. In this town she had met nothing but nice people, and a hopeful spirit floating in the air worked its magic on her, even in the deluge. This town held old history, yet it was all about a new national park, a gift to the nation. It was reverence for the old and expectancy for the new. Maybe that explained why so many artisans had gathered here, so many people came and were still coming.

She would be late meeting Luke. Should she walk in the rain?

Ever since she'd awakened, an image of him walked along with her, and she couldn't wait to see his face up near hers again. She had been in close proximity just the night before, but she already longed for his eyes, his words, his arms.

****

But when she saw Luke, instead of sweeping her into his arms or kissing her, he stood, solemn. Holding his hat in his hands in front of him, he barely smiled at her, and there was no affectionate greeting. Something was obviously wrong, but she didn't want to discuss it in the lobby of the hotel. Maybe Luke didn't want to let on that they were a couple. Maybe he didn't want to set tongues wagging. But nothing like that had held him back the night before, and the news was already out.

Once in the truck, however, he looked as if engaged in an internal battle. He glanced over and smiled at her, then patted her hands that she held in her lap. He began the tour by telling her where they were going, explaining that they would leave the Little River Gorge and climb Sugarland Mountain, then pass through Fighting Creek Gap on the way to Observation Point.

Whatever was wrong, obviously Luke didn't want to talk about it, and Janey felt lost as to what to do. Along the route Luke had planned, Janey faced forward as he drove winding roads that took them higher into the ether. At one point, the light around them dimmed, and the air filled with a dense but delicate mist.

He said, "We're in a cloud."

The rain had made the morning cool, but she rolled down her window and put her hand out. The mist was cooler still, and so fine it felt like a cold dash of liquid dust. "I've never been in a cloud before."

He finally smiled again, but just a little. "Today I'm hoping to show you many things you've never seen before."

Still with no mention of the previous night, they slid through the gap that opened up to a massive spectacle. A range of many crowns stood ahead, some of them crossed by long arms of fleecy cloud clinging to the slopes. Above, the summits seemed to float out of a foggy white sea, and below, lush green slopes planed down the valley.

As signs directed, Luke kept the truck in low gear as they drove down the backbone of the mountain to Observation Point. There they got out to stand and observe the vast view and watch the bank of clouds waft and wander. On high, a wind dashed in and blew Janey's hair off her face.

Standing side by side with him, Janey crossed her arms, hugging herself against the chill, and turned toward him. "Luke," she began, pulling strands of hair off her cheek and lips. "You're so quiet and subdued today. What's going on?"

He gazed over at her for a moment, then turned back to face the expanse. "I've never asked, but if you really want to know what's on my mind, it's—well, I don't know why you've come here."

She touched his arm. "I didn't know it, but now I believe I came here to meet you."

He turned to her, his eyes terribly sad. "Oh, Janey."

"Yes?"

He sighed and looked broken-hearted. But he firmly said, "I have to finish my work with you and then go home."

A bit confused but still believing all was well, she said, "Then I'll go with you."

He touched the back of her head and pulled her into his chest. Whispering into her hair. "You know that can't happen."

Janey pulled away and searched his face.

He continued, "Last night was wonderful. But we got caught up in a moment of letting everything go. It was an accident. You're from the city. I live on a farm. It's up to my brother and me to keep it going after our parents are gone. That's their legacy and ours too. A working farm," he said, "isn't for you, Janey." He remained, standing still, a rock against a current, solid and still. "It could never work between us."

Stunned, she turned her back to him and took a step away, then rubbed her upper arms more briskly. She heard herself stammer, "I'm sorry. I'm so sorry. Suddenly everything felt so…so right. I saw things so undoubtedly, so…so plainly clear. I'm sorry."

His hands on her shoulders, he said, barely above a whisper, "I'm sorry, too."

She gazed out at a view suddenly gone dark and full of confusing green dips and swells. Compared to sights she'd seen before, this spread of nature was vast. The colors changed under the brushstrokes of moving clouds, and on the ground beneath her, each flower and leaf was an artistic creation like no other, each petal and vein a tiny miracle.

The night before had felt like a miracle. She'd woken joyous, but obviously Luke had woken regretful. Cole had once cautioned her against thinking too much, but it appeared that Luke had done just that and had talked himself out of the wonder of the night before.

Did it have anything to do with Cole? Did Luke decide that involvement with a former fiancée of Cole's amounted to a betrayal of sorts? He hadn't struck her as one who would feel that way. Like her, he would know that no suffering and denial of happiness would bring Cole back, and that living onward happily would be the best way to honor his memory.

Back in the truck, they sat in silence for torturous moments until he said, "If we continue on this route, it'll take us into North Carolina, or we can turn around and go back to see Elkmont."

Still looking forward, Janey asked, "Is that where Cole is buried?"

"How did you know?"

"I just had a hunch. He mentioned that place to me."

"Well, if you want to know more about Cole's family, our family, at least a part of it, you'll find it in Elkmont. Is that what you'd like?"

At that moment, she didn't care, but she answered, "Yes."

Luke was now solely acting the role of a tour guide. Janey couldn't remember ever reading something or someone so mistakenly before. Her assumptions and how incorrect they'd been held her still. She was a stone, her heart aching but petrified in a grip. She tried to shake herself out of it, but the pain of his rejection was like a recurring stab, coming back again and again. It kept coming around in an endless cycle. What was she to do with the hurt?

Retracing their route, they returned to the Little River Gorge and turned, then followed a road that took them to see a closed-until-July Boy Scout camp, and on the hillside, the hotel there, also not open for the season yet. Nearby stood some occupied private cottages and a street lined with creek-side cabins and an unoccupied clubhouse. Luke said that locals called this place "Clubtown."

"The wealthy joined either the Wonderland or Appalachian Clubs, and the two groups didn't like each other much."

Janey managed to converse and not sound like a shattered soul. "Like the Hatfields and McCoys."

"No. That was family, and that was Kentucky. This was, I guess you could say, about snobbery."

All was quiet except for the humming of insects and the trilling of birds. Nature was already sprouting and pushing its roots and limbs back in, reclaiming what was once hers only. No wind in that spot, so the towering trees stood still like wise old sentinels guarding a sacred place.

He told her that most Elkmont land owners had sold their properties outright to the government, but others held lifetime leases. He explained how the park had taken over all of the privately owned property within the new park boundaries by way of eminent domain.

"They were forced out?" asked Janey.

"Most went willingly, but some fought it tooth and nail. The gover'ment compromised by letting 'em stay for the rest of their lives if they wanted."

Janey glanced around. "Most everything about the park is so special, I'm glad it's being preserved for everyone to enjoy. But I do feel for those who didn't want to go."

"When the park got started, back in '34, my grandfather saw the writing on the wall. He worked for the Little River Railroad Company, leading a team of loggers. He and his men felled the trees, laid 'em out on skidders, and then pulled them behind horses to the train that hauled them to Townsend for milling.

"He had a place 'round here, but he sold out early and joined my great-uncle in Gatlinburg, where they started buying up all the small farms abutting each other, while the prices were still dirt poor. They're both gone now, buried here in Elkmont, where I reckon they felt they belonged. Now my father and uncle own one of the biggest spreads of fine farmland in all of Gatlinburg Valley."

Despite it all, it was still pleasant to be around Luke. Listening to him talk and being with him brought on a sense of nostalgia and wonder. It reminded her of waking up when she was about twelve, early in the morning, before speaking, before moving, and feeling full of joy and anticipation that a new day had dawned and anything could happen.

She said softly, "I'd love to learn more about the history here."

"I can tell you lots, and you'll find many old-timers here willing to tell their tales."

"I eat that stuff up."

"Pioneer history?"

"Yes, really all of American history, but I have a penchant for Ancient Rome and Greece, too."

"I'm your guy for what went on here. I happen to be a history buff, too."

She looked around and felt the quiet. It was peaceful, yes, but Janey sensed some sadness and discomfort here.

Luke asked if she was up for a walk, and when she said yes, they headed off on a trail that took them through towering woods and a mist that lay over the plush earth like the vestiges of ghosts. Overhead, the tree limbs and leaves wove a lacy net, blocking all but flashbulbs of the sun here and there. Crickets and other insects whirred in tones, and birds frolicked in the trees. Otherwise they were alone.

Going off on one of her wild tangents, Janey couldn't help thinking this would be a good place to take someone and commit a murder. Dump the body and no one would find it.

They came upon what was left of an abandoned settlement. But all that remained were some mossy stone walls and chimneys. The forest here had been more aggressive, already spreading out like a spongy creature intent on absorbing the new and returning it all to wilderness, extending out to take back what had been taken from it before.

He led her to an old stone bridge crossing a small rock garden of a stream. Moss-covered and ancient-looking, this was the bridge Cole had told her about.

"Cole told me there was a bridge here that looks like it belongs in a fairy tale. This must be it."

Luke nodded.

They stood on the high point of the small, gently arched bridge, and Janey felt the presence of souls lost to time. She tried to imagine this a place of people and human energy and wondered what those early brave pioneers thought about, dreamed about.

"I need to tell you something," Luke slowly said.

Janey turned to him. She hadn't expected any further conversation other than information about the area. Still in so much pain from what he'd said before, she waited, scared to death, for more.

Facing her with his hat on, he stuffed his hands into his pockets. "Early this morning I went to see Louz, one of Cole's sisters, the one he was real close to. I told her you were here, and she told me something I didn't know before." Pausing for a moment as if catching his breath and preparing to tell a long story, he went on, "When Cole's ship was hit, it didn't sink all the way. The crew had to scuttle it so the Japs couldn't get it and steal information or whatnot. But the survivors had time to remove some of the bodies, including Cole's. In his jacket pocket were some letters that eventually made their way back here. A small bundle of them were addressed to you. Guess the ship was heading to port when it got hit, and Cole was aiming to mail 'em when he got on shore."

She had to let that settle for a moment. She had no idea there were letters she hadn't received. "Cole's parents had my address. Why didn't they forward them to me?"

"Well…I'm getting to that."

His reticence was evident. If he was having a hard time saying it, it must be something. Her skin chilled as she whispered, "Go on."

He looked askance and sighed heavily. "There's more. There was also a bundle of letters addressed to a girl back here. Name of Marlene. She and Cole had been high school sweethearts."

"So?" she asked, her head spinning but wanting him to go on.

"I hate to tell you this, but they were engaged, too."

"What?" Janey had to clutch her blouse at her chest. She swirled those awful words around in her head and dared them to make sense. "Engaged up until he left? But he became engaged to me!"

"I know."

"What else is there? How could this be?"

Luke looked pained but said, "I loved my cousin, and I love his memory. But like all of us, he had his flaws."

"He had a tendency to become engaged to more than one woman?"

"I don't know about that. But I have to tell you now that Cole was always real good with the girls. Some might have called him a lady's man, and I might have to agree with that. Girls everywhere swooned over him, and he knew how to get 'em to fall hard. Every time. Marlene was crazy about him."

"Wait a minute. Cole told me several times that he wanted a life away from the farm. He went to college so he could design buildings. He wanted an unusual life, nothing like going home and marrying a high-school sweetheart."

"I know what you're saying, and Cole did always talk about things like that. But when he came back here, he was with Marlene, like a couple. She was waiting for him, too."

It felt like submerging, sliding to the lowest of depths. Janey had to sit down on the edge of the bridge, even though it was dirt- and moss-covered. She let her legs fall into the air, into the void, as her heart sank to the lowest of all places. Cole hadn't been true. It had all been a lie.

"So they gave Marlene her letters but didn't send mine to me."

"Like I said, my aunt and uncle were all tore up. I'm thinking they didn't want to stir up trouble. They knew Marlene and still do. I reckon they wanted to protect her."

Janey laughed pathetically. "At my expense."

He crouched down beside her and said, in a soft voice, "I've been guessing you could see it that way, but they meant no harm. They were probably baffled about what to do with those letters for you. They were in no state of mind to make good decisions. But I'll say it now for my family—I'm sorry. It was wrong."

"So Marlene was the grieving fiancé at the funeral."

With reluctance she could see, he said, "Yes."

She smirked. "I can see it now. Had I shown up, it would have been most inconvenient."

"They knew of you but not that you and Cole were engaged. They assumed it was some kind of special friendship."

"At least now I know why they didn't contact me until they had to. But they could've sent me those letters."

He looked down, and she shook her head. "I couldn't make myself come here before now. Well, now I know why."

He said again, "I'm sorry."

"All my wonderful memories are ruined."

Luke seemed to be studying something on the stones beneath him. He peered up at her. "Did I do the right thing in telling you?"

"It makes no difference now, does it? The deed is done. Please don't expect me to comfort *you*."

"I'm sorry. I didn't mean it that way—"

She sat up straight. "On the other hand, why did you tell me about Marlene? I didn't have to know."

"If you even mention Cole's name in this town, someone is gonna say something about her and him. They were linked in these parts. Everyone saw them as a couple. I figured it'd be best if you heard it from me."

"I'm leaving tomorrow, and no one has said a word. I haven't let it be known why I'm here."

His gaze was soft on her. "Maybe I figured you deserve the truth—"

She forced out a weak laugh, halting him. "I guess I had some good instincts when I stayed away for so long, but my instincts have sure been wrong about other things. About you. About Cole…"

He seemed to consider her words, then dismiss what she'd said about him. "For what it's worth, I know Cole cared about you. He was writing you, and he did send your address to my aunt and uncle in case something happened to him. He made sure at least you would know."

She smiled ironically. "He cared," she said and then forced tears to stay put in her eyes, "but not completely. Not enough to tell me the truth. Not enough…"

He touched her arm, and she drew away. She didn't want him to console her, and she definitely didn't want him to touch her.

He pulled back and stared over the creek bed. "Would you like me to find out if my aunt still has the letters? Louz thinks she does. Do you want them now?"

"Yes," was all she said.

"For what it's worth, too, and probably not worth much to you right now, but I know...had Cole come back, he would've been happier if he'd gone to you. It's so obvious why he fell so hard and asked you to marry him. My guess is that once he met you, he changed his mind about Marlene but didn't have the heart to tell her in a letter."

Janey forced herself to nod, then finally stood, surprised her legs could hold her.

As they rode back, she had to sort through her feelings that lay scattered in the shifting shadows of a wooded winding road. The sun was out for one minute, then gone the next. Everything was clear—and equally muddled. Mountains leaning in and huge open sky above. Dark and light. Unbelievable but also true.

How had she been so wrong about Cole? How could she have fallen for someone his own family called a lady's man? Had any of it been real?

It had been real for her. But how was she going to live with this new awareness? How could she go forward believing in anything now? She had no idea if anything romantic that had ever happened to her was real. Todd hadn't even understood that she needed to come down here, and he'd essentially broken up with her. Cole was engaged to another girl when he proposed, and he had been for a much longer time. Luke had toyed with her emotions.

Now she wasn't sure if what she'd had with Todd was real, not sure what was real with Cole, and especially how she could've thought Luke was real for one moment.

Why hadn't he told her all of this before? If he

believed she deserved the truth, why hadn't he just laid it all out right away? Instead, he'd doled it out in pieces as sharp as broken glass. Even if he only found out about the letters yesterday, he knew Cole had been engaged to Marlene. He knew about that.

It hit her then: They'd never made it to the cemetery to see Cole's grave. But now she no longer cared to go.

****

When they arrived back in Gatlinburg, he pulled up before the hotel and prepared to get out and walk her in.

"Please don't," Janey said.

His face clouded when he heard her tone of voice, and his eyes swam with surprised pain. "I'm sorry."

"Please stop saying that. Cole didn't love me enough, and you're just sorry…" She caught herself and stopped.

The rest of the light drained from his eyes.

Opening the passenger door, she paused. "What happened to Marlene, by the way?"

Finally he answered, "She was tore up too. But she pushed through, and about a year ago, she married a good friend of Cole's, a fella everyone knows and she'd known ever since high school, too. He got out of the Army early with a Purple Heart. But he's okay again, and they just had a baby girl."

She stepped out of the truck. Her shock and anger was getting the best of her. Even as she said it, she hated herself. It wasn't Luke's fault, but still she said, "Well, when you see them, be sure to give them my congratulations." She resisted the urge to slam the door. Preserving what was left of her dignity, she closed the truck door quietly and slowly walked into the hotel.

Chapter Twelve

"I Can't Begin to Tell You" - Bing Crosby, 1945
Gatlinburg, Thursday, May 10, 1945

After she awakened, Janey thrust open her curtains to the view beyond. The mountains always looked like a painting, especially at this time of early morning, while the big russet sun spread peach light through the blue, this way and that. She had planned on spending a pleasant day here, perhaps finding a place to lunch outside, enjoying each step of the sun crossing the sky, and later, perhaps each time the candle on a table was lit, each time she heard a cork pop.

After she dressed in a blouse and skirt, she went down to the lobby and asked for help arranging her travel back to Philadelphia beginning in the morning. Another driver, a different driver, please. As usual, they were overly kind and helpful, advising her that she would need two full days to make it back. She had to arrive in time for work on Monday, and she dared not be late.

She hated the fact that something she hadn't known before had hurt her so deeply. Never had she expected to feel this way. Nothing good had resulted from her coming here; nothing had been resolved in her mind except that Cole wasn't who she'd thought he was. And Luke had turned out to be the same. She had gained only a sense of dismay and duplicity here. She'd wasted time and money and had made things worse.

Her anger gone now, she also realized she'd barged in unexpectedly into the lives of a family suffering a tragic loss, disturbed what peace of mind they might have been recovering, and complicated matters to no end. She'd probably upset them more than the truth had upset her.

Deciding to make the best of her last day here, if that were possible, she took a walk and could barely feel her body. Drained, she was merely a haze, nothing of substance left inside or out. She made herself move forward anyway. She avoided the area where she'd met those nice women, those fans of Luke's, who'd thought them a couple.

She could understand her pain over Cole. But why had Luke's rejection hurt her so? She was no longer enraged about any of it; perhaps her feelings had been imaginary. Perhaps she *had* gotten carried away. She certainly held a deep respect for Luke. It had been only that and some curiosity, she told herself. But curiosity had never before skipped her heart, tripped her up, or folded her stomach like this. Luke was different, nothing like any other men she knew.

She visited craft shops and tourist stores. She wanted none of it for herself but bought an embroidered handkerchief each for her mother and Tessa, a small knife for her father. Although some moments here had been pleasant, even exultant on that one night, she wanted to take none of it back with her *for* her.

She stopped to look at the horse-drawn "surrey with the fringe on top" that was available for hire. So gay, so in contrast to the way she felt. But she'd not regret seeing this scenery. She would go back to the city, but a piece of her would live on amid the blue light.

****

Upon her return, Luke was there waiting. He'd been sitting in the lobby and immediately stood when he saw her. He seemed hesitant but said a steady, "Good morning."

He was probably wary of her, considering how she'd ended the night before. There was a clearly discernible and ardent plea in his eyes.

Regretful about her behavior, she felt sorry for him in that moment. He hadn't made the decision not to forward Cole's letters. But he had told her about Marlene. And she told herself he couldn't help the way he felt or didn't feel about her.

"Good morning," she said and managed a short smile. There was only one reason he might have come back today. "Did you get the letters?"

He had to glance away. He said, after a few tense seconds ticked past, "Not yet."

"But they still exist?"

He nodded. "My aunt has them. They're somewhere up in the attic, where they put away all of Cole's things. They couldn't bear to look at them back then. But she's going to find them as soon as she can and gladly hand them over."

Janey shook her head. "I hope I didn't upset her, and I don't want to pressure her, but how long is that going to take? I have to leave here tomorrow morning."

Turning his hat around in a circle before him again, he explained, "My aunt and uncle wanna meet you. They feel awful about what they did, or should I say, didn't do, and wanna apologize to you in person."

Janey sighed.

"I know you're likely thinking it's too little, too late, and you'd be right. They know that, too. My aunt 'specially feels she failed to do the right thing in the face of Cole's death, and she wants to make it right. I know what you must be thinking—there's not much they can do at this point to make it right, but maybe you'd like to see the land Cole grew up on, the house he grew up in, and"—he smiled—"I can promise you a darn good, home-cooked meal."

Janey softened. "I'll need to ask for your help getting to Knoxville tomorrow morning."

"Of course, you have it."

She thought hard for a moment. "I guess, since I can't leave today...and please forgive me. I'm not completely cold-hearted, Luke. I can't imagine what it would feel like to lose a child. My reaction was excessive yesterday, and I'm sorry about it. I promise I don't overreact more than, say, ninety percent of the time."

He smiled, looking greatly relieved.

She continued, "If you think it's the right thing to do, I'll meet them. But are you sure it won't bring on more sorrow?"

"They're sure. They're pretty adamant about wanting to meet you."

After Janey put her purchases in her room and brushed her hair again, she left with Luke.

Gatlinburg, the town, quickly gave way to farms and fields and far-reaching green-as-green-can-be pastureland in valleys. They traveled east out of town toward Pittman Center, and soon there were more animals, orchards, and fencing than people and cars. Above it all loomed the Smokies, today as clear and distinct as if stamped indigo-green against the sky. The blue-smoke clouds of the Cherokees had quietly let go to the sun.

As Luke drove, Janey fell in love with Luke's hands. They were square and tan and manly as all-get-out. She wanted to kiss his fingers, even though farm dirt most likely lived under his nails. Then the lovely curve of his lower wrist—just beautiful. Then his shoulders, which were rounded with muscle from farm work, and she knew the skin was smooth even though she'd never touched it. Once she got to his neck, she couldn't fathom what was coming over her. How could she still be falling in love with this man?

Luke pulled off the main road and started an easy climb through a large apple orchard toward a cluster of buildings, a white-painted farmhouse and a red barn, cornfields and cow pastures, fenced-in corrals and smaller roads, fields of other crops in the distance spreading out like wildweed. He pointed out the shearing shed, which he said he'd built himself, and the horse stable, which he'd built with Cole one summer.

It struck Janey as the quintessential American farm, overlooked by the greenest mountains she'd ever seen. Beyond the first cluster came other buildings and another house and smaller barn, all recently painted. No old rusting farm equipment or weeds. This was not a poor farm.

As they passed the first house, Luke told her, "We Parkers live in this one, and we're headed to that one over yonder where the Huxleys live. But other than the houses, it belongs to the whole lot of us, equal." He grinned. "I hope you won't mind the outhouse. We cleaned it today, just for you."

Janey harrumphed laughingly. "Don't give me any

of that. This is a beautiful place and a lovely home. I can see why your family settled here."

"We had to find a place to hide out and make our moonshine down in the holler."

She smiled. "I'm not listening to you any longer."

As they pulled up, two young women were descending the wooden front steps, the rails painted green to match the shutters on the house. One was older and darker, and the way she held herself struck Janie as dignified and a bit defiant.

The other was shorter and was so blonde and bright-eyed she couldn't be missed, not even in a crowd. Almost the opposite of her sister's, her countenance was gentle and giving. Her pale hair had a quality Janey recognized, the same sheerness and shine, that floating quality of Cole's. A prickle moved over her scalp.

They opened her car door. "We're the welcoming committee. I'm Louise, but call me Louz," said the older one. "I'm the black sheep of the family."

Janey had to smile.

Louz sported dark curly hair, a little wild like Tessa's, with a sheen to it reflecting the sun. Instead of the smooth pageboy style of the day, she let her curls grow just past her shoulders, unruly and free, giving her a rather fierce and exotic look. If she were a flower, she'd be a blood-red rose. She looked to be about twenty-six, another woman past her prime, who also didn't appear as if she worried about it. She wore a confident and frank expression.

She pointed to her sister. "And that's Sylvie, the angel of the family."

Up closer, Sylvie, with that translucent hair and wide sensitive eyes, brought Cole back for a moment. A female, softer version of her brother. But if she were a flower, she'd be a sweet blue delphinium. She swatted at her sister. "My name is *Sylvia*, and I can speak for myself, thank you very much."

Their ease and humor made Janey smile. They reminded her of Tessa, and a little ache entered her bones. She was indeed ready to go home.

Louz said, "Our parents want to talk to you, but don't worry. They won't bite."

Sylvie said, "I'm sorry I can't promise the same for Louz here." She nudged her sister.

"I'm harmless too, you know," Louz said with a flip of her hand. Janey would soon learn that was a classic Louz move. "Please don't be nervous."

"Me, nervous?" joked Janey.

"Right," said Louz. "Our parents are the ones who should be nervous," she said a bit sternly. Then she glanced at Luke. "That was fast."

"At your service, ladies," he answered.

Louz took charge and ushered Janey onto the porch and inside the door, where Cole's parents waited, standing side by side just inside, wearing nearly blank but expectant expressions, and she detected the sadness in their eyes.

Just what Janey had feared. She was past her anger and now only hoped she wouldn't bring back bad memories. Obviously she'd already brought back regret. Louz introduced them as Margaret and Robert, two well-groomed older people who carried the weight of the world on their shoulders, seemingly. They were dressed in suits, as if it were a Sunday, and beyond the smear of pain in their eyes was nothing but honesty and humility.

They exchanged pleasantries and then offered her

coffee or sweet tea; Janey chose the sweet tea. "I've never tried it."

"Well," said Robert, "then you're in for a treat."

Louz and Sylvie disappeared into the kitchen beyond the dining area, visible through a wide archway and a swinging door propped open somehow, and Janey had no idea where Luke had gone. She sat in a side chair while Margaret and Robert perched on the sofa to the side of it in front of the window. They turned to face her and asked about her journey here, what she'd seen so far, and if she had enjoyed it.

The conversation was easy and pleasant, but Janey could tell they were using the time to prepare for what they really had to say. After Louz and Sylvie delivered the sweet tea and coffee, along with coffee cake on individual plates with forks and napkins, they set the tray down on the coffee table.

Janey tried the sweet tea. Yes, it was very sweet. "Delicious," she pronounced. "Thank you."

Margaret, who wore her gray-streaked hair in a coiled bun on top of her head, started by opening the side table drawer and pulling out a stack of four letters tied by a red ribbon. The envelopes were white but crumpled as though they'd see a lot of wear, but Janey also noted that they'd been smoothed and retied but not opened.

Cole's mother sat with her legs crossed at the ankles, her hands in her lap. She said, "I'm sorry it took a while to find them. But here they are. And I want to give you my sincere apologies. When we first received them, I knew I needed to send them to your address. I put the stack aside, and it got lost in the shuffle.

"At the time, we'd finally gotten some help putting Cole's things away in the attic, and the letters to you were up there mixed in with some of his other letters and postcards from his travels." She drew a deep breath, took a sip from her cup, and blotted her lips with a napkin. It took Janey a few moments to realize she was battling tears. "But the honest truth of it is…we didn't know what the right thing was to do. We weren't altogether ourselves."

Robert blinked hard and joined in. "We should've sent them right away. Cole wrote those letters to *you*. They belong to *you*, and I wish I'd made sure you received them. I'm sorry you had to come here to find out about them."

"We're not proud of our poor decision at the time."

"Yes," said Robert. "We should've acted differently." Then he handed over the packet of letters.

Janey took them and laid them gently into her lap. After a few moments of silent contemplation, she tucked them away in her handbag. "Thank you. I accept your apology. In all fairness, I should've come here before now. Then I would've known."

"We can't apologize enough."

Janey patted Margaret's hands. "You already have."

A half minute ticked by. "So, you met Cole in Philadelphia, I assume," said Margaret.

"Yes, just before he left." Janey stopped herself; she shouldn't have mentioned him leaving. They didn't need to start re-imagining that. No embellishments. Tread lightly, she told herself.

Robert added, "You saw him after we did."

"How did he look?" asked Margaret.

She'd never tell any of them that he'd looked scared. "He was dashing in that uniform."

After a short spell of silence, Luke reappeared.

146

"These women here are fixing to make a feast for you. In the meantime, would you like to go out and meet some sheep?"

Janey welcomed the chance to escape for a moment and clear her head. "Certainly."

Outside she could breathe better. Luke took her back out into the sunshine and to the truck again. They both got in. "It's almost shearing time, but first we're tagging the spring lambs. You might like them. Girls usually do."

Janey smiled. Luke drove to a gate, got out and opened it, then closed it behind them and steered into a pasture full of sheep voluptuous with grayish-white wool so thick Janey wondered how they could tolerate the heat. "I bet they're ready to get that all off."

Luke said, "You bet. They'll be happy after it's done. But these mama sheep aren't going to be real happy about us taking their lambs. They don't understand we're just fixing to tag 'em and bring 'em back. So you stay in the truck."

Janey watched as he first skirted the herd that seemed to be huddling together. A black-and-white dog took the opportunity to come sniff Janey's hand that she had let hang out of the window. Half the dog's face was white, dominated by a big blue eye, the other half was black, surrounding a big brown eye. Like every unexpected thing that had happened here, Janey had never seen another dog like him.

"Hello, boy," she said. He put his paws on the side door and lifted himself up so she could scratch the top of his head.

In the meantime, Luke had picked up two lambs and now placed them in the truck bed enclosed with slatting.

"You've met Hank," Luke said as Janey continued

to love on the dog. "The best herding dog around here. He's a right smart dog, and he can run circles around most people in these parts."

"Hank?" Janey questioned with a laugh. "He's such a beauty, I expected a prettier name."

"Funny you should say that. Sylvie doesn't like the name either. She calls him Laurence, like a laurel wreath. She names everything for flowers."

Janey scratched Laurence under his chin. "Yes, Laurence, you need that sweet name."

Luke rolled his eyes.

He kept moving lambs over and over, going farther into the herd until the truck bed was nearly full of bleating babies already longing for their mothers. Janey kept turning around and saying soothing words, trying to comfort them.

Luke rubbed the dog on his back and sent him back to the sheep, then opened her door and handed her a very small lamb—it had to be one of the youngest. Tiny leggy body, sweet planed face and wide eyes, pink nose and tongue, so soft to the touch it broke Janey's heart.

"Runt of the pack. I figured you might like this one."

"Ooh, it's so sweet," Janey cooed. "Dear, dear, little one," she said as she stroked its head.

"That's a girl, by the way," Luke said. "But don't name her."

He moved around and jumped into the passenger seat. "Back when Louz and Sylvie were knee-high to a grasshopper, they used to name the lambs, until they learned better."

Janey sniffed in the earthy, grassy scent of the lamb as she touched the space between her eyes. "Why? What happens to them?"

"These are in fact gonna be kept for wool, but it's never a good idea to name or get attached to any farm livestock."

He started the truck and drove it over a grassy bumpy road to a corral near the Parker house, his family's, where they met up with Luke's younger brother, Tim.

Luke introduced him to Janey, and the young man, who appeared to be about twenty-one, could scarcely look at her as his face flushed tomato red. Janey sized up the situation quickly. Although he had a burlier build than Luke's and a charming baby face, too, he was painfully shy. The opposite of Sylvie and even more so of Louz.

Before he went around the back of the truck to unload the lambs, Luke whispered to Janey, "We Parkers and Huxleys come in all varieties."

Janey stepped out of the truck and passed the lamb over to Luke, then kept her distance, not wanting to get in the way as he and Tim, who'd vanished momentarily and then returned with a ledger book, pencils, and metal tags, gathered the lambs together inside the smallest of the corrals that she could see.

The ground inside was a mix of grass and packed dirt covered by what looked like a fresh layer of straw. Janey entered carefully, not wanting to soil her shoes. But she couldn't resist trying to comfort the smallest and most frightened of the lambs. She petted their heads and whispered soothing little nothings.

His eyes crinkling at the edges as he squinted against the bright light, Luke said, "Just like Louz and Sylvie."

The sun had long reached its apex and was sliding down the sky. Leaves rustled in the breeze and chipmunks came out of hiding. Birds called and beat the air with their wings. Everything around her was fully alive and in motion, but she felt sad that Cole had ever left this lovely place only to die in the bowels of a ship under attack. She couldn't bear to think of it. As she gazed up to the highlands, shielding her eyes from the sun, even breathing caused her pain.

But she turned back toward Luke.

Despite it all, she liked being around him. Of course he was charming and funny, but there was something about the way he looked at her, as if a question always projected from his eyes, as if he wanted to know her better. Understand her. And she, in turn, wanted to uncover the question and know everything about him. The pupils of his eyes were as black as ink but also alive with something like an old-soul spirit. He met her gaze in a way that was as baffling as it was becoming familiar.

Pulling herself together, "What's the tagging for?" she asked.

"Identification, so we can keep track of 'em—their gender, age and such, immunizations, and health concerns."

Janey never knew she'd love animals other than cats, but she wished it were possible to take a lamb home with her. Of course it wasn't, but she knew Tessa would love them, too.

Luke said, "Tim can take it from here."

Next he drove to the horse stables and helped her out. As they headed inside, he said, "We let 'em out in the mornings and evenings when it's cool. They're resting in their stalls now."

In the first stall was a chestnut with a white face. "This is Maisie, my favorite mare. I usually take her when I'm moving the sheep up and down. But the others"—he gestured to three others in stalls—"I take turns riding them, too, so they'll get some exercise. That big bay over there, that's Old Chuck. He likes getting out better than all of them. Too much female company in here."

Janey stroked Maisie's face and lingered on her muzzle, letting her huff out warm breaths onto her hands. She glanced at Luke. "Wait a minute! Didn't you just warn me against naming farm animals?"

He blushed and smiled. "You've caught me out. Horses are different."

Focusing again on Maisie, she said, "There's no crime in being soft-hearted. I understand. When I was a girl, I had a love of horses, even though I'd never been around them. I collected those little ceramic horse figures—I'd find them in trinket shops and on street market days. I pestered my poor parents until they finally took me for a pony ride in one of the parks. I was about twelve. When I finally got near a horse, I was terrified. I hadn't pictured them so *big*. I got on because I wanted to be brave and it had cost my parents, but I can't say I enjoyed it."

"Would you ride now if you had time?"

"Probably," she answered.

"You'd have to trust me. Believe me that I'd choose the right horse for you and wouldn't let anything happen to you?"

Without thinking, Janey quipped, "Well, you strike me as trustworthy." But even as she said the last word, she slammed face-first into a memory. That night. And what he'd said to her yesterday morning.

Luke didn't seem like the same man who'd acted as

if he was wildly in love with her one night and then told her it couldn't work between them the next morning. Or maybe she still didn't know all the facets of him. She gazed and caught his eye, a strange look in them. He was probably remembering that night and the morning after, too.

But Janey finished with, "I think I'd give it a go. I wouldn't be able to resist getting up in those highlands."

"I'd have to get some notice you were coming," he said and winked. "There's a rustic cabin up there. I'd have to clean out the cobwebs, run off the rats and bats, and spruce up the outhouse."

"Sounds wonderful."

"And I have to warn you—I don't usually bathe or brush my teeth when I'm there. No woman has ever set foot up in that shanty."

"Not even Louz?"

"No, she doesn't care for rodents. She's girly even though she pretends not to be. Cole and I used to torment her. Once, we put a dead carp in her book bag."

"You did not!"

A goofy reminiscent smile. "Yes, we did."

"Did you ever do it to Sylvie?"

"Nah," he answered. "We couldn't bear to do it to her."

"I guess chivalry is still alive then!"

He looked pleased, as if she'd sent him a signal. But if she had, she wasn't aware of it. "Yeah, I'd get you in the saddle. There's an old saying like that. You gotta get back on that horse, or some such."

"Hmmm. Not sure I've ever heard that one."

"I still have lots of tricks up my sleeve." He gazed out beyond the stable doors in the back, up toward the high ridge that loomed over their land. "Wish you could stay longer. I'd promise to keep surprising you."

"Everything about this trip has been a surprise."

He shook his head. "And not all of it was good. I hope you'll look back and remember some pleasant moments."

Luke would probably carry the guilty burden of what Cole had done to her for some time still. And if he were as nice as he seemed to be, he'd regret what he'd done, as well. "I will, Luke. I will remember the good moments. Like this one."

He stepped forward, reached out for her hand, and took it softly in his.

Her body felt limp, and her mind became muddled. Was it just a gesture of how sorry he felt for her? Or something more?

"Cole's parents, your aunt and uncle, are very nice people, Luke. They're lovely and kind despite their own suffering. I hope they'll feel better about everything now that they've given me Cole's letters. It was a good idea to come here. I'm glad you asked me. Thank you."

"Are you feeling better about coming to Tennessee now?"

She shrugged. "In a way, yes," she finally answered. "But now I know Cole wasn't free to propose to me. Maybe it was never real."

"Oh, Janey," Luke said, glancing her way, his voice grainy as if it was difficult for him to say the words. "Like I said, I believe Cole did fall for you—it's obvious why he did. But he should've told you the truth about Marlene. In some ways, I wonder if Cole wasn't exactly himself when he made such a bad choice in Philadelphia."

"I hesitate to say this, but…I think you'd want to know. Of course I don't know how Cole was before, but in Philadelphia, although he was the most handsome and charming man around, deep inside I came to believe he was unprepared and a little…scared."

"And why wouldn't he be? Going off to war and all," said Luke.

"Right. I think he needed that weekend with us together."

"Thanks for giving him that."

For only a split second the words swept through her. *Thanks for giving me a wonderful time too…and then taking it all back the next day.* But she didn't say it.

Luke said, "Maybe everyone was doing the best they could under the circumstances and it's nobody's fault."

"I agree."

"I'm still sorry for Cole's deceiving you. That part wasn't right. But I get why he'd wanted to marry you. In my mind, I guess I'll always see you as Cole's girl."

She couldn't stop herself. "You didn't seem to feel that way two nights ago."

He dropped her hand and looked away. Slowly he said, "I know."

"So is that why you took it all back the next morning? Why you acted and still are acting as if nothing happened?"

He couldn't face her for several long minutes, just gazed away into nothing, it seemed, his mind churning up a storm, she guessed. But he finally did have the courage to face her. She had to hand him that. "I don't know," he eventually said, torment etched into his face. "That night was beautiful, but…"

She waited.

He looked lost, then finally said again, "I don't know."

Janey heaved in a huge breath and let it out in a long line of frustration. "Never mind, Luke. Your idea was probably the right one. Let's keep acting as though it didn't happen."

His face fell in a surprisingly defeated way and he opened his mouth to speak, but at that moment, the shadows of two figures leaned into the stables, and he quietly took a step back. "Here comes another welcoming committee," he finally with a sad, half-smile. "Meet my parents."

As he made the introductions, Janey moved forward and took the hand of a man whose looks he'd passed on to Luke. Will Parker had a similarly shaped face and smiling look about his mouth, but his brown hair had turned into something of a gray bird's nest. "Pleased to meet you," he said.

Jean, on the other hand, wearing a printed cotton shirt dress and sensible shoes, looked shy and hesitant but was equally friendly. "Welcome," she said.

"This is the friend of Cole's I was telling you about," Luke said to them.

In their eyes the same pain that none of them could hide roved over their eyes. It felt for a moment as if all she'd done here was bring more torment to these people.

"Any friend of Cole's is a friend of ours," said Will. "We'd ask you over for supper, but Jean's been canning all day, and we were planning on just whipping up some eggs."

Jean said, "I'm sure Margaret and Robert and the girls are fixing you a feast."

"No doubt," said Janey.

****

When she and Luke returned to the Huxley house, Margaret had made dinner, Sylvie had helped her in the kitchen, and Louz had set the table. Tim disappeared as fast as he could after declining the invitation to join them for dinner.

Luke said, "It takes him a while to warm up to people. Plus, he don't, uh, *doesn't* see a lot of sophisticated city ladies like you."

Janey snorted and passed her hand in the air. "This is a beautiful place. Your family has a lot more than mine does. We run a diner. There's nothing sophisticated about it."

Supper consisted of fresh fruit, fried chicken, mashed potatoes, spring greens, and southern-style biscuits so buttery they didn't need any added. Margaret doled out huge servings, saying, "All of you girls could use more meat on your bones."

"That's too much!" Louz protested as her mother dropped a huge dollop of mashed potatoes on her plate.

Luke said, "I'll eat what you don't."

"It's so completely unfair," chimed in Sylvie, pointing at Luke. "He eats like a bear just out of hibernation and still stays a bag of bones."

Janey smiled. But she'd been in Luke's arms. He hadn't felt like a bag of bones. He was sturdy and stalwart and warm.

Luke countered with, "Don't be such a grouch. Louz is starting to change you."

Louz dropped her fork. "What did I do to you?" she said to Luke. "Sylvie called you a bag of bones, not me."

Luke shook his head and dug into his mashed potatoes, stirring extra butter into them in a circle.

"Yeah, but you can handle it, Louz."

Sylvie threw a haughty glance around. "Would everyone please stop trying to protect me? I'm seriously working on being a snot, like Louz."

Robert pointed his fork at Sylvie. "Enough. This is a dinner table, and we have a guest. Behave, now."

Sylvie faked contrition. "Sorry, Daddy."

After that, Luke and Robert talked about the lambs, how many they had counted and tagged, and their growth and health in general.

Louz shifted in her seat, then asked, "Could we please talk about something else? Poor Janey here is probably fighting off a bad case of the fuzzies."

Janey laughed. She hadn't heard that expression before. "I'm fine."

"We want to know all about living in the city," said Sylvie excitedly. "I lived in Maryville and went to college there, but I've never taken a step beyond Knoxville."

"Knoxville is nice," said Janey.

"But it couldn't be as exciting as Philadelphia. I want to know all about it."

Louz rolled her eyes, but the four females kept talking about places and people, while the men continued to discuss the crops, market prices, and how they would handle harvest season. They hoped that many of the local men who'd been fighting in Europe would come home now, safe and sound, and they could employ some of them.

Janey loosened up and enjoyed herself. Occasionally she noted eyes on her and glanced up to see Louz, wearing a studious expression, watching her as if trying to figure out something.

But after dinner it was Robert who asked to speak to her again, back in the parlor room on the sofa. She could tell something else was on his mind, maybe something he'd had to think about before saying it. Both Luke and Louz stood aside, talking quietly between themselves but within hearing range of Robert and Janey.

It took a while for Robert to get ready to speak. Margaret sat beside him but didn't start talking either. Minutes went by, interminable and silent.

Finally he got to what Janey sensed was hanging over him. He held his clasped hands down on his lap and cleared his throat. He swallowed, and she could see the Adam's apple move in his neck. His attempt to mask the fear in his voice gashed an instant slice through her heart.

"What was between you and Cole is private, and you don't have to tell me anything you don't want to," he began. "Luke told you about Cole's engagement to a local girl at the time he left here." He had to pause. "And he said it was a surprise to you."

She tried to keep her voice light. "Yes. He hadn't mentioned it."

His worry and confusion seemed only to worsen. "I just hope…I mean…I'd hate to think that my son…" He swallowed again, as though his throat had gone dry.

"That our son," Margaret added in the moment of silence.

Then Robert continued, "That our son could have wronged you in any way or hurt you or deceived you. Cole always had a bit of the outrageous in him while he was young, but he grew up into a good man."

Janey nodded.

"I hope he didn't leave any lies behind."

Janey could see the hesitancy in his eyes, the fear

that his memories of his son could be tarnished.

She touched his hand. By then Louz was watching, listening. So was Luke.

"Please don't spend a moment of time worrying. Despite our differences in backgrounds, Cole and I found we had a lot in common. He was a little lonely, away from home, and I guess I was lonely at the time, too. But there was nothing of romance between us. Cole and I struck up a fine friendship. Rest assured, we promised to write and remain friends for life, but that was all."

Relief spread on Robert's face like the opening of wings.

****

Luke drove her back as the stars came sparkling out of the ink sky and the moon began its slow rise. Out of the darkness inside the truck cab, she heard Luke's voice. "You're one amazing woman, Janey. It's easy to see why Cole fell so hard. Thank you for what you did back there."

After a moment, she said, "You heard."

"Yes, and so did Louz."

"Do you plan to say anything to the contrary?"

"No. I see no reason for them to believe other than what you said. No need to cause any more pain." He paused, drawing in a deep breath. "And for sparing them the truth, I greatly admire you." He said in a softer voice, "Fact is, you're one of the finest people I've ever known and I reckon one of the bravest."

Janey shook her head. "Again, I've certainly given you the wrong impression. I'm not brave at all." She stared through the windshield as the headlights beamed two wedges of light before them.

Todd came into her mind. Would he forgive her

when she went back? Did she want him to? It was difficult to imagine going back and picking up where they left off.

She said, "Right now, I feel pretty terrified about what lies ahead."

Luke pulled up in front of the hotel but didn't immediately hop out. "What do you mean?"

She shook her head. With no idea why she was saying this to Luke, she stumbled on, "Suddenly I'm afraid of going back, of the decisions I have to make when I get there, even going back to work—and I don't know why. Despite what I've learned here, it's been an escape, in a way. But it's also shown me what a foolish romantic I was just a couple of years ago. You've given me way too much credit again. Right now, I'm wary of everything the future holds."

He gazed her way with quiet resolve, and his eyes held sincerity. "Janey, I do understand."

His kindness intensified the sorrow, and a little sob seeped from her mouth. Heat and pressure gathered under her eyelids. She couldn't remember ever feeling so overwhelmed. But she fought back, swallowing the stinging tears.

He sat still without saying anything, and she was aware that he did nothing but watch and wait for her, should she want to talk more about it.

Slowly her composure returned, and she leveled her head.

She had embarrassed herself. It felt as if the day had played out over a hundred hours. Massive waves of emotion had washed over her and yet had left her dry.

Luke grabbed her hand and gently squeezed, and it came back. The way he'd held her that night. And the kissing, Luke's kiss. The memory hadn't faded, but it was almost impossible to believe it had happened; the night had taken on a fairytale quality.

Even harder to believe was that he'd been just as thrilled as she'd been that night, and then he hurt her. She supposed she had read him all wrong, and still, she longed for him. An irrational desire. It had been so easy and natural, for that short while that now felt like a lifetime ago, and then he'd changed overnight.

Luke was sweetness; he was also pain.

That reality came back again and again. If only they'd been allowed to hide away from it all and simply get to know each other and fall in love for months and months, years and years.

He said, "I'm so sorry this happened to you."

Her eyes still smarting, she gazed over his malleable face and said, "I know, but I'm being a baby. Look what you and your wonderful family are having to endure. I'll get past it, but what remains for those of you who knew Cole and loved him best, well, I guess it never goes away."

"It'll get better, though. We come from rugged stock. We'll always go on, we'll laugh and smile. Like Cole would've wanted."

"You're the courageous people," Janey said softly. "Not me."

"Yes, you too," replied Luke.

Chapter Thirteen

"Dancing in the Dark" - Artie Shaw, 1941
Gatlinburg, Thursday night, May 10, 1945

In her room, she set her handbag aside and decided to begin packing. She made the mistake of sitting on the edge of the bed first, however, and then couldn't move another muscle. It didn't come from physical exhaustion but more the emotional kind.

It was absolutely time to go home and try to get her mind back.

She swung wildly between two poles: sadness for Cole's family, all of them, and wishing she could do more to help them, and relief that, despite it all, she was going away. There was nothing left to do here. One feeling pulled her one way, and the next pulled her the other.

After opening her suitcase atop the bed, she began to empty the drawers. Folding her clothes, putting in her shoes, all but what she would wear the next day.

Finally she finished packing, retrieved the packet of Cole's last letters, and set them on the bedside table. She started to undress, planning to get into bed and read them, probably read again and again until she fell asleep.

A rap sounded on the door. Janey rebuttoned her blouse and opened the door to Louz, standing there waiting, a look of anticipation on her face.

"Louz!" she barely managed to get out. She had no idea what this sudden appearance meant.

"Janey," Louz answered, "may I come in?"

"Of course," Janey answered and opened the door all the way.

"Never fear," Louz said. "I'm not here to cause any trouble."

Louz had changed into a full-skirted, off-the-shoulder cocktail dress in shimmering navy, She'd added a fake beauty mark on her cheek, and on her face, nothing else but lipstick. She looked exotic, not rural in the least.

Janey swept her arm toward the bed, the only place in the room to sit. "Sit here on the bed with me."

Louz's eyes grazed over the packet of letters on the bedside table. "I see you're settling in for some reading, and I promise not to take long."

Janey enjoyed Louz. "Take all the time you need."

Louz sat and crossed her legs. "I want to thank you for saving my parents, but I know. I asked Luke if there had been more between you and Cole, and he said he couldn't say but doubted it. Poor Luke. My dear cousin cannot tell a convincing lie. It was written all over his face. So, yes, I do want to thank you for what you said to my mom and dad back there. Even though they don't deserve it. They should've sent you the letters." She sighed. "But I know something's missing here."

Janey thought she could discern Louz's meaning but didn't want to presume. "You're going to have to spell it out for me."

"I knew Cole the best of all. We were the black sheep of the larger family, you know. I still am, as I told you. Cole and I were always far too selfish and adventurous for our own good. Always getting in trouble. Making promises we couldn't deliver on. I'm no saint, and Cole certainly wasn't one. So don't think of sparing me. I already know you must have been waiting for him. Were you?"

"Yes."

"So how serious was it?"

Janey, feeling a bit invaded and puzzled, held onto her upper arms. Louz was demanding the truth, and she was an adult who seemed more than strong enough to take it, so why not tell her? "It was serious."

"How serious?"

"We were engaged."

"Just as I figured." Louz's eyes shifted elsewhere for a moment, then she stared back at Janey. "Today must have been horrible for you."

Janey sat down. "I'm fine. I've weathered worse." Even as she said the words, it hit her again. She hadn't been able to will away the ache of betrayal just yet. "Sure, I've found out that Cole wasn't exactly honest with me. He never mentioned Marlene or anyone anywhere else. I just assumed he'd told me all I needed to know. But I'm still certain Cole cared for me. My memory has shifted in some ways, but I still had the most romantic three days of my life."

Louz leaned back on her elbows. "You know, for Cole, every moment was a chance to do something extraordinary. And he wouldn't have spent three days with you if it hadn't been extraordinary."

"Thank you."

"We're so much alike. *Were* so much alike," she corrected herself wearing a melancholy expression, which she quickly whisked away.

"I understand Cole better than anyone. Truth be told,

two fellas in the army are writing me now. I guess you could say I've led them both down the primrose path. I sort of promised myself to both of them. I just couldn't stand seeing either one of them off with a broken heart. I couldn't hurt them then, but I'm going to have to crush one of them soon. Now that the war's over in Europe, I would think they'll be coming back. And I'm going to have to face the music."

Janey wasn't used to such honesty, especially from someone she'd just met. "You don't mince words, do you?"

"I have no patience for subtlety."

Janey smiled.

"And if I were you, I would've told everyone what Cole did to me. My sense of indignation would've gotten the better of me. I'd have to find someone to blame. Other than the dearly departed, of course. I always had such a soft spot for Cole." Louz seemed choked up for a moment, her chin quivering, but quickly checked herself. "I'm not nearly as kind as you are."

"The last thing I deserve is praise. This trip—well, I feel pretty stupid now. It certainly hasn't gone the way I thought it would. And…"

Louz waited.

"I have a guy back home. He didn't want me to come. And my boss didn't want me to leave right now either."

"Lordy. Who's the guy?" Louz asked.

"Someone I've dated for a year. He's pretty angry I came."

"Will he get over it?"

"I don't know. I left on shaky ground."

"Do you love him?"

The question, so penetrating, held her silent. No one had asked her if she loved Todd, not her parents, not Tessa, not any co-workers. They simply assumed. She had to ask herself now, and came up unsure. The happy times with him felt so long ago in the past.

"I'm fond of him, but I'm pretty sure we're not an item any longer."

"Fond? An item? That's a pretty tepid way of describing it."

Janey shrugged. "I'm kind of lost right now. Most of this trip has been completely the opposite of what I hoped for. I wanted to close the chapter of my life that held Cole in it, but now I have more questions than answers."

"And now there's another complication, isn't there?"

Did Louz know about that night on V-E Day with Luke? Local people had seen them together on V-E Day; she had to have heard. "What do you mean?"

Louz passed a hand in the air. "Never mind." She looked down at her nails. "Cole never tried to hurt anyone. He was just kind of...impulsive," she said gazing up again. "He lived every moment and he lived it to the max. But he definitely put himself first. Like I said, Cole and I inherited the self-centered characteristic that comes out of the family. Sylvie's so saintly she's almost not human. Tim, too. And no one will ever live up to them. Only Luke got the best of our blood. He's kind and unselfish but also very human. He's not perfect, but he's special."

Janey nodded.

A sudden spark of energy lit Louz's eyes. "Come out with me," she said abruptly, reminding Janey of Cole so much it stabbed. "It's Friday night, and everyone's still celebrating the Armistice. I know some places that'll be hopping. Come on. Worrying and waiting has gone out of style."

Janey gazed around. Her eyes landed on the letters, but she darted her glance away. She shrugged. Why not go out? Why not let loose and have some fun? It was her last night here after all, and she answered to no one. "I just might do that."

"Good girl," Louz said, "but I must warn you. Being seen out with me might besmirch your reputation."

"I think I can handle it. Besides, I'm not worried about my reputation. After all, I'm leaving tomorrow." She had to ask, "Are we going to a square dance?"

Louz laughed. "Contrary to public opinion, this town has a few hideaways not awash in mountain-man music and moonshine. I know exactly where to take you."

Janey changed into her dress, the same one she'd worn in Knoxville with Luke, and her best shoes, sling-back pumps with small crisscrossed leather straps across the toes. They walked away from the hotel, and Louz locked arms with Janey, enveloping her in a buttery sultry scent.

As their steps rapped the sidewalks, Louz said, "There's a hidden bar the tourists don't know about. An old former speakeasy. They actually do have moonshine there, but the Tennessee whiskey is excellent."

"Isn't moonshine illegal?" Janey queried. "I've sure seen a lot of it around here, and I've been meaning to ask."

"Illegal, yes, but most people, including the cops in this town, don't enforce anything like that. They might partake of the moonshine, too. Some of them, I mean. Their wives have no idea what their men are up to."

"It all sounds so very small town."

"Small town with big secrets, you know. But it's a nice place. It has many niceties but also some oddities. Even I like living here."

They ducked in behind some craft shops and then some heavy shrubs and entered what looked like a private home, but inside was a dark room and a long bar, a mirrored wall just barely illuminated behind it, the place heady with cigarette smoke.

With just a bit of light from candles and a subdued glow from wall sconces, the club was dark but not dreary. The scrubbed wooden floor and a single rose in a bud vase on each tiny table made the atmosphere spare but not boring. The backdrop—a wall painted in swirls and shades of magenta and sapphire—was interesting but not too interesting. It didn't take the focus off the music.

The bartender glanced up and tipped an imaginary hat. "Good to see you, Louz."

A man sitting on one of the barstools spun around. "Well, look what the cat dragged in." Then he saw Janey. "Sorry, miss. I didn't mean you."

"Louz's reputation precedes her," said another man.

Still another man appeared. "So who's this?"

Louz answered, "Janey from Philadelphia."

"What brings you here, Janey?" The man was tall and redheaded, with more freckles than an appaloosa.

Louz cut him off short. "Good Lord, are you really going to start with an interrogation?"

Changing tactics, the man, spreading his arms wide, said, "I'm offering you ladies anything you desire for the evening. What else could you ask for?"

"Maybe some class, Jimmy," said Louz, straight-faced.

Jimmy laughed, however. It seemed they all enjoyed Louz's sense of humor.

Then Louz introduced Janey to the men standing around them and moved on to the two bartenders, one a lady named Iris. The men seemed to be waiting for Louz to pick the evening's companion from amongst them. Pressed into her cocktail dress, Louz became a different person at night, as if she came truly alive after the sun went down, or maybe it was the club. When someone came up to the bar, she offered him a dazzling smile.

She whispered to Janey, "It's fun fending them off."

They sat at the bar. "Hit us with the best you have, Iris," Louz said.

Iris, who had bobbed blonde hair pulled back in victory rolls and wore the tightest pencil skirt Janey had ever seen, pulled out two shot glasses and plunked them down on the countertop, then filled them with an amber fluid. With honey-glazed skin and hair so silky it gleamed, Iris reminded Janey of an unusual animal. She asked no questions—and Janey sensed she was not so much disinterested, just lost in silent observation.

Louz clinked her shot glass with Janey's. "This, after all, is moonshine. You can't come to Tennessee without sampling some moonshine." They both downed their shots in one long gulp. Janey's throat burned, and her eyes teared up. She fought off the coughing and found herself smiling. She'd never taken anything straight before—what a heat going down!

"I knew I liked you from the start," said Louz. "We're going to get along just swell, you and me."

"I wish I had more time, but I'm leaving tomorrow."

"So you say."

Janey didn't know how to take that. A few men stopped by to greet Louz and introduce themselves to Janey.

Everyone was speaking to each other and flitting about, but their peering eyes rarely put Janey and Louz out of sight. They were the only two women in here alone, but more men and couples that Louz didn't know poured in.

Louz said, "It seems the tourists have found us."

Someone turned up the jukebox music, and happy people started dancing to jazz. Janey hadn't expected to find jazz fans here. Until now, any music she'd heard had been banjos and fiddles.

Something about that sultry music brought on an influx of feelings. Janey didn't feel the way she'd expected to feel about Cole here. Now he did feel more like a long-lost friend she'd helped along his way. And she would be leaving tomorrow with no idea what had really occurred with Luke. To her, it felt as real as this wood floor and the solid earth beneath her feet. But apparently it hadn't meant much to Luke.

Louz barked over the noise, "Let's dance."

"With each other?"

"Why not?"

"Of course. Why not?" Janey exclaimed.

They joined a throng of dancers cutting up the rug, so to speak. Big-band music felt more expected, rhythmic, and easy to dance to with a partner. This jazzy music was no such animal. It produced an intense beat that made Janey want to jump off the chair and dance like a spinning top gone haywire. The next song, a soft and sexy one, made her want to sway her arms and move her entire body like a snake. It seemed to give her permission to do anything she wanted.

"You're fun," screeched Louz over the sounds of glasses clinking, loud talk, and even louder music.

"*You're* fun," Janey said back.

"So am I," shouted a young man with raven-black hair slicked back. He inserted himself between Janey and Louz.

Louz nudged past him. "Sorry, Sam. This is a private party."

"You're breaking my heart, Louz. Like you always do."

"I'll take a raincheck, however," Louz said.

"Promise?"

Louz swatted at him. "Good Lord, will you just leave?"

He slinked away but wore a smile. Everyone seemed to know Louz, which came as no surprise to Janey. They all seemed to enjoy her, too, even though she was decidedly unconventional and bold. It was as if the war had changed things for women. Women had kept the war effort alive by working on just about everything on the home front; they'd held families and factories together. Women served, too, some even flew planes. And now it was finally coming to an end, but women had tasted power and freedom maybe for the first time, and none of them were going to be the same again. Even in a small tourist town surrounded by farms and ranches.

She and Louz ended up talking to some other young women, old schoolmates of Louz's, who treated Janey as if she was part of their inner circle. If she had to come up with one word to describe the people of Tennessee, at least this part of it, she would say, "friendly." Every one of those young women asked Janey questions about herself and seemed genuinely interested in what she said. They answered her questions openly, as if they'd known her for years.

Soon Louz was ready to move on, saying, "Let's blow this joint."

Louz led her to another hidden place with no signage, behind one of the new luxury hotels, and into a lower level private club, filled with the elite of the tourists, where the Champagne was flowing. On the stage, a band made up of mostly older men had set up. Dressed in identical black suits, the bandmembers had polished their shoes to a gleaming shine matching the spotless, mirror-like piano. Surely it would pass a white-glove test.

Surprising her, they started with a fast big-band type of tune that stirred the place like a whirlpool, pulling in everything around it. It whipped up something inside Janey, too, a longing that needed to be released. But who did she long for? Not Todd, not Cole, and she wouldn't allow herself to think it was Luke.

She applauded with vigor as the first song flowed into another. This was an older crowd, a place where perhaps the wealthier tourists made their own night life. In the pauses between songs, Janey could hear the ladies' bangles and bracelets clink as they talked with their hands and called each other "Darlin'."

Women in this place wore black cocktail dresses, with skyscraper-high heels on their feet. Men who looked like a mix of dandy and mobster completed the scene.

When a Champagne cork popped like a shot, the

place stilled for a moment, but then everyone returned to whatever remarkable dance step, perhaps the Lindy Hop or the Shim Sham, they'd been doing or whatever interesting subject they'd been talking about.

Sometimes Janey overheard the words "Nazi" and "Hitler" but not often. People seemed to drown their worries about the war in the Pacific in whatever wild concoction or deadly moonshine they'd been drinking and the vivacious conversations occurring about the club.

She lost track of Louz and slinked over to the Champagne cart, where a young waiter filled her a flute. As she waited for the foam to die down and she could ask for more, she glanced up at the man, who was really no more than a boy, maybe not even old enough to drink, yet here he was, surrounded by mostly older folks.

Janey said, "I imagine you hate these little soirees."

The boy's eyes slowly went wide. He forced a laugh and focused down as if embarrassed. "Not so, miss."

"Oh, come on," Janey said. "I'm surprised you haven't learned how to sleep standing up."

He really smiled then. "No, ma'am."

During a break, Louz introduced her to the bandmembers, and they talked it up until they started playing again. These men struck her as seasoned and worldly. Not a one asked her why she was here, why she was single, or any personal questions.

Her favorite, the bassist named Royce, was rotund like his instrument, the oldest of them, a happy rapscallion sort who said he'd grown up in Slidell, Louisiana with six brothers and one sister named Delia.

"You're like Delia," he said to Janey. He smelled of spearmint and wore a flower in his buttonhole. He moved his large body like a dancer behind his bass as he played. Graceful, at ease, as if he had been born to it. His wise eyes said he could read her like a sheet of music, and it didn't bother her a bit. "She was like a little ol' island surrounded by a sea of bad boys." He paused. "You know some of them bad boys hang out in these clubs, don't you?"

Janey decided to make light of his comment, but she wondered if he meant to warn her about anyone in particular or just men in general. "You're not old enough to be my father."

He smirked.

"Are you trying to tell me something?"

"Nothing in particular. Just want to make sure you got warned." He cocked his head. "You gonna be able to handle the heat?"

Janey hitched a hand on one hip and gave him a haughty stare. "I'm practically a glacier."

He laughed with an open mouth.

Janey saw Louz coming. By then Janey was yawning and thinking about all the traveling she was to start on the next day, even though the place was still so lively, fun, and friendly.

Louz stated firmly but with a smile, "I think we need to get you out of here."

They left the bar and passed through the hotel, exiting by the front doors. Outside was a small but lovely manicured outdoor sitting area, steps leading down into it. Janey barely remembered seeing it on the way in. Now she really wanted to get a closer look. Had there been a little pond?

She grabbed the night-damp staircase railing, and then somehow she slipped or something and she was on the bottom step. Stunned, Janey told herself she almost never fell, not even when she was a kid climbing trees and fences. Maybe the stress of traveling and everything that had transpired here was taking a toll.

But the path was slick, and she felt dizzy. Was she getting sick, or was it that shot of moonshine? Louz had her arm now and steered her determinedly down the sidewalk, past a rush of passersby who almost shoved them aside as most of the crowd was heading in the opposite direction. Then it seemed they were on the street. Janey lurched forward.

There was a half-second of engine sound and a scent of exhaust. Something hard hit her in the abdomen and she lost all air in her lungs.

She heard Louz scream. And then she was sliding down, down, and down more, until the pavement met her knees, a descent into something like death, she was aware of pitiful gasping sounds emerging from her throat just before everything went black.

Chapter Fourteen

"It Could Happen to You" - Jo Stafford, 1944
Gatlinburg, Thursday night, May 10, 1945

Swimming upward through dense waters that became lighter and brighter and then breaking through the surface into a blinding light, Janey must have regained consciousness within seconds. It couldn't have been long, because Louz was just then getting down on her knees and fanning Janey's face. Louz's eyes were wide as saucers, her smiles and laughter suddenly snatched away. She looked terrified.

Janey inhaled and felt air enter her lungs. She could breathe. That was good. She was still alive.

All the color had left Louz's face. Janey just then remembered the scream. Louz had screamed.

"I'm okay," Janey said, directed by some kind of natural instinct to reassure.

She had a sensation of floating now, as if she'd lost bodily weight and her ties to the earth. But really, she was okay. She couldn't have landed very hard, because she wasn't in pain. She didn't hit her head.

Louz sounded out of breath. "I thought you were dead, for a second."

Janey sat up. "I just fainted." Quickly she became aware that her right leg was under her body and the left one lay straight out.

A small crowd had gathered. She could hear, "Is she all right?" "Should we call for a doctor?" and such, but she focused on herself.

"Give her some air!" someone shouted, but Janey, although somewhat blinded by a bright light, could see others gathering in the surrounding darkness, pushing in.

Dear Lord, what happened?

As she pulled her leg out from under her, a sharp pain pierced through the right ankle joint as though a knife had gone through it. She gasped and took a hard look at her ankle, but it appeared fine.

Louz wore a mortified look. "Are you sure you're all right? I can't believe this. Just stay put. Maybe you shouldn't move. I'll get help."

Janey peered around at all the unknown faces, peering in. "No, don't leave me here alone. There's no need for any help. I can get up."

"Are you sure you aren't hurt?"

"I feel fine."

"Someone's calling a doctor and the police."

"The police?"

"You were hit by a car."

Janey shielded her eyes. The bright light was coming from headlights that hadn't been there before—or she didn't remember before. A man was standing by, looking as terrified as Louz did. His arms were crossed and his eyes were wide with fear. He had to be the driver.

She heard him say, "She stepped right in front of me. Just like that. I couldn't stop in time."

She started to get up.

Louz asked, "Wait, wait. Are you sure you can stand so soon?"

"Yes."

"Here," Louz said. "Let me help you, then. Get up slowly and lean on me."

Janey got up and stood, despite the pain in her ankle, which she didn't put any real weight on. Instead, she put her body weight on her left leg and let Louz hold her steady and balance her. Louz asked people to move aside.

With Louz's help, Janey hobbled up to standing and realized she was barefooted. What had happened to her shoes? "This is what I get for drinking that moonshine."

"Don't say that," Louz whispered. "Don't blame yourself or I'll beat you up even more."

A moment later a police car pulled up, and two officers got out. One questioned Janey, and one questioned the driver, whom Janey could now see was a forty-ish man, well-dressed in a suit. His car was a late-model Buick.

The officer was very kind and took Janey's name and local address, and Louz told the officer that the crowd had pushed a lot of people out into the street. Janey said she hadn't seen anything coming.

Louz insisted, "He didn't have his headlights on. He turned them on only after he hit her."

The officer, a man in uniform and hat, looked to be in his late twenties. The other officer was older, maybe in his forties. The young one interviewing them made notes on a pad, and then glancing up, said, "By the way, hello, Louz."

"Pleasure meeting you this way."

The older officer approached. "First things first. We have to get this young lady to a doctor."

"I'm not hurt," Janey said. "I'll just go back to my room. At the hotel. I can get there with Louz's help."

The young officer insisted, "Not so fast. We need to make sure you're not injured. Just give us another moment, and I'll take you in the patrol car."

He went about asking a few people questions and asking others to move on. But there was still a small crowd of concerned people watching their every move. Louz whispered under her breath to Janey, "Sorry about the attention. They mean well."

She helped Janey circle around to the back of the patrol car, and both got into the back seat and waited longer, until the younger officer finally slid into the driver's seat. All the while a heavy liquid-like weight was filling Janey's right ankle and moving down into her foot.

The young officer put on his lights but not his siren, thankfully. Were the lights really necessary?

As he turned around and headed to the hotel, Janey tried telling herself that her ankle didn't hurt. This throbbing pain couldn't be as bad as all *that*. To distract her thoughts, as they pulled away she glanced out the back window. *What in the world?* Was that the older officer cuffing the driver?

****

Louz helped Janey past the lobby and up one flight of stairs to get her settled in her room, and just after that, a doctor showed up. Apparently the hotel staff had called him. Or maybe the officer had. She didn't know and didn't care. She just wanted this over with.

An older, portly man, wearing glasses pushed down on his nose, greeted her with a smile. "Now what have you done with yourself, young lady?" He had a teasing manner but soon became serious. He asked questions such as what day it was, who the President was, and the like. Where she was hit in the abdomen was amazingly not even sore, so he was most concerned that she'd lost consciousness for a moment. But she was fully oriented and alert, so he concentrated on her ankle next. She told him where it hurt, right in the joint.

He finished feeling it up and down and then began flexing and extending her foot. "Does that hurt?"

"Yes."

He stopped. "Well the good news is I don't think it's broken, but it could be. It would be best if you got an X-ray in the morning, just to be sure."

"I think I just twisted it."

"Hmm, maybe. But you still need an X-ray tomorrow."

Janey shook her head. "That's impossible. I have to leave for Philadelphia first thing in the morning. I'll get an X-ray when I get home."

"That's not my advice. There's no way to tell for sure if it's just a sprain unless you get an X-ray, and if it's broken, it needs to be stabilized right away. You'll need a cast and crutches."

Then he took Janey's temperature, pulse, and blood pressure. "You have a slight fever. Have you been feeling a cold or a sore throat coming on?"

Janey swallowed and for the first time realized her throat was scratchy and dry, uncomfortable. "Maybe, yes," she said.

"You'll need a swab of your throat tomorrow, too," said the kind doctor.

"I'm sorry, but I have a job in Philadelphia. I have to be there Monday morning."

"That's not going to happen." A different voice. Only then did Janey realize that an older officer, not the one from the scene of the accident, had entered the room behind the doctor and was speaking to her. "Sorry to break the news, but I'm just telling the truth."

"What?" asked Janey.

Louz said, "Hello, Sheriff."

He tipped his hat. "Miss Louz." Then he looked at Janey again. "I'm Sheriff Snearl."

"Pleased to meet you," Janey said, although she wasn't pleased in the least. This was becoming more and more a debacle, an unnecessary one, at that.

The sheriff, a middle-aged man who looked as much farmer/rancher as almost everyone around here, said, "We need to take a sworn statement from you tomorrow at the station."

Janey's heart sank. "I can't do that. Sorry, but I'll lose my job if I'm not back in time. I'll give you a statement tonight, if you wish." Wincing from the pain in her ankle, she tried her best not to show it. She had to get everyone out of there. "Please, I'll be happy to tell you anything you want to know. But I did tell the story to the officer on the scene."

Snearl turned to Louz again. "We need a statement from you, too."

"Okay, but Janey needs to go home tomorrow."

The doctor piped in, "I understand she has a job, but I think she might be coming down with something, plus she has an injured ankle. It's my best judgment that she stay put for a while."

Louz repeated herself: "She has to go home."

Snearl said, "I'm sorry, but we really need her to stay."

Louz turned coy. "Why, if you can take a statement now?"

No response. Louz's charms weren't going to work on this sheriff man. Straight-faced again, Louz continued: "She's a friend of our family. If she says she can't stay, she can't stay. We'll vouch for her."

"There's going to be an investigation. We need to record her statement before she goes away." He turned back to Janey. "You ladies been drinking?" Sheriff Snearl asked with a grin.

Louz answered quickly, "Of course we've been drinking. Everyone's out drinking to celebrate the war's end. We had one shot of moonshine. That doesn't mean we deserved to be hit by a car."

"You were hit, too?" the sheriff asked with another grin.

With arms crossed now and her color high, Louz answered tartly but in a way that said she was only trying to help, "Certainly not. I'm speaking for my friend here."

Janey took a gulp of water. Someone had placed a glass on her bedside table. "I'm okay speaking for myself. The doctor has checked on me. I might have a cold coming on. No big deal. But there's nothing wrong with my head, and unless I'm being detained, I'm leaving tomorrow."

The doctor stood his ground. "That's not a good idea."

"I appreciate the concern," Janey said, "but I really do have to get back home. It's very important that I do."

The doctor and the sheriff stared at each other, the doctor rubbing his chin. "It looks like you're outnumbered," he said kindly.

Janey leaned back into her pillows. This couldn't be happening.

Louz and Snearl talked more, while the doctor gave

Janey two aspirin tablets and wrote out an order for an X-ray and a prescription for something "for pain" should she need it. Handing those things to Janey, he said, "Keep that foot elevated, don't walk on it except to go to the bathroom, and try not to put your weight on it. Put ice on it if it begins to swell."

Louz took the order and prescription and laid them on Janey's bedside table. "These are useless. There's no drug store in town, and you'll have to go to Maryville or Sevierville for an X-ray."

Janey stared at the ceiling. "I can't do that. There's no time."

How could this have happened? Her mind was racing. How could she not show up Monday? How could she let them know if she didn't make it? She'd have to make some long-distance calls. Why, oh, why had she come here?

She heard Snearl's voice. "I'm sorry for the trouble, but we'll be seeing you tomorrow, Miss Nichol." Then he started to leave her room.

She had the awful urge to yell after him, "No, you won't!" but stopped herself.

Lost in her worries, Janey realized that Luke had come into her room too. She felt his presence before she saw him, and it was reassuring, although she couldn't pinpoint why. Just an inexplicable feeling.

Luke was talking to the sheriff. After the doctor left, too, Louz seemed pensive. "I just remembered—I must have jinxed you. Remember when I asked if you were really leaving tomorrow? I don't know what got into me, but now…it feels…prophetic. I feel terrible now."

Janey lifted her head and said to Luke, "I'm still leaving here first thing in the morning."

Luke looked taken aback. "I just promised the sheriff you would stay."

"Why did you do that?"

"To get rid of him for you."

"Great. But I'll be good as new in the morning."

He pointed to her right ankle. "You sure about that?"

Boy, did it smart. Janey took a hard look. Her ankle had ballooned, and now all of her lower leg down to her toes throbbed like the dickens.

Silence as all three of them stared at her ankle, watching it getting worse before their eyes.

"I'll get ice somewhere," Louz said and headed for the door.

Luke paced the room, rubbing his chin, his brow furrowed, deep in thought. Janey watched him without caring if he noticed she stared. Why was he so troubled about this? She found it too difficult to turn away.

Even when she told herself to stop looking at him, her eyes moved from his head, lingered on his shoulders and his back as they tensed, and let go while he paced. Then she found his hands, which made her teary. A strange sensation on her skin felt as if his touch was still there. How could that evening on V-E Day have meant so much to her but not to him?

He stopped and gestured to the bed. "May I sit?"

Janey nodded, and he let himself down easy, as if she was made of glass that might break.

He seemed at a loss for words, and a look of pathetic guilt and regret took hold of his expression.

She asked him, "What's going on here? Why are they blowing this all out of proportion?"

He shook his head. "You won't believe it."

"Try me."

He almost laughed. "There have been feuds around here that go back to the Civil War days. This has something to do with that."

"You don't say."

"That's the unbelievable part. But it's true and quite quirky. There are some folks around here who still hold grudges."

Her mouth fell open. She shut it purposefully and said, "You're right. It *is* unbelievable."

Luke kept explaining. "Sheriff Snearl and the man driving—Jones, he's new back in town but has deep roots. He's building a hotel here, and he and Snearl are on different sides of some old family feud. So now you're caught up in the crossfire. Somehow you fell right into it."

"Can't you do anything?"

"I tried. Our family—we've never taken sides or gotten all swept up. But he wouldn't listen to reason."

"Can he really keep me here?"

Luke considered it for a moment. "If I were you, I wouldn't test it. He can do pretty much what he wants. He's got a lot of power in these parts."

This situation was getting more insane by the minute. "Wow," Janey said, slightly shaking her head. It was unbelievable, but when she made herself believe it, she also felt an undeniable optimism that she could work it out. She had to. "Who else could we talk to? There has to be someone who'll see how bizarre this is and let me go. Is there a judge here or something?"

"I think the sheriff has the jurisdiction in a situation like this. And, well, unfortunately he has legitimate grounds for concern. Apparently some bystanders told him Jones was drunk—"

"Are you serious?"

He nodded. "If he wasn't fit to drive, then he was negligent."

"His car wasn't damaged, was it?"

"I doubt it."

"So there's no reason for all the hoopla."

"Some of the bystanders said his headlights weren't on when he hit you. Others say they were. People are contradicting themselves all over the place."

Janey laughed pathetically. "Why can't they just leave well enough alone?"

"Because the sheriff wants to get to the bottom of it. He told me they're still interviewing people on the street. If it looks like Jones wasn't alert enough to drive and even forgot to put his headlights on, Snearl will probably throw the book at him. They don't like each other."

Janey raked her hands through her hair. "This is insane. I have to leave. At Walker Scott, they made a special exception for me, letting me take off even though I'd just started a new position, one with even more responsibility than I had before. I can't let them down. I have to be back on Monday."

Luke sat and studied her. His eyes wide open, he hid nothing, she was sure. Maybe he wasn't even capable of hiding anything. When he looked at her this way, it was like listening in on a private conversation with whatever he said to his soul. She'd already lost her anger, and as Louz had said, Luke was a good man. Then again, all the bad news she'd heard about here had come from Luke. So why had she lost her anger?

Probably because Luke showed no pretense, and even when he'd broken bad news to her, it felt more like giving her the truth that she deserved, not with any intention to hurt her. She admired the simple way he expressed himself, as if his words came straight from his mind with no forethought.

"This feels so unfair. I'll take responsibility for myself. If I don't go, I might lose my job. Will you help me?"

"I'll do the best I can."

His gaze changed to something more wanting, even though it landed softly on her as it always had. But she saw it. He felt something for her. He'd always seemed free to reveal his caring nature and even his vulnerability. Now he was not exactly hiding something, rather holding it back. She wished she could reach out and touch his face, tell *him* everything was going to be okay.

Instead, Janey laid her head back on the pillows and stared at the ceiling, studying some tiny hairline cracks in the paint she never would've noticed before.

Luke was still there. Just above a whisper, he said, "I bet you wish you'd never come here."

"You sure hit the nail on the head," she said into the ceiling. She couldn't quite fathom she *was* here, having this conversation. She felt like someone who'd accidentally awakened out of a deep sleep to find she'd stumbled into the wrong world. Tripping into the street, a car plowing into her, being detained by a sheriff... She was the smart sensible city girl who had it all under control. She was never late for work; she didn't call in sick. She was close to her family; she helped her parents in their diner. This, *this* could not be her life.

Luke finally spoke again, "You should never have gone out with Louz. She's well known to be trouble."

"She's your cousin."

"That doesn't mean she's not trouble."

Janey scoffed. "I happen to like her."

"Everyone likes Louz, and I love her. But the truth is, she can get others in trouble, too."

"She didn't force me to drink that moonshine. I did that all on my own."

"How did you happen to get in the street?"

"I was dizzy, so everything's hazy. I remember some flowers and a garden, steps, then seeing the street. Sort of."

"Try to remember. How you happened to be in the street. It could be important."

Janey sighed. Some things were coming back, rising out of the haze in her brain. "I think I was trying to get out of the crowd, but in truth, now, I have no idea."

****

After Louz returned with ice and made her an ice pack, Janey convinced Luke and her to leave and go back to the farm. The hotel staff had been warm and friendly and had left her alone, as she requested. She turned off the light and tried to sleep. But her ankle was worse. She couldn't get her mind off it. She stayed in bed as long as she could before she rose and hopped to the bathroom.

She removed her clothes down to her underwear, bra, and slip. That was all she could manage. More of the evening was coming back.

On the way back from the bathroom, she lost her balance and had to put her right foot down to get steady again. The ankle throbbed and ached even worse, with more frequent shooting pains.

Back in bed, Janey reapplied the ice pack. She had to get some sleep, and the swelling had to go down by the morning. But her ankle was getting even more puffy. The ice didn't seem to have had any effect. She tried moving only when necessary.

She turned off the light and rolled slightly onto her left side, keeping her right foot elevated on a spare pillow. She'd never imagined the trip turning out this way. Finding out about Marlene, that wild night with Luke, the missing letters, getting in a fight with a car...

With no warning, a chill came over her body and it felt as though someone threw cold water on her brain. The letters. Where were the letters from Cole?

She sat up and turned on the bedside light. Not on her bedside table where she'd left them. She opened the drawer in the table. Nothing there, either.

She peeked under the covers, which was nuts, then made herself get up and make a quick look around her room. Nothing. Anywhere.

What in the world? Where were Cole's letters?

Chapter Fifteen

"Paper Doll" - The Mills Brothers, 1940
Gatlinburg, Friday, May 11, 1945

In the wee hours, finally, she lost herself in a sleep that denied her aching ankle, forgave the clouds that had swept in to cover the stars, and blocked the sounds of cars in the parking lot below and the main street beyond.

She awakened not sure where she was, her head filled with the confusing sludge that follows an almost sleepless night. In a rush, she remembered. That had to have been one of the craziest nights of her life. But it was over now. Finally she could begin the journey back.

A knock on the door made her roll over on her side. The clock read just after 7:00. She and Luke should leave for Knoxville soon so she could get on a train there. He'd probably come to pick her up.

Oh, dear Lord, the pain in her ankle! The ice in her pack had melted, and the pillow was wet. Now her lower leg ached and was also freezing cold.

Someone knocked again. She said loudly, "Coming."

The door was locked—she would have to get up. She tried to get to the door by hopping on her left foot but had to check herself a couple of times, and the pain of any pressure put on her right foot made it feel as if every bone was fractured.

She opened the door to find Louz and Luke standing there, both wearing the same inquisitive look.

"How is it?" Louz asked, not bothering with any pleasantries.

"Not good."

Louz helped her back to the bed. Janey winced at putting her legs back up. Not until then did she realize all she wore was her underclothing and slip. Louz didn't seem to notice, and Luke was trying to act as though he hadn't either.

"It doesn't look like you'll be catching a train in Knoxville today," said Louz. Luke was still standing by.

"Please don't say that."

"How many trains do you have to get on and off to get home?" Luke finally asked.

"There were quite a few stops on the way here. I suppose it'll be the same going back."

"You won't be able to do it," Louz insisted. "You can hardly move from here to the door."

Janey looked at her ankle. She hated to admit it, but even she wasn't sure she could handle train travel with her ankle the way it was.

"This is a disaster," she said. What would Mr. Walker do? What would Lorraine do? She might have to kiss her promotion goodbye. Everything she'd worked for! Her eyes smarting, she had to look away. "I might have to make some long-distance calls."

"And you have to get that X-ray and make your statement to the sheriff," Luke added.

"Thanks for reminding me," Janey said and smiled to let him know she wasn't mad at him. "I'd almost forgotten."

"You can't get it all done without our help. Then,

191

after that, you have to rest. There's no way you can leave today," ordered Louz.

"But my job…"

"I'll take you." It came from Luke.

Janey looked up at Luke, hard. "What?"

"We can start driving after the X-ray and the sheriff. I'll get you to Philadelphia by Monday morning, even if I have to drive all night."

Janey shook her head. "But you're busy here. What about that?"

He answered, "I'll get a kid from town and make Louz and Sylvie help with the sheep."

Louz poked him. "Mom already treats us like slaves in the house."

"Seriously," Janey said, "what about the gasoline?"

"Farmers get all we want, remember?"

"Oh, okay. Still…it's too much to ask."

"You didn't ask. I offered," Luke said. "So we better start rolling, get on the road as soon as possible."

Pensive, Janey faced away and focused on the wall. When she looked back, she caught Luke gazing down at her partially clad body like someone might admire a painting. But was there also some lust in his gaze? At least he was human.

Yes, Louz, you were right. He is human.

"It's no one's fault but mine—the moonshine part, that is," Janey finally said. "You shouldn't have to turn your life upside down."

Luke glanced away toward Louz. "It's also partly Louz's fault."

Louz poked him again.

Looking back at Janey and keeping his focus on her face, Luke continued: "I want to do it. It's not an obligation. I want to take you, but I gotta go make some calls."

She stopped arguing. She couldn't help but feel uplifted at the thought of getting back on time. But she shifted uncomfortably on the bed. "I'm not sure I can let you do that, but I do want to get started on all the other things, as soon as possible."

Louz stayed in the room to help Janey dress and finish packing while Luke went to the front desk, checking her out of the hotel and making phone calls. With help, she could move slowly.

In a rush, she remembered the letters. She grabbed Louz's arm. "My letters from Cole. They're missing."

"You're kidding!"

"They were sitting right here on the bedside table. I was going to read them, but then you turned up."

"You must have moved them."

"I didn't."

"I'm going to take a look around anyway." Louz moved to the dresser and opened the top drawer, then searched the drawer and produced nothing. "You're right," Louz finally said. "They're not here. Someone must have taken them. But for now, we have to go get that X-ray.

Janey let the letters leave her mind as she slipped her left foot into one of her tie-up, low-heeled traveling shoes, then tried absentmindedly to put the other one on her right foot. Due to the swelling, she couldn't squeeze it in, and she let out a little yelp.

"Don't push it," said Louz, playing the nurse. "If it's broken, you could make it worse."

"It's not broken. I'm sure of it."

"By the way," said Louz, "I went back and looked

last night. But I never could find your shoes."

****

In Maryville, Janey had to go to the emergency room. A different doctor, who reminded Janey of a rabbit with his dominant nose and upper lip, came into the treatment room and introduced himself. Not unattractive but not handsome either, he did have interesting eyes, blue-gray with a darker ring around the irises.

The X-rays showed that Janey had a simple fracture of one of the bones in the ankle joint, a clean break but a break, nonetheless. After the doctor returned with the news, he told her she needed a cast, but the ankle was too swollen to apply it today. Again she had to tell another person that she had travel plans and it was imperative that she keep them. On the drive there, she'd already decided to take Luke up on his offer. In a private vehicle, they could do it. They could get her back in time.

But the doctor nixed those plans. "I'm going to stabilize it with a wrap today, an adhesive bandage." He opened a pale yellow can and pulled out a roll, four inches wide. "No more ice. You'll need to come back tomorrow. If the swelling is down, then we'll apply the cast."

Janey's heart plummeted into her stomach, and her thoughts came in a swirl. Would she be able to work with a cast on? Would they let her? She wouldn't be able to move around as fast, obviously, but she could still do her job. "Can't that be done in Philadelphia?"

"You need to stay off it and come in daily. No trying to walk on it, or the break could get worse. Young people's bones heal quickly, but there's always a chance of further damage if you do too much."

"Even with the bandage on?"

He nodded. "Keep the bandage on, of course, and keep the leg elevated to prevent swelling."

"I'll be careful. I can do that while heading back, though, can't I?"

"You've had a shock to your system." He pointed at her foot. "Do you want that ankle to heal right or not?"

She stilled.

"You need to stay put." He pointed at her now. "That's doctor's orders."

She wished Luke and Louz hadn't heard that. She might have been tempted to tell them she'd been cleared to go.

The good news was that she no longer had a fever, and her throat was clear. So that problem had been alleviated. The doctor left, and that was that. Only Louz said, "I'm glad we heard what he said. You wouldn't have told us, would you?"

Janey shook her head.

"You are one determined lady, willing to bend the truth a bit to get your way," Luke said with a little smile.

"Only here. I used to be an honest Abe. But Tennessee has pushed me to my limits."

"And this Tennessean is beginning to read your mind," said Luke.

Janey was sitting on the treatment table, already worn out, already disbelieving *again* that this wasn't just a nightmare. A few tears sprang into her eyes. "I've never had a broken bone, ever," she said to Luke and Louz, who were standing to the side of the table, not moving, not talking, just solemnly observing now, all admonishments evaporated, as she swiped at the tears.

Then came a couple of pathetic sobs, her nose running, and huge tears rolling down her cheeks, ruining what little makeup she'd been able to put on this morning. She was pathetic. With all the pain and suffering around the world, here she was crying over a fractured ankle. What a baby she was being! But Louz and Luke didn't say a word. Louz handed her a handkerchief. Luke came forward, took the back of her head gently in his hand, and pulled her cheek in against his chest, which made Janey cry even harder.

By the time she'd been fitted with crutches, it was going on 2:00 in the afternoon. At last, she was discharged from the Emergency Room.

In Luke's truck, Louz squeezed in the middle of the bench seat, and he started the engine, then looked over past Louz to Janey. "Now for the hard part."

Louz chuffed out a laugh and said, "Smart aleck."

"How could it get any harder?" Janey asked, then saw a way out. "Besides, the doctor said I need to rest. Maybe I don't have to go see the sheriff after all."

That was met with silence.

Janey asked, "Do I really need to go?"

Luke sighed. "I'd advise getting it over with."

"For once, I agree with my cousin," said Louz. "And I have to go anyway. They know where to find *me*."

****

After exchanging some dollar bills for change, Luke pulled up to a pay phone, where Janey talked to an operator and dropped coins as instructed. Then she made calls to Tessa and to Walker Scott, letting them know about her injury. The factory was working around the clock, so she left a message with one of the weekend supervisors, who promised he would get it up to the office building first thing Monday morning. Janey asked Tessa to call Lorraine on Monday morning, too, just in case she didn't get that message.

After Janey had given her the short version, Tessa said, "I should come out there."

"No! Aren't you in the middle of finals?"

"Yes, but it makes me feel ill that you're hurt."

"I'm fine. I called *you* because I expect you to remain calm. Imagine if I told Daddy. It's up to you to convince him I'm going to be okay. Don't you go batty on me."

"I can't help it. It's tough to picture you down there dealing with this by yourself."

"Don't worry about it any longer."

"But you're having to go through this alone."

Janey gazed toward Luke and Louz, waiting by the truck. It was amazing how adversity brought people together, and it was further amazing how close she felt to both of them, as if they'd known each other a lifetime. They were treating her like family, and after all, the accident had been her fault. But no one said a word of admonishment to her. She and this family had recently been through a lot, and they understood each other.

"Not to worry, Tess. I'm not alone," she finally said to her sister.

Chapter Sixteen

"This Is No Laughing Matter" - Charlie Spivak and his Orchestra, 1942
Gatlinburg, Friday, May 11, 1945

She sat in a small room at a table in front of Sherrif Snearl and another man called Williams—a district attorney or something like that—who had slicked-back silver-and-black hair and a small face. Louz had already gone in and given a statement while she and Luke waited in silence, both of them grim-faced.

In the room they used for interrogations, a woman had been brought in to put everything down on paper. Sitting against the wall was another, younger man who, strangely, reminded Janey of a smaller Todd.

Everyone greeted each other pleasantly. It seemed they were all friends.

Rationally, she knew she was there to give a statement, that she wasn't under arrest or a suspect in a crime, and yet it felt that way. There was a strange atmosphere in a police station, even a small-town one, and she found herself somewhat nervous until she managed a way to mentally brush it off.

Since the accident, Janey had become more clear-headed. A lot of the night before had come back, sharp and detailed, but not everything.

Behind them in the room, a window blocked the sun,

except for bands of light that cut in between the Venetian blinds and made eerie-looking stripes on the opposite walls. Stripes, like prison uniforms.

The presumed district attorney introduced himself and asked, "Ready to begin?"

So he would be conducting this interview. The quiet before her reply was long and tedious. Janey held tightly to her purse in her lap like a shield. How had the case of nerves crept back over her? She had only to tell the truth.

After she had stated her name, birthdate, and current address, the DA said, "Tell me about the events leading up to the accident last night."

"Well, I went out to a place with Louz. I had one shot of moonshine. Then we moved on to another place, and we danced some more. I started not feeling well."

Williams leaned back in his chair, but his eyes never left Janey's, his bottle-brush eyebrows unmoving. "Would you say you were intoxicated?"

Janey snorted out a laugh. "I didn't feel drunk, but in truth, I've never been one to drink, and that was my first moonshine."

Williams' eyes showed sympathy. "Don't worry about it. You're not being accused of any wrongdoing. You're going to be fine. Okay?"

Janey nodded.

He rocked forward and made a note on a pad that sat on the table and then set his hooded gaze on her again. "Go on."

"On the sidewalk, we were sort of fighting our way through a stream of people all out doing the same thing we'd been doing, and most of them were heading in the opposite direction. Before I knew it, I was in the street, and that's where I was hit."

"What else do you remember?"

She held his gaze and didn't blink. "Nothing. Until I woke up."

Williams tilted forward and toyed with a pen on table. "What about just before you were hit—did you see any sign a car was coming?"

"No."

"Did you see headlights or hear a car?"

"Not really. Maybe a hint of an engine sound."

"Do you remember anyone shouting at you or warning you in any way?"

"No."

"Were you pushed into the street?'

"I don't remember any deliberate shoving or pushing. Even if I got pushed out, it was an accident. I'm sure of that."

"What else?"

"I don't think there's anything else. But those last moments are still unclear. I don't remember seeing any lights, but truth be told, I've never drank like I did last night, and I don't know if that had something to do with it or not. I heard the driver say I stepped out in front of him, and I think that could be true. I could've stepped out in front of him."

Williams's face was a sheet of nothingness. But it was obvious by the look on the sheriff's face that this was not what he wanted to hear.

The DA went on, "It's important for you to remember about the headlights. Louise Parker's statement is inconsistent with yours. Did you see any headlights?"

"Not that I can recall, but as I just said, most of the night has come back to me, but the part right before the car hit me is still sort of—blank."

He waited for a moment, his face still unreadable. "If you'd seen headlights, do you think you would've realized a car was coming?"

"I don't know. Maybe yes, maybe no."

Williams and Snearl sat quietly for a moment, and Williams's tapping of his pen on the tabletop began to sound impatient. After a few protracted moments, they excused themselves and stepped out of the room, and when they returned, Williams didn't come back.

Snearl said, "Sorry for the trouble, Miss Nichol. You're free to go," and nothing more.

He stayed behind to help her as she swept out of the room and headed down the hall toward the front. She was almost out of the office area, when she heard, "Miss Nichol."

Turning, she saw the man who resembled Todd, the younger man—or officer—or whatever—who'd been in the office and had not said a word.

"I'm Officer Bates, by the way."

Janey nodded.

"I must apologize for all this," he said in a clear, low voice. "I'm sorry you had to come here—I can see it has unnerved you... What else can I say?" In his eyes was the softness of a true apology.

She raised her chin. "Thank you."

"Thank you for coming here and being so honest with us."

"Gatlinburg has old feuds, I hear," said Janey.

Bates nodded. "True. It's kind of a weird tradition."

Janey tilted her head toward a waiting area, where Luke and Louz were waiting. "Thank you."

Back in the presence of Luke and Louz, Janey

inhaled deeply and released the police experience in a long stream of breath. On the road again back toward Gatlinburg, she took in the scenery, which seemed to change with each cloud passing overhead and each turn in the road, making her pensive and reflective.

Despite it all, she had learned something here. She felt changed, permanently altered. As though the experiences here had revealed a new layer of herself that now couldn't be sealed again. True, some of it had been heartbreaking, but other things had been illuminating. Here she'd finally learned the truth about Cole. Betrayal was an awful pain, but she had endured it and accepted it. She'd never been injured like this before, and yet she was managing, along with the help of nice people.

She'd experienced a magic-filled accidental date and felt something she'd longed for all her life but didn't know it. She'd finally felt what she was really waiting for. But Luke didn't feel the same way. And still she felt pulled by a magnetic and mysterious current toward the man, even though she knew currents could be dangerous. They could take you to all sorts of perilous places, and then drown you. And still, here she was. She was enduring it because she had to, but getting over Luke was not going to be easy.

At least she wasn't alone. Tessa's worries were unfounded.

She told Luke and Louz what had happened with the sheriff.

Luke chimed in, "He was itching to get something on Jones, but you nipped that in the bud."

"Even though I think Jones had forgotten to turn his lights on, the charges probably won't stand because you didn't corroborate."

"Sorry."

"No, it's okay," Louz said and passed a hand in the air. "I didn't care about nailing Jones, but the sheriff sure did."

"I hope he doesn't hold a grudge?"

Both Louz and Luke laughed. Then Louz said, "Just try not to have any more contact with him."

"But no harm done," Janey said, backtracking. "It wasn't exactly a social call, and Bates did apologize for the whole thing." She wouldn't go on and tell them how she'd felt. What did it matter now anyway?

Janey focused on the road ahead. It hit her again that she wouldn't be leaving today. That was the really bad news. She had to reach deep for her voice. In a pitch barely above a whisper, she managed, "Guess I have to go back and check into the hotel again."

"That's not where we're going," said Louz.

"I hope the hotel will have an available room."

"Forget it," Luke interjected. "We'll have none of that," he said. "We're not leaving you alone there."

"I'm fine alone."

"Like I said, forget it. I'm driving, and I've already made the decision."

Janey didn't like people making decisions for her. This situation had already made her feel helpless, and normally she hated that. But in this instance, she didn't mind having someone, whom she knew wished her only the best, making some decisions on her behalf.

"You're going home with us," Luke said. "And that's that."

Chapter Seventeen

"Star Dust" - Artie Shaw, 1940
Gatlinburg, Friday, May 11, 1945

Apparently Luke had already called his aunt and uncle and told them what had happened at the Emergency Room. He and Louz had made the decision that she would stay with the Huxleys in Sylvie's room.

"Then where's Sylvie to sleep?" asked Janey.

"She'll move in with me," answered Louz.

"That's way too much trouble. I can take the sofa."

Louz rolled her eyes. "It's already been decided. We're in charge now. Sylvie's so annoying she might be dead by the time this is over, but I'll try to suppress my urges."

"I have a sister, too," Janey said. "I love her to death, but she talks too much. My father calls it her flapdoodle. I have to take breaks from her here and there."

"Sylvie not only talks too much, she's almost always in a state of dreaminess, off in the clouds. And she tells you her every thought. It's exhausting."

Luke flicked eyes over her that shined, fully alive. "As I said, our family has something of everything."

Janey smiled. "I hate that I'm putting Sylvia out of her room."

"End of discussion, please?" said Luke.

"We've heard the last of this," Louz stated with

finality. "Don't be like Sylvie and talk too much. That's an order. I learned from the doctor back there that orders are all that work with you."

Janey grinned but kept her mouth shut. It did feel comforting that she wouldn't be lying in a hotel room with no one around. It was nice to think someone would be nearby. "I can't thank you enough."

"Don't thank us yet. Prepare to have huge plates of food pushed on you. My mother will bake, like it's a party. And Sylvie will drive you batty with endless chatter, believe me," said Louz.

The skies cleared, and the sun came out. It was a good sign.

****

Back at the Huxley house, Margaret and Robert were waiting at the door, smiling and enthusiastic as if this was cause for celebration. Sylvie was dolled up in a pink-and-black, floral-print rayon dress with substantial shoulder pads and a small belt at the waist. Her face was beamy. "I'm so glad we'll have you for longer." She bounced on her toes.

Janey smiled.

Louz whispered to her, "Don't worry. I'll make sure you get some peace."

Janey got to practice climbing steps on her crutches and easily made it up onto the porch.

Margaret said, "Come in, come in. I'm so sorry what happened to you, dear." She sent an admonishing glare to Louz. "And even sorrier that it had anything to do with Louz."

Louz rolled her eyes, and Janey said, "It's okay."

"We're so pleased to host you," continued Margaret, and Robert nodded.

Inside, Janey had to manage a full staircase, but did so as though she'd been born with crutches. Luke went up step by step behind her to assist if needed, or in worst case, break her fall should she falter.

They showed her to a bedroom decked out in ruffles and hues of blue and pink. Of course this was Sylvie's room; it reminded Janey of Easter. The window curtains had been pulled back, allowing sunshine in. Everything had been polished and dusted. On the bedside table was a vase filled with freshly picked wildflowers—such a nice touch. Their kindness was humbling.

As all three women helped her unpack and get settled in, she lowered herself to the bed and lifted her legs. The ankle was less painful with the bandage on it, and the doctor had given her some "ease medicine."

A buzz in the air, and then a dark thing passed between Louz and Sylvie.

Sylvie screeched, "It's a bee!" and began swatting at the air and crouching. "I hate bees!"

"Good job, Mother," said Louz. "You managed to bring in a bee with the flowers."

"Oh, dear," said Margaret. The bee swerved in the air very close to her face. She screamed, too.

Louz laughed out loud, and Janey couldn't help joining her. As her mother and younger sister continued to wither and back away, Louz followed the bee to the window and gently trapped it against the glass with a cupped hand.

Janey finally stopped laughing. She looked at Sylvie. "I never would've guessed it. You're a farm girl, so I wouldn't have thought…after all."

"I'm terrified of bees and wasps, even moths," said Sylvie. "It's Mom's fault. She passed the fear on to me."

"Don't get stung!" Margaret ordered Louz, who gently captured the bee in her hand. "Sylvie, open the window."

"Do I have to?"

"It's not even the stinging kind!" insisted Louz.

While cringing and keeping as much distance as possible between her and the bee in Louz's hand, Sylvie opened the window a few inches, and Louz released the bee.

Just then the door flew open and Robert and Luke barged in wearing fraught expressions. "What's all the screaming about?" demanded Robert.

Sylvie and her mother broke out laughing.

Louz glanced at Janey. "I told you this was going to be a trial."

When Janey stopped laughing, she hated to admit that she was tired. The others seemed to know it. Everyone left except for Louz, who sat down on the edge of the bed.

"I'm going to leave you alone, and…I've been pooh-poohing it, but I do owe you an apology."

Janey replied, "You do not."

Louz sighed hugely. "I wanted you to stay longer, but not this way. I'm so bullheaded and used to getting what I want, I fear my wishes might have grown into an unconscious but full-blown conspiracy to keep you here."

"Nonsense," said Janey as she laid her head back on the pillow.

"My will is strong, but enough talk," Louz announced and pulled the drapes closed. "Take a nap."

As Louz was leaving the room and closing the door behind her, Janey stopped her. "Louz?" she asked. "Why did you want me to stay longer?"

Louz smiled. "I'll say it again. Enough talk already."

An hour or so later, a current in the air flowed across her face and neck. Instinctively, she opened her eyes and turned sharply toward the side of the bed. Luke was peeking inside her door. He gazed upon her as if she was a rare species. She wasn't alarmed, but instead, it felt warm and only a little bit intrusive.

In a low voice, he said, "I'm sorry. I didn't mean to wake you."

She cleared her throat and whispered, "It's okay."

He took a step in. "Crazy, but I got worried. I needed to check on you. Make sure you're okay. Is your ankle hurting? Do you need some aspirin?"

Janey sat up and leaned back against the headboard. "I'm fine. This family would never let anything happen to me. I've never been doted on so much in all my life."

"They probably feel like they owe you somewhat, but they wouldn't be doing it if they didn't really like you. You don't realize how exceptional you are."

Janey laughed. "There's nothing exceptional about me. You, the people here, your family, now, they're exceptional."

"I don't believe your modesty. You must have to fend off men all the time."

"Not so," she said laughing again. "I'm well past my prime."

"According to who?"

"Almost everybody, to tell you the truth. Besides, before the war it was raining men; now they're few and far between."

"But you're a looker, plus you have a quick wit."

A little laugh escaped her. "I don't think I've ever

received so many compliments, either. I could get used to this. Even if I don't believe them all, you can keep them coming."

"My cup runneth over."

"This is an odd conversation."

He laughed silently. "I agree with you. I told you it was crazy, but I had to see you. And I had another reason." He reached inside his jacket and retrieved a bundle of letters he'd had in there. Her letters!

"You took them?" she asked.

"Yeah, when all those people were in your hotel room, the letters were lying out in clear sight of everybody, and I was afraid someone might not be able to resist temptation and would take them. So I got them out of there. I didn't open them," Luke said and handed them over.

Janey ran her hands over them. True, they hadn't been opened. "Thanks for holding onto them for me. Ever since I've been here, I've caused trouble. And now with this injury, I hope I haven't disturbed your peace of mind."

He harrumphed pathetically but with a smile. "You've disturbed my peace of mind ever since I first laid eyes on you."

Even in the low light, she could see his calm but anticipatory expression. And the way he said self-effacing words laced with humor always gave her pause. "I'm going to take that as another compliment."

"Yes," he said almost silently, "you should."

Again, she didn't know how to take his praise and attention. She couldn't stop feeling drawn to him. *Perhaps things you've lost feel sweeter somehow.* She couldn't shake the feeling that meeting him and that night together were the beginning of her real life. For the first time she'd breathed in the same way with a man, in the same inner world, even though their pasts were so different. It felt as though he'd been with her all night. She had the urge to touch him again, kiss him again. And she should care nothing about him.

How did other people do this? How did they endure ambiguity and heartache? Why did they keep trying? She asked herself these questions, although her body had already answered them. Stunned by her own weakness for Luke, she couldn't move for a moment.

It emanated from him, too. But she felt certain he'd never act on it again, especially not here. He whispered, "How's the swelling?"

This was safe territory. "Better, I think. The bandage is loose. So it must be going down."

"That's good news," he said. "I'll let you get back to sleep."

"Leaving so soon?"

He hesitated. "Do you need anything?"

I need you, her mind screamed, but she shook her head.

He moved toward the door. "Feel better, Janey."

She stopped him again. "Luke, if I can get the cast tomorrow, would you still drive me to Philadelphia? I hate to ask, but if I can get back to work by Monday, it would mean a lot to me."

"Of course I'll take you. We can drive straight through."

"It's just that I have a new post, a recent promotion." She stopped herself from explaining further.

"I understand."

"I want to leave for the hospital as early as you can

manage."

"Just tell me when to be here."

"Daybreak?" she asked. "I don't want to wake everyone up while it's still dark."

"Not to worry. Farmers and their families tend to get up early."

She paused, then said, "Thank you, Luke."

But before she could figure out why he'd really been there, he left. And oddly, as he took each step, it felt as if he were slipping away with something important.

Janey flopped down on her back against the pillows. They'd spent a lot of time together by then, but she still couldn't figure him out. She looked down at the letters in her lap. This time, she didn't leave them out—she put them in a drawer. Even after she tucked them into some of her clothing and went back to bed, something was nagging at her. Luke seemed as truthful as could be, but it was odd that he took the letters during those chaotic moments in her hotel and didn't mention it until now. Was there another reason he'd taken the letters?

****

By the time supper was served, Janey felt rested and ready to go downstairs. But the worry over her job had not left her yet. She had no idea what her future would be at Walker Scott now. Of course they would understand that breaking her ankle was unexpected and not her fault, but still, they needed her. They'd probably bring up someone else in her absence to help. What if it turned out they liked the new secretary better than her? It was hard to think about that. Janey had a house to take care of, a mortgage, and bills. And she read in the paper that women everywhere were already beginning to lose their wartime jobs. The job market would be flooded with them. Plus there were many good secretaries on Fourteen who could be promoted and would be thrilled to take her place.

Luke had left the Huxley house, and a tiny twinge of disappointment coursed through her. But of course he would go home to eat with his own family.

At the dinner table, Louz filled her mother, father, and sister in on all the details of the day, and Janey described her interview with the police and the sheriff's reaction.

"I'm glad he didn't get what he wanted, especially if Jones didn't deserve it. Serves him right," said Margaret as she served the fruit bowls.

"At least he didn't abuse his power," said Robert. "We're wary of him. We didn't vote for him, and he knows it."

"How does he know?"

They all laughed. "He knows," replied Robert.

When Margaret brought out the pork chops, she served everyone and then started to cut Janey's into bite-sized pieces.

"Mother!" said Louz. "There's nothing wrong with her hands!"

Margaret stopped, looking perplexed. "But I want her to conserve her energy."

Janey tried to stifle a laugh. Even Sylvie was covering her face to keep from busting out.

Louz said, "Good Lord, Mom. She's not an invalid."

Robert peeked up from his food. "Don't use the Lord's name in vain, Louz."

"Good *Lord*?"

"You heard me."

For the rest of the evening, Janey sat and ate quietly,

simply enjoying the playful comradery and sense of humor that circulated among this family. A meal like this was something she'd experienced only rarely. Her parents always worked the dinner hour, which meant wolfing down something on the run in between customers or grabbing a few bites at the end of the day. Sure, they'd shared Thanksgiving, Christmas, and Easter dinners, but it was nothing like what the Huxleys enjoyed every day.

Over dessert, they lingered and talked until the night air rolled in and darkness lifted out of the ground.

Luke rapped lightly on the door frame and walked into the dining room. At first sight of him, Janey momentarily lost bodily weight and her ties to the earth. How could this be? How had this man and one night with him affected her so? He was a shepherd, which almost sounded like a joke. Their lives were opposites. They shouldn't have been attracted to each other at all.

But the sight of him struck her through with powerful feelings of vulnerability, intense pleasure, and then disbelief and some shame. It was getting worse each time she saw him. The very short glance she took filled her with all that and more. She kept imagining she was back there on that V-E Day night, his arms around her, his scent, the way he kissed her—like a dying man, dying for what they had together. And the way she could feel his heart beating despite what else they were doing. His beating heart always there, as if in her hand, and the sensation of rightness, perfectly centered, surrounding her, and emanating all the way inside. His was a tender soul, and yet the fiercest one she'd ever known.

With a great smile of satisfaction, he handed Janey a fresh bouquet of wildflowers in a Mason jar tied with a ribbon. "No bees in this bunch, I promise."

Sylvie screeched, "Did you check? Are you sure?"

He smiled. "I checked."

"Will you calm down?" Louz admonished Sylvie.

"Thank you," Janey said to Luke, finding herself so appreciative of the kindness shown, it moved her. She smelled the flowers and gazed up at Luke, who seemed appreciative, too. She said in barely above a whisper, "I didn't peg you as the wildflower-picking sort."

"You haven't seen nothing yet," he said. "I've got another surprise outside."

Janey grabbed her crutches. "Oh, please, do show me."

They excused themselves, and the others seemed content to let them go outside by themselves.

On the lawn area in front of the house, Luke had set out three bent-wood porch chairs. "I figured you'd like some fresh air. There's no moon tonight. The stars will be putting on quite a show here."

He helped her down the steps, out onto the mown grass, and to her chair. He'd placed a pillow on the back. He pulled the second chair in front of hers and placed a pillow on that one, too, so she could put her right leg up. They stood facing each other in the muted light coming from the windows, the stars wheeling overhead in a slow, age-old swing.

Before he helped her settle in, he said, "I think you'll find that farther away from city lights, the sky will be breathtaking."

Night had fully fallen, and it sounded like a jungle. She guessed it came from croaking frogs and screeching owls or hawks, crickets singing with their legs, and the steady thrums of other insects, and in combination, it was so loud they had to talk over it all.

"I can't get over this sound. What is that loud surging...like a pulsating...rumble of sorts?"

"You're hearing lots of tree frogs, too, but that'd be the katydids."

"What's a katydid? Some kind of cricket?"

"It's not a cricket. It's more like a green grasshopper with long antennae. I'll go find one for you, show you up close."

"No, no," Janey said laughing. Luke had still not lost the country boy in himself, and he could be so insistent. "No, please don't do that."

"It's no trouble. When we were kids, Cole and I used to catch them all the time."

"No, it's not that," she said still laughing. "I don't want to see one close up. I really don't want to. I don't like creepy crawly things."

"Like Sylvie."

"Well, I don't usually scream the way Sylvie did. But I share the same sentiment toward insects."

He smiled and shook his head. "Girls."

She shook her head. "Boys."

They both laughed then.

Janey said, "I've never heard anything like it. It's just amazing. This is so thoughtful of you, Luke, to bring me out here."

"Anything for you."

She sank into the chair and rubbed her arms.

"I'll get you a sweater," he said. "It's gonna get colder."

Janey scrunched down and looked upward. It took only a minute or so for her eyes to adjust, and then the sky exploded with brilliant points of light, diamond white light.

Luke returned and said, "Here." She sat up again, and he slipped a wooly sweater over her shoulders. "This was made from one of my sheep's wool."

She turned her head and buried her nose in the sweater, pulling the scent of the earth into her nostrils. "It's wonderful. Thank you."

Up in the sky above, more darkness mixed with more specks of light. The longer she looked, the more the billions of stars seemed to emerge. Amazing, like jewels on black silk, like sparkles on black sand beaches she'd only heard of and imagined but never seen.

The kindness shown her by this family—a family that had recently lost someone so horribly—touched her in a tender place. She had reminded them of Cole. Louz and Luke knew that Cole had lied to her. She figured they never forgot, would never forget. How did they do it?

And this sky. So lovely, too sweet a gift to bestow on the war-torn planet below.

Do we deserve it?

Luke said softly, "Each one of those suns out there could have planets orbiting them. Think about that. And just the sheer size of it all. Our sun is probably small in comparison to the others. It always strikes me as amazing every time I take a good look."

She peered deeper, glimpsing more and more. "It's astounding. I've never seen so many," Janey whispered as the same feeling of savoring a perfect place and time came over her as it had on *that night*. It was a glorious, rare moment, and she was surprised to find herself so happy. Luke had made her fall back in love with nature and with life in general.

Janey said, "I do wonder what might be found out

there someday."

"I've read that, in the future, we'll put a man in space. That someday it might be common, like gettin' on a train. Would you go?"

"If I had a chance to go into outer space?" She thought for a moment, her practical sensible side battling with her adventurous side. "Hmmm, good question. I'm not sure. I'm quite fond of this planet. Would you go?"

"Hell, yeah. I wouldn't be able to pass up the opportunity."

"You're brave, then. An adventurer."

"Not really brave. I'm more afraid of what's going on here than anything that might be out there."

Janey nodded. "Because of the war. Yes, I see what you mean."

"So once this war is over, and the scientists can get back to their work on space, I'll convince you to go with me."

She wasn't sure if he was flirting or just musing. Luke had no guile about him, so she took it at face value. Just daydreaming, she convinced herself. He'd let himself be with her that one night, but she doubted he'd ever do it again. For just a moment, it was on the tip of her tongue. *Did that night mean anything to you?*

It was a mistake to remember those vivid, tender moments of falling in love. She couldn't look at him and see the same expression he revealed that night, or she'd end up crazy again. She imagined that he touched her hand, and then squeezed it. The silence between them was not silent; instead, it was full of everything people say inside and hope the other can hear. She knew what he was feeling, and he knew what she was feeling.

"I made a mistake," Luke said out of the darkness.

Not knowing what he was referring to, Janey held her breath.

"When I blew off the experience on V-E Day with you, I made a mistake. I awakened in the morning, feeling like I'd had the most amazing dream of my life, but I convinced myself that it couldn't have been real. I truly believed in that moment that I was just playing a substitute role for Cole, that I was his imaginary replacement, and you couldn't possible care about me in that way. I was wrong. I'm sorry."

Janey finally breathed and had to take a moment to let it sink in, what he'd said, and then to gather her own thoughts. "Why, Luke, why? Why didn't you believe it? For me it was the most real thing that's ever happened to me. I find it hard to believe that we could have read things so differently. In the morning I felt even stronger about it, but you woke up and blew the entire thing off."

He sat up in the chair and turned toward Janey, his forearms on his thighs, his hands hanging down between his legs as he leaned forward. Janey couldn't look him in the eye, not yet, but she could still hear the pleading in his voice.

"Like I said, I was wrong. I never thought I could ever hold a candle next to Cole, especially with a woman. I guess I got struck through by a serious case of nerves, and then I acted on it, like an idiot. I wish to God I hadn't done it. I wish I'd given you the benefit of the doubt, but my own doubts overwhelmed me. I should've kept my mouth shut and let things unroll as they had started to."

Finally Janey took a glance. Luke's face was almost as tormented as the moment when she'd told him she knew Cole. She had to look away. "Why are you telling me this now? Why the sudden change of heart?"

"It hasn't been sudden. Over these past few days, we've spent a lot of time together, and I see that you're one of the last people on earth who could fool herself into thinking she was falling in love if she wasn't. I see you as true, through and through. Honest to a fault. Trusting, maybe to your disadvantage. I didn't know you that night or the next morning. But now I feel I know you well. You're beautiful and smart, Janey, but you're also a girl with a lot of common sense."

Janey almost laughed. "Sometimes, yes. Other times, no. That night I left it all out there."

"And then I crushed you. I ruined it."

Janey didn't respond. He still wasn't telling her how he felt about her. As if reading her mind, he said, "That night was as real to me as it was to you. It's like it was preordained—it was beauty and joy and all the hope two hearts can hold. I felt the way you did, and I still do. I fell in love, too. Please tell me I didn't ruin it all. Please tell me that you can forgive me."

Janey continued to stare at the sky until the stars blurred before her.

"Janey, please look at me."

She made herself look again at his pained but lovely face and keep her eyes on him.

He said, "Please tell me what you're feeling right now."

Janey tried to gather up some words that would begin to say all she felt inside, all the conflicting emotions, all the confusion and the doubts that *she* now had. "You were so adamant that it couldn't work between us that next morning. You shut me down without much of an explanation. Now I understand what you were going through, but that doesn't exactly comfort me. Your feelings now have shifted twice in only a matter of days. I don't know what I can count on, Luke. I'm sorry, but I just don't know how to deal with this now."

He gulped so loud she heard it. "I deserve that, but I'll prove to you that this is my—these are my true feelings that are not gonna change again. Please let me make it up to you."

"To what end?" Janey had to say in a whisper. "As you pointed out that morning, showing *your* common sense, we come from different worlds. If we are to be together, if we can get past all of this, and I'm not sure we can, one of us would have to give up our world for the other. There's an obvious geographical problem."

"I love the way you talk," Luke interjected.

Janey went on, "You already told me you're inheriting this land, and it's obvious you love it. It has been in your family for generations. I'll be the one who's expected to drop what I have and come here. And I have a loving family, too, back in Philadelphia. They need me too. I help my parents all the time, and I'm very close to my sister. It would be difficult for me to leave her. Plus I have a great job and recently got promoted. I have a lot to give up as well."

Luke looked down at his hands. "I feel that, in time, all of it can be worked out."

She turned her head away then. "By that, do you mean that I will have to work it out, that I will have to be the one who gives up my life from before?"

He didn't answer at first. Rather, he sort of hung his head. Janey felt sorry for him, sorry for both him and for herself. Maybe this was just an impossible situation, and Luke had been the first one to point it out. Maybe he was the wiser one after all—he'd begun to think of the complexities from day one, while Janey had avoided them.

He didn't respond for long minutes, and then he finally said, through a long sigh, "I don't know. I don't have all the answers yet. But I do believe that you and I can work it out. We'll find a way."

Janey gazed back at the stars. She had no response to that. Putting off problems and decisions didn't make them easier to address. In fact the protracted time could make them even more difficult to get past. But she couldn't say that, not on this night, right after Luke had just said exactly what she had wanted to hear. It was terrible—she had wanted him to say what he just did, to pledge his love, but now that he had, she was pointing out how the situation was probably too complicated for it ever to end up right for both of them.

The spell broke when Hank came running up, tail wagging, tongue hanging out, a big doggie smile on his face. Luke stroked him. "The sheep are all corralled for the night, so he can take a little break now."

That sounded like a good idea to Janey. Maybe she and Luke should take a break from this discussion, too.

Hank/Laurence, eyes all lit up with excitement, put his paws on Luke's lap, where he received lots of loving and scratching before coming and getting more of the same from Janey.

Just like that, the time for talking had come and gone. She felt as though she had stepped down to a solid place, when she'd been floating on wisps of nothing solid above. But the turbulence remained inside her.

They sat in silence then, but it wasn't the uncomfortable kind of silence. Something of quiet happiness and contemplation, reveling in the beauty of nature, came back over Janey in a gentle wave, and she was certain Luke felt it, too. It was as though peace reigned on earth here, at least for the moment. As though they were as far away from the carnage as the earth was from one of those distant suns. And out here, she could breathe so deeply. It felt like a cleansing, so pure it had a feeling of rebirth about it.

For that moment everything in her life felt a bit astounding. Especially the way she felt with Luke. Never had she seen anything like it coming.

She kept her gaze upward and let herself get lost in the smattering points of light. Human lives were no more substantial than the dimmest of the celestial bodies arcing through the emptiness, only one day to grow old and die. But each one was also distinct and unique. There was something of a miracle in each one of them.

She hoped this planet would soon receive a miracle. In the form of peace.

Sitting next to Luke that night, for a moment, everything seemed possible.

Chapter Eighteen

"Let's Get Away from it All" - Tommy Dorsey, 1941

Gatlinburg, Saturday, May 12, 1945

In the morning, she got up before dawn and hobbled her way to the window, where she pushed the curtains aside. She wished there had been moonlight so she could look out over this land while it was bathed in silver light. Instead, it was just the darkness spilling more stars. She liked this family; she liked the people in town—except for the sheriff and even he was okay, just misguided by an old family feud—and the land was lovely.

You could live here, she heard in her head as if a spirit had bequeathed it to her. She found herself considering the idea as never before. Everything so far in Tennessee had taught her something.

As dawn was beginning to break, the slightest blue-violet color easing into the pitch black of the eastern sky, she quickly readied herself and began to pack. When she ran across Cole's letters that Luke had secreted away for her, it was a shock to realize that she'd forgotten to open them. Again. Or maybe she wasn't ready to read them yet. Maybe she was beginning to avoid reading them.

She packed the bundle of letters again.

The Huxley family had arisen and dressed to see her off and had also made a hearty breakfast. When it was time to leave, Margaret kissed her on both cheeks. "I wonder if you should be taking off so soon, but it's your choice, of course, my dear."

Janey could hardly meet Louz and Sylvie's eyes. Both looked grief-stricken. They said goodbye and hugged her while pushing back tears, and Robert told her she was welcome to come back any time. "For any reason," he finished.

"We figured you'd stay longer," said Sylvie. "I haven't even started to tell you my ideas. You see, someday when we're not needed on the farm like we are now, I want to move to a city. Maybe Philadelphia."

Janey's eyebrows lifted in surprise, but why wouldn't Sylvie want to leave? Many people wanted to leave home, and many of them wouldn't appreciate what they'd had until after they did leave.

Margaret said to Sylvie, "Stop it. She doesn't need to think about that right now."

"I'll write you about it."

"I hope you do," Janey replied.

Louz came closer. "And you must come back here to visit. You let me lead you astray only once, you know. I have much more where that came from."

Janey gazed around at all of them. A whirl of sadness and gratitude encircled her heart. "You've all made this a very special journey for me. Your generosity is just so…generous." She was getting tongue-tied. "Thank you from the bottom of my heart."

"Don't be a stranger," Louz added.

"Expect many letters in the mail," said Sylvie.

"Safe travels, my dear," said Margaret.

Still taken aback by how close she felt to them after such a short time, nevertheless she got in the truck, faced forward, and checked her ankle. Even though she'd been up and moving about on her crutches, the swelling hadn't returned. Sure a doctor would cast it this morning, she imagined the long drive ahead.

Did she dread being around Luke, or did she welcome it?

As they drove to the hospital, the sun was still rising, painting the sky in lovely shades of salmon and purple.

At the hospital, the doctor confirmed that her ankle could be cast. Some swelling was still present, but he felt it was safe. While he was applying the cast, at first she was flooded with elation, but stunned all over again when he said, "I want to see you back here tomorrow morning."

Would this ever end? Even with nightmares, you eventually wake up. "Why? I can follow up with a doctor in Philadelphia."

"That's quite a long haul, isn't it?"

She indicated Luke. "I have my own private chauffeur."

The doctor shook his head. "I'd like you to stay off the leg for one more day. All that moving around and letting your leg hang down all day could cause a return of the swelling. And if that happens, the cast could cut off the circulation."

This time, she didn't argue. *Cut off the circulation?* That sounded scary, but she wouldn't let that happen. If anything went numb...she could seek help.

After the doctor left, Luke said, "Don't even ask."

"Please take me anyway."

He slowly shook his head. "It's only one more day."

"One more day means risking my job. No one's taking care of me, Luke. I'm not inheriting anything but a rundown diner I don't want. I take care of myself, and I need my job."

"You can't work if you can't walk."

She lifted her hands helplessly, then rubbed her temples. "This is beginning to feel like a well-executed scheme to keep me here."

"Ah, shucks, I hoped you wouldn't figure it out. I've bribed all the doctors."

She smiled despite herself. "Funny."

"Come on," he said. "You know you need to stay for one more day. And I promise to make it worth it."

Janey couldn't answer or act the least bit pleased. Disappointment was a deep ache in her bones. Looking down at her leg, she said, "I wish all of this would go away. Now I have to go back and unpack yet again. I feel like I'm living in an endless circle."

"I understand," he said gently. "But why not make the best of it? We have the rest of the day together. The truck's got a full tank, and there's lots of drives we haven't taken yet."

She looked up. "The doctor just said I shouldn't take any long drives."

"I could take you on a short one. Let the forest do its magic. Any idea what you'd like to see?"

"I can't imagine."

"Wanna go to a place where they make moonshine?"

"Don't those people have a reputation for shooting strangers on sight?"

"I'll bring my gun."

Janey's eyes grew huge.

He laughed. "Just kidding."

"Thank goodness."

"But I could get you drunk on moonshine, for real this time."

"You're a bad influence."

"Maybe I'll get you so drunk you'll step out in front of a car again. Break your other leg. Then you'd have a matching set."

She smiled. She couldn't help herself. "I think I'll pass."

He rubbed his chin. "I'm just thinking. Yeah, with two broken legs, you'd be stuck here for a long, long time."

"You'd get sick of me."

In all seriousness, he said, "No, I wouldn't."

Janey smiled. It was amazing that even after that brutally honest conversation the night before, under the stars, they could still enjoy each other. Even though nothing was settled and in fact nothing was even remotely agreed upon and they had no idea how they would go forward, they could still have fun. Suddenly resigned to stay for one more day, Janey remembered something Cole had told her about. "Aren't there some caves around here?"

Luke's eyes sharpened as if he'd just seized upon something. "The area is riddled with 'em. You're not thinking of going down in a cave, are you?"

"Of course not. I wouldn't go in one even if I was fully functioning. But it'd be interesting to see how they appear, how the earth opens up, learn how they were discovered, that sort of thing."

"Then I know the perfect place. And it's only a short drive. I'll take you there and then straight back to the farm for more rest."

So, in the middle of all this mess surrounding her,

even then, perhaps a happy day could happen. "Sounds like it'll be worth it. Thank you, Luke."

"If you thank me one more time, I'm gonna…"

"What?"

"Never mind."

On the way, Luke entertained her with stories of childhood exploits while she examined her snow-white cast and listened. "I'd tag along with Cole and his buddies sometimes. We never let Tim go."

"Maybe that's why he's so shy."

"No, he was born that way. Tim lives more in his mind than the rest of us, but he loves our land. Not sure he could do it on his own, but us together, we'll keep it going."

Then he went on with his stories. "The older boys I knew were fearless. Once Cole and his friends found a dead mama bear. Apparently got hit by a car and crawled off to die. They carried her two cubs back to the road and flagged down some help.

"They always explored and made pretend rafts, then tried floating 'em over the rapids. Those rafts always cracked apart. They also found caves and slithered down deep. The grown-ups never knew the half of this."

"Did you go into the caves?"

He shook his head. "A little ways. But I found out I like things above the ground better than under it."

"Pioneers used to use caves as cellars, didn't they?"

"Hmmm, I reckon they might not have used these caves for that. They're pretty rugged 'round here. I'm taking you to some just off the road a bit. Easy to get there."

Slowing down along a deserted strip of dirt road surrounded by dense forest, he seemed to be searching for something. Were they really to stop in the middle of…nowhere? Befuddled, she realized that's exactly what Luke was doing.

Her face must have shown her hesitancy. He said, "Trust me," as he engaged the hand brake and opened the door on his side. He came around for her, and she took his hand, and in his face and gaze, she saw a serene sort of happiness. It was as though he could always find a reason to smile.

He helped her out and get steady on the crutches. They headed in and almost immediately came upon a barbed wire fence. Luke spread the wires for Janey and helped her get the crutches through first. As she followed, Luke assisting her, she shot him an admonishing glare. "This is private property, I presume."

He nodded. "I have no idea who owns it. No one's ever around. We came here for years and were never told to get off."

Janey said, "There's a first time for everything. If we start taking bullets from some outraged landowner, you'll protect me?"

He smiled. "With my life."

Luke took the lead again, and in only a few minutes, the trees fully enveloped them, and only a faint trail remained. But it was almost flat, and Janey could handle it.

In this place, the air lay soft on her skin like a gloved hand, and everything smelled good in the forest, even some stagnant-looking ponds with their animal-like muskiness. But the rest was all grasses and wild daffodils, birch woods, and oakmoss. Here the forest was dense with trees as tall and straight as a Philly skyscraper. They looked like an army protecting a consecrated place.

Janey was doing well on her crutches until they came to a stream. It was small and shallow with plenty of rocks to traverse for the crossing. She said, "I'm not supposed to get the cast wet."

Luke responded, "I'll get you over."

First he took her crutches and rock-hopped over to the other side. Then he came back and surprised her by lifting her in his arms. She had an instinctual urge to bury her face in his neck. Like *that night*.

"I want you to admire my lightness of foot," he said with a chuckle. Then, not attempting a dry crossing on the rocks, Luke started sloshing across the stream, making a ruckus, and raising droplets in the air and laughing.

She laughed, too. "Look at you! Now your feet are wet."

"I couldn't chance stumbling and letting you down. I'm carrying precious cargo, and I want you high and dry." He set her on the ground, then suddenly pulled her close and pointed downstream. "See that?"

A black bear with a cub drank from the stream at the water's edge not that far away.

The bears looked shiny and silky as their coats reflected the sun. They didn't seem bothered by the presence of humans, but a shiver ran down Janey's spine. They were, after all, wild animals, and she was a city girl. She couldn't help thinking, *Lions and Tigers and Bears, Oh, My!* from the song in *The Wizard of Oz*.

Janey asked, "Should I be scared?"

"Believe me, the mama bear knows we're here. If we don't get between her and her cub, she won't do anything about us."

They stayed and watched. Luke's breath was on her neck, warm and gentle, and she didn't want the moment to end. The two of them, holding close and watching a lovely sight of nature's glory, together, breathing as one. If only she could freeze time. But all good things come to an end, unfortunately, and the mother bear and cub finished watering and disappeared into the forest.

"The cub was adorable. Now I understand why teddy bears are so well-loved by children."

Luke hadn't let go of her. He whispered in her ear, "I told you I'd show you bears."

She turned and melted into him, and she had the feeling that real living had once again come to call. He lifted her face to him, then kissed her on the lips, then more deeply, and then more deeply still. Their mouths melded into each other's, and for a moment, the earth and everything else fell away. She could've stayed in the moment forever.

When Luke finally pulled back, he said, "I'll never forget this," the same thing he'd said that night.

No, her mind screamed, rapidly switching into protective mode. *Not again.* She still didn't know how she felt about Luke's swift change of heart; she hadn't had the time and quiet to process it. And lingering in the back of her mind—he'd had a swift change of heart after that night, too. Could she trust him to be the stable, loving man she'd always wanted? She wanted to trust him, and yet there was a small fear that he might be just toying with her. It seemed he was unattached and had been for a long time. Why? Did he enjoy being the town's ever-so-likeable and fun eligible bachelor? Was this a game?

She pulled back. "Why are you doing this to me?"

Her heart, beneath her ribs, beat hotly and painfully, and her chest suddenly grew tight. She said helplessly, "You have to stop doing this. How can you do it again? Making me fall for you again. You broke my heart; you told me it couldn't work. Last night, you seemed to have changed your mind. Completely. I won't allow you to-to—" Janey choked, almost losing her wits, then checking herself. She must have sounded pathetic.

With his eyes pleading into hers, Luke replied, "I made a mistake pushing you away like I did. Like I said, I just couldn't believe you could go for a fella like me."

She found his eyes. "That's unreasonable."

He took half a step back. "Look at me, Janey. I don't have much to offer."

"You have everything."

"I've always lacked that firm belief in myself as anyone special. Cole and Louz, now they're special. But not me."

He looked at her as if fighting an internal battle, one side waged by the sensible part of him, the other side by the emotional part. "On that night, I figured you were still in love with Cole, and I was an easy guy to stand in for the night. But now I'm certain you're not in love with him any longer. I think you've moved on, and now I agree with what you said that night. You came here to meet me. Do you realize that for the last couple of days you've hardly mentioned Cole?"

"You're right. I'm not in love with Cole any longer and haven't been for a while now. I was in love with a memory. Frankly, I don't know what to feel about Cole anymore."

He nodded slowly, before his jaw flinched as he continued, "I can't apologize enough, and I understand how confusing and all over the map I must seem to you. I'm very sorry for what I said that morning. At the time, it seemed the most sensible thing, that you were just lonely, and I was there. And it kind of bothered me to take Cole's girl. If it weren't for the war, he might be here with you."

"I wouldn't have even met Cole if not for the war. Sure we had a whirlwind of a romantic weekend, but Cole lied to me. Even if he'd lived, I wouldn't have been able to forget that."

"I see that now—you know who you are and what you want. You have to respect a man's honesty and character to love him completely. I was wrong about you in the beginning. I didn't know you well enough then to see, but I do now."

"You hurt me, Luke. It's hard to trust you again, too."

"Please give me a chance."

Reluctantly she shook her head. This conversation was beginning to feel like an endless circle. "I don't know if I can. It's more than just trust."

"What then? I'll do anything to prove..." He stopped as though struck by the pained expression on her face. She was suffering too, looking at him and the way he was pleading with her. "I know I hurt you, and I'll never do it again. You can count on me, Janey."

"I want to."

She had to look away for a moment when he said, "Please..."

Gathering her bearings, she almost felt faint. Then, looking away to the earth and the forest, to ground her, she felt like a lost soul, one who had lost her way in the woods and was looking for some sign of safe passage.

Eventually setting her gaze on his face and in his eyes again, she said, "I feel rather lost right now. I keep thinking about what you said on the morning after that night. Our lives are very different and wouldn't mesh together easily. You were right about that. I doubt you'll be moving to Philly, and if I come here, I'd have to give up being close to my family and my job and my house. I would have to let go of many things that mean a great deal to me, and all for what has transpired over only a few days. And it could end up like it did with Cole."

"It's been five days, and each day I've loved you more."

"Five days? That long?"

In the dappled sunlight, circles of shade played across his face. He said, "Besides, I'm not Cole. I figured you could see that by now. Guess I have more to prove to you, or I haven't shown you well enough."

Shaking her head incredulously, Janey pleaded, "I wish I could walk in your shoes for one day. To feel so sure of things. When I first came here, life seemed simpler, but it's not. It's more serious, and yet it can be ridiculously wonderful. I haven't told you this before, because it might sound batty, but that night seemed like an old recurring dream of mine that came true. In the dream, I was dancing with a man I was passionately in love with. But I couldn't see his face until that night. All of a sudden my dream was coming true and the face was yours."

"Janey, that's the sweetest, most adoring thing anyone has ever said to me. You're the woman of my dreams, too."

She swallowed, wishing she could just jump into trust again, let herself fall for him all over again. She said, "I'm confused. I'm sorry, Luke, but you can't expect me not to shy away a bit. You pushed me away when I was at my most vulnerable."

"I know."

Questions reeled around in her mind. She could get over the recent pain, or so she thought, but could she trust him? That night she'd opened up so fully, and the morning after, he'd just as fully closed the door. How do you trust someone completely after that? Especially since it would turn her life around if she decided to be with him?

Luke stroked her arms, easy as a feather, and his expression was one of quiet desperation mixed with hope. She'd never known a man who allowed his feelings to show so clearly on his face. Luke was that guy—the one who didn't hold back, who was ready and willing to give his all.

He said, his voice tremulous, barely above a whisper, "If you let yourself believe in me, I promise not to hurt you ever again."

"No one can make that promise, Luke." Her own words were like sandpaper in her throat, but she'd always been a truth-teller, and she could see that Luke was too. "Let's be sensible for a moment. Even people who love each other can inadvertently hurt each other's feelings."

"I'll amend what I just said: I'll never *purposely* hurt you."

"Did you purposefully hurt me that morning?"

He hesitated. "No. I thought I was doing what was best for you."

"This is what I mean. Even the closest of souls can see things in different ways. I know you weren't purposely hurting me back then. You were just being honest about the way you felt. I hadn't seen it coming, that's all. It took me completely by surprise."

"I wish I could go back to that morning and do and say wholly different things."

"I do, too," Janey said. "But unfortunately, it doesn't work that way."

"You get one chance and that's it? That's what you believe?"

"No, I'm not that harsh."

"I'll never see you as harsh, Janey," he said eventually. "You're the forgiving kind. Even with Cole, I can see that you've forgiven him."

She gazed away then. "I don't know. I just don't know what I believe right now."

It seemed as though both of them had run out of words, too scared to say more, and the earth was still moving, time was slipping away, and they had to get on with it. Besides, it was getting hot, and they had the rest of the day to talk more.

Reluctantly they pushed on.

Only steps farther, the forest opened enough to let a beam of light illuminate a small clearing. They walked past some very old, cut wood on the ground and a small ladder, almost grown over by moss and clover. Then an outcropping of rock, near the center of which was a gaping crack in the earth. Bigger than what Janey had imagined.

Luke pulled out a penny and dropped it into the black space of that hole in the ground. Janey heard a ping, then another ping that sounded farther away, then another and another and another until there were none.

"It goes down in levels. When we were boys and first found this place, the rest of us boys quit going on when we reached the second level down. Cole carried a lantern and went in until he couldn't get down any farther, but he told us he saw a gigantic open room below him. Said it was pretty spectacular. The walls were too steep to get down into it. I think he was the first human being down there ever."

"That's remarkable."

"Yeah, some other people know of this entrance, but we also think no one else has discovered there's so much down below. You'd have to be experienced and have the right equipment to go down into that big chamber Cole saw. Once he said that when the war was over, he was gonna come back and buy up this land, then see if he could develop the cave into a tourist attraction."

"You're kidding," Janey said. "He told me nothing about plans for coming back here. He had fond memories, yes. But he told me he studied architecture to get away from here."

The moment those words left her mouth, Janey regretted them. Luke looked devastated. And she'd just given credence to her theory about hurting even the one you love.

She backtracked. "I don't think he wanted to get away from family. Rather, he wanted to go on adventures."

Luke nodded. "That was Cole. Big dreams and big plans always on his mind."

"Obviously he really loved it here, despite what he said to me."

Luke sat still and barely moved for a moment, but soon he had already recovered. "Wait up here for a moment. I'm fixing to bring you something that's over a million years old. Like those stars last night. You like ancient history? Well, this is earth's ancient history on display."

"You don't mean you're going in there!"

"You bet I am. I have to fetch that penny."

"Be serious for a minute," Janey said. "Please don't go in there for *me*."

"I can reach what I want without going very deep. Maybe even the penny, too. Second or third level down. It's right safe—I know. I've been here before."

"Things can change, you know."

He laughed. "Not around here they don't. No," he said with more seriousness, "this place is a hidden gem— I bet that when Cole went down, no other person had gone down there in the last few centuries. There was no evidence even the Cherokee had ever found it. And I doubt anyone's been here since Cole."

"Wait, are you sure about this? You don't even have any equipment."

He nodded. "I'm barely going in. Just to the first level to look around. I remember it down that far, clear as day."

Janey could tell that Luke was going to do what he wanted, no matter what she said. She stopped arguing with him, and within minutes, he dropped into the hole, and she heard him land. A solid thudding sound. "What I'm looking for, it's not here on this level. I'm gonna go just one more level down," he shouted up. His voice echoed into nothingness.

Then it disappeared.

"Are you okay?"

His voice was farther away, and if it echoed, the cave must have claimed it for its own. She heard only once, "You bet. Just arriving at the third level."

Janey glanced around and hoped the bears hadn't followed them. Despite what Luke had said, she would've been terrified if she'd seen them any closer. Still gazing about and then at the gaping hole in the ground, she thought about what Luke had said. If she stayed here, maybe the Parkers would buy this land. Maybe they could develop this into a place where it was safe to host visitors, scientists, ancient historians, and the like. Maybe she could use her organizational skill, love of history, and people savvy to help make this cave a tourist attraction and center for research.

She hadn't heard from Luke in a while. She moved herself over to a rock with an almost flat top near the opening in the ground. She let herself ease down on it so she could peer down. What was taking him so long?

"Luke?" she yelled.

"Yes," he said from the hole. A hollow sound from far away, it echoed eerily, getting slighter and slighter until it vanished into the atmosphere.

Relieved he could hear her, she called out, "Are you soon to come out? I have a creepy feeling. What are you looking for anyway?"

"Something for you. They're called stalactites and stalagmites."

" I remember those from science class," Janey said into the hole.

"Just give me a moment," said Luke.

The sound of rocks falling against other rocks emerged from the hole. Crumbling sounds. Not the kind of sounds one would want to come out of a cave.

"Luke? Come up, please. I hear rocks moving."

"I'm trying something. Give me a little more time," he called back.

The sun was bearing down. Janey's brow began to sprout little beads of perspiration. She removed a handkerchief from her pocket and patted her entire face. She watched a woodpecker high in a tree, gazed about for bears, and wished she had some water.

A few minutes later, she heard Luke's voice. "Janey?"

"Yes."

"I can't get out."

Joking again. He never stopped. "Of course you can. Get up here! You're making me nervous."

"I'm serious. I can't get out."

Heart suddenly thumping, she gasped and asked, "What are you talking about?"

"Never mind. I have another idea."

"What?" she called down. "What's going on? I'm getting scared now."

She heard more sounds of rocks moving and Luke grunting. "What are you doing?"

After another long moment, he answered, "When I was down here before, Cole or one of those other guys must have boosted me up. It's steep, and I don't remember it that way, but I must've had help. Still, I figured I could get out by myself, 'specially since I'm bigger now. I've been trying. But I can't."

"Truly? You can't climb out?"

"Truly."

"Promise this isn't a prank."

"It's not. I wouldn't joke about something like this."

She gazed about helplessly. "What would you like me to do?"

"I'm thinking you should probably go for help."

"Oh, my God!" She broke out in a bigger sweat.

Again, she had to shake her head.

"I'll keep trying. But can you drive? Never mind. You can't drive with a cast on your leg."

Starting to panic a bit, she asked, "Please don't take any risks. You could cause a cave-in."

"I won't."

"So what now? Do you have any rope in your truck?"

It took a few moments before he said, "No. This is hard to believe, but I don't see any way out of here. Nothing has worked. So I guess you should go back to the road and wait there until someone comes by. No, forget it. I wasn't thinking about the creek."

"I'll get over it," she said feeling determined. She wasn't one to shy away from a challenge. "I'm more concerned about the road. It looked deserted."

Despite it all, he sounded cheerful. "Someone will pass through. That road is used by farmers."

Janey stood and gathered the crutches. "I can't believe this is happening. Can it get any crazier? I'm really leaving you in a hole in the ground?"

"Don't worry, baby. I'll be fine down here. It's just me and a million years."

Chapter Nineteen

"Don't Fence Me In" - Bing Crosby and the
Andrews Sisters/Roy Rogers/Gene Autry, 1940
Gatlinburg, Saturday, May 12, 1945

Still in a state of disbelief, though not really—no
doubt Luke wouldn't ask for help if he didn't need it—
she steadied herself on the crutches and headed out. Luke
was stuck, and it was up to her, even in her reduced and
belabored state, to summon help. She had to do this, and
she had to do it right. No missteps, no further accidents
or delays. No bears.

Breathing hard despite trying not to, she had no
difficulty until she reached the creek. She made a fast
scan up and down for any sign of bears or other creatures,
and then, fueled by determination, fear, and adrenalin,
she searched through the clear water for flat rocks and
set her crutches on them. Then she used the crutches to
help balance herself while she took a first step onto a flat
rock, the water running over it. She did the same thing
over and over again and proceeded cautiously, step by
deliberate step.

Maybe it was the flood of emotions, but something
drove her across fairly quickly and without more than a
slight waver once about half way across, she landed on
the other side. Then she continued swinging herself up
the path until she reached the barbed-wire fence, which

proved more difficult.

She slipped the crutches underneath to the other side, noticing that the crutch tips had gotten muddy and grassy after leaving the creek in a wet state. Balancing on one foot, she reached down and spread the wires, then put her left foot through. She grabbed a crutch and set it upright to lean on and tried to lift the casted leg through. She ended up having to put some weight on it in order to keep her balance, faltering on the way. Her left knee scraped on the wires and sprang dots of blood.

But she felt no pain, only the thrill of success and even more determination. She'd worn pedal pushers instead of a skirt, which helped a lot, but the fabric snagged going through, too, and she noted a tear in them now over her lower thigh. Some blood bloomed there, too.

No matter.

On the other side, she came to the road in a jiffy. Then—nothing, not a vehicle in sight. Nothing but Luke's truck. Not even a squirrel chirping or bird fluttering by to keep her company.

She waited. And waited longer. She thought she could see the grass growing and feel the world turning.

Someone, come on! she screamed inside her head. It was the warmest day since she'd been in Tennessee, and her hands were sweaty on the crutches, her mouth parched. She didn't think there was anything to drink inside Luke's truck, but she swung herself over to look inside anyway.

All to no avail. She stood on the road again and searched up and down, willing for something, someone to appear.

What was Luke doing now? She couldn't imagine

being alone down in a cave with no one around now to call up to. If the wait was long for her, what must it feel like to him? And it had to have crossed his mind that she might not have made it to the road and they might both be in peril. Would he wonder if no one was coming to help them? Would he try other ways to get out and make things worse?

She had to stay out in the sun on the road. If she waited in the trees off the road a bit, she might not be able to move out of the shadows fast enough to stop a car should one come by.

Luke had faced this so calmly and bravely. That made her worry more. Was he really terrified inside, only society demanded that a man not show fear? Were there animals in caves? She knew there could be bats, but were there also insects and snakes and maybe more creepy creatures? Surely they would terrify her, but he could probably handle them. What was happening to Luke now?

She had asked him to take her to caves. He'd done this to impress her, and now he was paying for it. How she wished she'd asked him to take her someplace else, anywhere else.

The cut on her knee was bleeding more now, and she pressed the torn fabric on it to stop the seeping, getting blood on her hands. She wiped them on her pants and kept putting pressure on the wound.

Her hair crossed her face, and a strand flew in her mouth. She had to use her bloody hand to free her hair. Dear God, she must look a fright, she thought—a woman alone on the side of a deserted road wearing torn bloody pants and clinging to muddy crutches, and on her leg, a now-dirty and somewhat wet cast. Her face probably appeared frantic, and a little blood-smeared, too.

She gazed upward. It was such a pretty day, but her thoughts were getting bleaker.

It might have been no more than twenty more minutes, but it felt like at least an hour when finally a truck appeared on the road. It was an old farm truck with two shadowy figures inside. She waved wildly, although she needn't have done so. They seemed intending to stop anyway.

She flooded with relief.

The truck pulled up, and a young boy wearing a look of confused concern stuck his head out of the passenger window.

"A man is trapped in a cave. We need help."

The boy, about thirteen and wearing overalls, hopped out. "You're beat up."

"I had a tangle with the barbed-wire fence and lost. But I'm fine. Please go after him."

"Where is he?"

The other man pulled off the road and got out too. An older guy with a white beard. The boy said, "That's my grandpa. He should stay with you. I'll go."

She nodded toward the trail she'd arrived on. "Take the trail in. It's gets fainter but goes to a small creek. Cross that, and a little way in, you'll find a bunch of rocks. The cave's there."

By that time the older man had come up. The boy said to him, "She's okay. Just some scrapes."

The old man had obviously heard her directions. "I don't know that place. Reckon I'll go." He peered at the boy, who was itching to accompany him. "You stay with her."

"I'll be fine alone," Janey inserted. "I've been

standing here for a long time alone. I'd much rather you both go find him."

The old man asked, "That Luke Parker's truck?"

"Yes, he's the one trapped."

The old man nodded once. "You look bushed. You get on in the truck and sit still, wait for us there."

"Do you have some water, by any chance?"

"In the truck, there's cold coffee in a Thermos," he answered and started to leave.

"Not for me," she said, stopping them. "For him."

"Is he hurt?" the old man asked while the boy darted back to the truck and retrieved the Thermos.

"No," Janey answered. "Not when I left. He was fine, just alone."

They both quickly disappeared.

Janey swung her way to Luke's truck and let herself in on the passenger side. God, it felt good to sit on the seat. But there was no such thing as relaxing. She kept watching the road in both directions for more vehicles and then turning back and looking to see if the boy or his grandfather had returned.

It wasn't long before another truck came by, this one coming from the opposite direction. She stuck her arm out of the window and motioned. This one stopped, too. Janey managed to hobble out and describe the situation to the man behind the wheel, who appeared to be another farmer. He started to park and get out.

"There's already two others in there to help, but they're probably going to need some rope."

The guy put his truck back in gear. "I come from nearby. I'll go fetch that rope."

Janey waited in Luke's truck again, not nearly as frantic as before. Help had come. Luke would get out—

246

it was only a matter of time. But she wouldn't relax until she saw him again, safe and sound.

Soon after, the boy ran up to the truck, panting and sweaty. He must have run the entire way, but he said, "He's doing fine. He wanted me to come tell ya and check on ya."

"That's great. Thank you. Another man is coming— he's bringing a rope."

The boy said, panting, "I'll be heading on back to Luke then."

Janey rested her head on the back of the seat. In a rush, she became aware that her temples were pounding. She rubbed them and tried to wait patiently.

Luke stuck in a hole had temporarily overshadowed the conversation they'd had just prior to that. Now that she felt his entrapment was almost over, it came back.

He'd asked for her trust again. He wanted her love. She'd kept falling for him even when she'd willed herself not to. There was so much to love about Luke. The way he made her laugh, the way he made her feel— adored, and even more than an equal. Like something precious. And that feeling of really living since she'd met him was unlike anything before.

Could she forget how wonderful it was to be with him? His presence was calming and relaxing and fun, yet it touched her in new places. Somehow his honest and vulnerable heart made her reach for him. His pull was powerful, and he seemed willing to wait ever so hopefully for her to find her way back.

But it meant giving up the life she'd built. And he'd rejected her once in a most painful way. Love wasn't supposed to hurt. Could she get past that?

Whatever her decision, saying goodbye and

returning to Philadelphia would feel like being dragged in the wrong direction. And yet she had to do it. It was the safe course, the sensible one. The one no one except maybe Luke would question. It was the acceptable one. But was it the right one?

As her mind wrestled with questions she couldn't answer, the time dragged. It seemed like the rest of the day, but it was probably only a half hour or less before the second man came back, a big loop of rope slung over his shoulder and a canvas bag of other supplies in his arms. He'd brought a teenaged boy with him, too. They spoke to Janey briefly, but all three of them were anxious for them to go in and find out what, if anything, was happening and offer help. They too disappeared into the woods.

While she waited yet again, she pushed aside all those questions she couldn't answer and placed her focus solely on Luke's rescue and safety.

When he and the others finally emerged onto the road again, Janey had to wipe her eyes. She took deep calming breaths. She knew he'd be okay, but the release of seeing him out of there was overwhelming. She got out of the truck and joined the others standing around, talking about it.

Luke didn't come and hug her, but the look in his eyes showed that he'd been more concerned about her than himself. He quickly noted her torn trousers, bloody hands, and leg cuts. "Are you all right?"

"Fine. A little blood goes a long way. It's not nearly as bad as it looks."

He nodded, but she could see that he felt awful. His face hung slack with a barely detectible quiver in his cheek, one probably only she could see. Luke stood solemnly, talking to the men, who didn't seem ready to leave yet, and he was also thanking them profusely. But his eyes always returned to find her.

It turned out the first boy and his grandpa hadn't been able to do more than offer moral support and company to Luke until the other man and boy came and could toss down the rope to Luke and hammer it into the ground with a stake on top. After that, Luke scrambled up and out in no time.

Janey was surprised by how calm they appeared, even Luke. It seemed they hadn't been worried in the least. But still, they had to rehash every moment.

It was over. Luke was safe.

Therefore it startled her when a police car pulled up, with Sheriff Snearl behind the wheel.

Stumped, Janey couldn't imagine why he was here. Had he heard about Luke being in the cave and had come to assist and make sure all was well? News sure traveled fast around here.

Snearl stepped out of the car, hitched up his pants, and began a swaggering walk in their direction. He said in a joking manner with a grin to Janey, "You again?"

Janey said nothing, just smiled.

He said, "It seems you been spending too much time around Louz Huxley."

Snearl was enjoying himself. "Just relax now," he cautioned everyone, beginning to show signs of conducting his public duties. "Tell me what's going on here. I heard there was some trouble."

Luke's jaw clenched. The man with the rope said, "Luke here just got hisself a little stuck down in a yonder cave, but we got him out. Easy."

"Well, I'm glad you're all in one piece." Snearl gave

a cursory glance at Janey. "How 'bout you? Those injuries anything serious?"

She shook her head.

He said, smiling ironically, "You're a bit accident prone, aren't you?"

Janey laughed. "You can say that again."

Snearl frowned, pensively. "Maybe these parts don't suit you so well."

Janey shook her head. "I'll be the judge of that."

The sheriff turned to Luke. "How'd you happen to get in there?" he asked, gesturing toward the land.

Luke seemed to have regained some calm and motioned with his hand. "Down that trail there."

"Hmmm," said the sheriff, rubbing his chin. "That's real interesting. Let me see…" He paused. "I hate to have to tell you this, but as I recall, this land don't belong to you."

Luke simply stood.

"And as I also recall, there's a sign in there, on a fence, that says 'No Trespassing' on it. Or something like that. Did you see something like that?"

"Yes," Luke answered. "Sure did."

"Well, I got bad news for you, Parker. Wish you hadn't ignored that sign."

"I been coming out here for years, even since I was a kid."

The sheriff furrowed his brow, then said, "But you never was caught before. News about this is going to travel fast as a running wolf. I gotta do the right thing here."

Janey spoke up. "It was one of Cole's favorite places, and I asked Luke to bring me here. It was my fault."

Everyone stilled at the mention of Cole's name. Four men and two boys, paralyzed. But they ignored it as if they had to.

It took Snearl only a moment or so to get past it, however, and he stared them all down, rubbing his chin again, a bit of determination on his face now. He said to Janey, "Don't say it was your fault. I'm not arresting a perfect stranger in these parts. You didn't know any better."

"It was my fault," said Luke.

The other men, still standing by, said, "But no harm done." and "Everything's A-okay now."

Janey, who'd been as tense as a taut string, told herself to relax, but it did no good. She just knew something wasn't right.

"Glad you're not injured, Parker." The sheriff turned to Janey. "And you, too, little lady."

Janey nodded, but Luke said, "We're fine. Not needing help any longer."

The sheriff focused on Luke again. "But I have some bad news for you, I'm afraid," he said, dead serious now. "I have to put you under arrest."

At first Luke laughed. No one moved. Then Luke's face fell as it seemed to dawn on him that the sheriff wasn't kidding. "No you don't *have* to," Luke said. "For trespassing? Are you serious?"

"Serious as can be, I'm afraid," said Snearl. "This here land belongs to folks who are on the other side of the feud around these parts. It belongs to the Joneses. They're on the other side, not mine. If I don't treat what you've done seriously, they'll take it personal."

Luke laughed wryly. "This has to be a joke."

"Unfortunately," said Snearl. "It's not."

Chapter Twenty

"Prisoner of Love" - Perry Como/Billy Eckstine/ Ink Spots, 1940
Gatlinburg, Sunday, May 13, 1945

Another morning meant saying another goodbye. Just as she'd done the day before, Janey awakened and packed in Sylvie's room at the Huxley house, and they all had to endure another painful parting. Janey, full of emotion, still felt as though she were sleepwalking. Everything from the day before still loomed alive on the back screen of her mind, and the present couldn't overcome it.

Yesterday had not left her all night. Driving with Luke, visiting the Emergency Room, then going to the cave, Luke's entrapment and rescue, all ending with the sheriff, who really did arrest Luke for trespassing. Then he was taken to Sevierville, where the county jail was located.

Yes, the sheriff had really done it, which infuriated the Huxleys and Parkers alike, even as they understood it. Janey met Luke's parents again under the most trying of circumstances. And yet they couldn't have been kinder. Robert and Margaret, Jean and Will, all were infuriated that Snearl would do something because people on the other side of an old argument might find his leniency wrong enough to complain about. Normally, a trespassing charge would not be cause for arrest, unless some real harm had been done. Usually a warning or, at worst, a ticket would have been issued.

But Sheriff Gilbert Snearl whisked Luke off to jail out of town and made sure that he spent at least one night behind bars just so it would "look right." The old man and the boy had driven Janey back to the Huxley house, where she had to break the bad news.

After all had been said and done, both families and Janey had to retire to bed that night realizing that there was nothing more they could do.

Late, past midnight, when everyone else was asleep or trying to sleep, Janey let herself out the front door silently. She'd learned to move easily and quietly by then, despite the crutches.

She took herself down to the lawn where she had sat with Luke and looked at the sky only one evening before. A slim claw of a crescent moon hung there now.

The magic of being out here with Luke wrapped back around Janey. Despite the tension around her at present, the world had never felt so immense in its grandeur and mystery, and yet it felt as though it was right there in front of her to simply reach out and touch and hold and feel in the person of Luke. Deep where she reached, her heart spoke in a newfound voice: *Thank you.*

But although she asked the night sky for an answer, all she saw were the many shades and sizes of stars, and hazes of distant galaxies, all so mysterious, and at that moment, still so far out of reach.

****

In the morning, although it was a Sunday, Robert and Will headed out in Will's truck for the Sevier County

Courthouse in Sevierville, the county seat, to see if they could get Luke out, while Louz drove Janey in the family car, a 1940 Chrysler Windsor coupé, first to see the doctor in Gatlinburg, who'd agreed to open his office and check Janey's leg one last time. He finally released her to return to Philadelphia, and they made one final stop before leaving the area.

Louz drove to Elkmont and, once there, down a dirt road almost to its end. Off to the left and up the slope along the road, through the trees, were gravestones.

"I hope you don't mind if I don't come with you," Louz said solemnly, then painfully brightened. "I prefer the living."

"It's okay, Louz," Janey said as she opened the car door and stepped out.

"Janey," Louz said, stopping her and leaning over so she could see Janey's face. "I'm not cold. I just can't go there yet. I'm not one to visit graves, especially this one."

"It's no problem. I'm fine going alone."

"The marker up there now is just temporary. My parents will get another one when they can do it. They haven't been able to face it yet, but believe me, we'll put up something special."

Janey nodded and worked her way up the short gradual incline. And there it was, a kind of hardscrabble, haphazard, cleared area of mostly old stones, some of them listing over and host to mosses and lichen.

On the opposite side she noted ones that looked newer, and so she skirted the edge of the graves, noting some of the gravestones. Several for infants born and died on the same day in the 1800s. A man aged thirty-six years "husband of Mary, father of Jacob, Jonas, and Juliana." A woman who'd died in childbirth, buried with "infant."

People here had led such tough lives, had looked death so much more often in the face, and at much earlier ages.

Cole's grave, marked with only a simple metal cross that gave his name, birthdate, and date of death, was before her now. Janey stood still, not knowing how to feel. But this was what she'd originally come for.

"Cole?" she whispered.

She cast her face toward the sky and closed her eyes, letting sunlight bathe her face. But for only a moment. She was running out of time, and she could see turbulent thunderclouds gathering to spoil many picnics and strolls with lightning.

She tried but couldn't say she felt Cole's spirit. As she'd suspected on the night she heard of his death, she believed it had been present then, but surely, by now, it had already departed this earthly realm. At the foot of the grave, a small clump of yellow wildflowers had popped up. Janey reached down and picked one, brought it to her nose, held it for mere moments, and studied the precision with which it had been born.

A small gust of wind, soft as the breath of an angel, came through just then, and she let it take the flower from her hands and fly it to the faraway.

When she returned to the truck, neither she nor Louz spoke for a while.

They were headed to the Sevier County Courthouse too, so Janey could try to see Luke before she left. After that, Louz would drive her to the train station in Knoxville. Finally, it seemed as though Janey would really and finally begin her journey back.

Sylvie, Margaret, Jean, and Tim had stayed behind

on the farm to do chores. There was no such thing as a day off on a farm. No matter what, animals and fields had to be tended to.

On the way to Sevierville, Louz remained uncharacteristically quiet. Janey had the feeling that Louz's thoughts had moved from Cole to Luke.

Janey let her be for some time, then eventually said, "It really was my fault. I wanted to go to the caves."

"Nonsense," Louz said as she gripped the steering wheel, then seemed to finally ease off and relax at least somewhat. "This stupid feud is still alive and thriving, it seems." She shook her head. "Man, do some people hold a grudge for a long time, but that's so Tennessee." She smiled. "I have to believe the sheriff will get his comeuppance. It was a fluke he got elected in the first place. Too many men not around to vote and women too overworked to go to the polls. He'll get voted out next time. No doubt about it."

Janey gazed forward as the road threaded onward in front of them. "What will happen next?"

"We'll get Luke out, probably later today or tomorrow. We'll tell everyone, and most of them will see it for what it is, Snearl scared of an old feud—in fact, they might even laugh about it—it is *so* ridiculous. Then we'll go back to the farm and our work and keep pushing onward. I'm not worried about any of us...except maybe Luke."

Louz glanced at Janey, who didn't know how to respond. Louz seemed to be asking a question, but Janey still had no idea how to answer. She said only, "I have to see him. They must let me see him."

"Never fear. I'll raise all kinds of hell if they don't. Besides, I used to date an attorney here. He's off in the war right now, but I made friends with many of his associates while we were an item. I can call in some favors. And my father and uncle can do that also."

Janey asked, "Is the attorney one of those men who's coming back for you?"

"No," answered Louz.

"Will you write? I want to know all about everything."

Louz grew pensive again. "Me, too," she finally said.

****

The courthouse dated back to 1896 and was made of brick, with a regal tower and a majestic four-faced clock. They located the jail, where Janey and Louz had only about thirty minutes to convince the authorities there to allow Janey in to see Luke and then go on their way.

But Louz was very persuasive and dropped some names, and Janey was ushered in after only a short wait. The visitation area was full of women and children waiting for Sunday visits, so the warden on duty took Louz back into the cell area.

Luke stood behind bars, his hands clinging to them, his face peering through, just like in some old western movie. Janey almost laughed. Ridiculous indeed! Alone in a cell, he followed her with his eyes, then smiled despite it all. "Well, you sure are a sight for sore eyes."

All her senses came alive at the sight on him. She swung herself over to him, balanced herself with both crutches under her shoulders, and took his hands on the bars. If only she could rip out those bars. "Right back at you," she said.

"So what's new?"

Janey squeezed his hands and smiled. "Just like you

to joke around at a moment like this. It's a good thing you haven't lost your sense of humor."

His gaze was the same, still mostly concerned about her, and his demeanor so sweet and calm as ever. "I'm looking at it as another milestone in my life. I've never been in jail before."

Janey smiled. "I'm to give you some messages and must do so before I forget. Your father and uncle are here working to get you out and they won't stop until they do. They hope it will be later today. Louz drove me here. The other ladies and Tim are taking care of everything back home."

"Okay, I kinda knew that already."

"But everyone's okay, just a bit worried about you."

He laughed a little. "It's probably worrying them more than it's worrying me. How about you?"

"Everyone keeps telling me it wasn't my fault."

"Because it wasn't."

"But I know you were trying to please me and maybe also stall for time."

"I was that obvious?"

"You went in there because of me."

He sighed. "But just like that night when you got hit in the street, you took on all the responsibility. That's what I'm doing now. It's right, and it's true." He reached through and touched her hair, moving it off her face. "Please don't be so hard on yourself. I made the decision to go in there."

Janey nodded reluctantly, then glanced away from his face for the first time and took in their surroundings more fully. It was all a bit ludicrous. And their time together was slipping away, so fleeting. Knowing she could not stay there for long, Janey had to hold onto his hand and the bar as though clinging to life. "I don't have a lot of time."

"You're leaving?" he asked, suddenly solemn.

She nodded.

"For good?"

"I don't know."

He shifted his weight, his face and eyes emitting love and a hesitant but hopeful sheen. "Listen to me, Janey."

She stopped him. "I need to tell you something first."

He waited for her to start.

"Back home, there's a man I met about a year ago, after Cole died, although we're not really together any longer. But we *were* together. The problem is that he loves me more than I could ever feel for him. And I definitely loved Cole more than he felt for me. Maybe I'm not cut out for love and marriage. Maybe for me, it's always going to be unbalanced."

He said searchingly, "You just hadn't met the right man yet. Until you came here."

She had to ask the world to stop spinning for a moment and wait for her to catch up.

"I'm the one, Janey," Luke said, velvet in his throat.

Again, she was not believing it. It was like getting a marriage proposal in a jail. From a man behind bars.

"I'm the one. Come back to me."

Her throat was clogging with happy sobs, her eyes filling with uncertain tears.

Tennessee had grown on her. A lovely dance of human interplay had gone on here. For others and for her. Some of it serious and romantic; some of it ridiculous, as Louz had just said. And here, Janey had started really living again, in a way stronger than the magic of Cole. Here, she had run headfirst into excitement and nonsense, too, but always it was real. Luke had lifted her up into believing that all things could be better than they'd ever imagined.

"I'll make you smile every day, and I'll also let you cry if you need to. I'll be there through thick and thin. I'll love you till you can't hold any more, till the day I die. If you have love, you can center your life anywhere you want to, Janey, and I'll be beside you every step of the way doing all I can to make it beautiful every single day. You'll also be free to do whatever you want. Hell, you can even grow mushrooms if you want, go to work somewhere. I won't hold you down."

His face was torturing her. This was what she'd always wanted, this feeling of complete immersion, lost in someone she loved and awash in the feeling that he felt the same way, all else abandoned. She reached out to touch his face, her hand grazing over his chin, then his cheek, and then stilling over his lips and moving upward to his eyes, which he closed as she touched them.

She wished she could love away his pain. His face, the most complete face, the most human face she'd ever known… It would always be a part of her. It would come with her now, wherever she went. She wanted to touch him and kiss him—and did so through the bars.

His face molded first with pleasure, then with the most hopeful of hope. "You take my breath away," he whispered.

His kisses were heated, his skin like velvet, and she needed this. He was kissing and caressing away what she needed to forget and making her believe what she wanted to believe.

"Do you trust me again?" he asked.

"Yes," she answered. Then made herself say the only words she could be sure of in that moment. She would never forget being here with him, and yet it was already beginning to feel like a part of her past. "But for now, I must go."

This time, they kissed slowly, and it was alternately tender and desperate—the push and pull of letting go.

"I'm asking you to come back here, to me. For a life, with me."

"Even though, as you once said, I don't fit here?"

"I was wrong. You fit just fine. And hell, all of us are intruders here. This place probably should've remained wild."

"Right now...I'm just not sure."

He looked away; she could see the pulse in his neck. It took him a while before he pulled his eyes back but said without an ounce of regret or recrimination, only tenderness and love, "I understand. You know where to find me. I'll always be here, waiting."

She started to leave, but his voice halted her steps. "Janey?"

She spun around.

"I almost forgot to give you this."

He held something in his palm. A broken off piece of stalactite or stalagmite about three inches long. Shiny white like marble, an ancient treasure that he probably shouldn't have taken. But it was what he'd gone into the cave for. She'd forgotten all about it.

She reached out and took it slowly. "I'll cherish this, Luke. Thank you."

"Janey," he said, stopping her again. "Just one more thing."

She waited, fighting the urge to run back and into his arms.

"Don't forget to look up at the night sky."

Chapter Twenty-One

"I'm Beginning to See the Light" - Duke Ellington, 1945
Philadelphia, Saturday, May 19,1945

Since arriving home, Janey had first set out to make things right at work. She'd arrived on Tuesday night, but despite the fatigue from travel and getting around on crutches, she arrived at Walker Scott at eight o'clock sharp on Wednesday.

When Lorraine arrived, she walked off the elevator and stood still in her tracks. "You weren't kidding, were you?" She approached Janey, who had been on her way to make coffee but had stopped to balance on her crutches. "You really broke your ankle."

"A car had something to do with it, but yes."

Curiosity all over her face and peering closer at Janey, and at her leg and cast, Lorraine asked, "How're you feeling?"

"Ready to get back to work. Do you think anyone will object to me hobbling around here on crutches?"

Lorraine laughed. "I doubt it. Just don't hurt yourself any further. They need you to work. Besides, it certainly shows your dedication to the job."

"I was worried, especially since I didn't make it back on Monday."

"As everyone can see," Lorraine quipped, "there

were extenuating circumstances."

"How has it been around here?"

Lorraine moved to her desk and plunked down her handbag on top. "Not so bad."

"I'm sure you're just trying to be polite and let me off the hook. It probably made for a lot of extra work for you."

"I can take care of both Mr. Scott and Mr. Walker, in a pinch. I sent some of his"—she gestured toward Mr. Walker's office—"typing to other secretaries. Another gal came in to do backed-up filing and answer the phones while I was in with one of the top dogs. The adding machine acted up, but it's all right now."

"I know it's been a trial for you, and I'm sorry. Thank you."

"In truth, it made the days go by quite quickly. No need to thank me. Thank *you* for coming back. You could've stayed out till the cast comes off."

She turned toward Janey and adopted a classic Lorraine pose, leaning her hip against her desk, legs crossed at the ankles, her head cocked to one side. "But enough about all that. Just glad to see you back. Are you steady on those things?" She pointed to the crutches.

"I've gotten the knack of them. I'm more than ready to resume my duties."

Lorraine lowered her voice. "What happened down there?"

Janey almost laughed. "Too much. You wouldn't believe it."

"Did you do what you needed to?"

Janey shrugged. "Not completely, but I'm getting there."

"Well, that sounds very mysterious."

"Funny you should say that. I guess I solved one mystery, but I got lost in another one. And there was a bit of an adventure, too. Come to think of it, maybe two or three adventures."

"Well, I'm impressed and very curious."

"Once I figure it all out, you'll be one of the first to know."

"That's all I can ask for," Lorraine said as she pulled out her compact and checked her makeup in its mirror.

"Is Mr. Walker sore at me?"

Lorraine snapped the compact shut. "I don't think so. And once he sees you and realizes you're back working hard for him again, it'll all be soon forgotten. Besides, you have some pretty convincing stuff on your person to show him how complicated things became."

"Funny, again. Complicated doesn't even begin to describe it."

"Are you aware you have a smile on your face?"

Janey shrugged and kept on smiling. "Parts of it were pretty weird and hilarious. I arrived just as the victory in Europe was announced. Then…well, it's too much to tell you right now."

"We should go out for a drink one night."

"I'd love that. Thank you, Lorraine."

"You missed quite a party here on V-E Day. It was rather wild and rowdy around here, too. You would've liked it. Some people actually let loose."

"No!"

"Mr. Walker smiled."

"Oh, my."

"Oh, my, indeed."

"Well, we have one more victory to go, don't we?"

Lorraine raised an imaginary glass. "Here's to that."

****

By the end of the day, Janey got herself back into the swing of things, and Mr. Walker showed her some kindness, asking if she was really ready to come back to work. Before she knew it, she was jumping up and moving quickly with the crutches whenever he called. She could shoulder a lot of responsibility. It did seem that things would go back to the way they'd been before, and her absence would be all but forgotten.

Forgotten by everyone, it seemed, except Janey. In quiet moments she caught herself looking beyond the big picture windows in the fifteenth-floor conference rooms, gazing at the sky and wondering if it looked anything like this in Tennessee. A woman's voice made her think of Louz's. Music made her remember dancing in the street. And every great smile made her think of Luke's.

But she finished out the week as though nothing had changed. Tessa picked her up at the station, and she went to see her parents that very first night of her return. She must have been projecting unconscious signals that said, "Don't ask me," because even her nosy family left her alone.

On Saturday morning, she scheduled nothing so she could take the day to finally read Cole's last letters. All along, she had to admit to herself, she'd been avoiding it.

But it was time. She curled up on her bed with Cheese at her side and opened the first one, barely breathing. The contents were most likely going to be unremarkable, but the build-up to reading them had raised her expectations. She squelched those, instead convincing herself that she really didn't know what to expect.

In the first letter, Cole described another ocean passage the ship had made. Surprising her, he had written some eloquent paragraphs about it. Over countless swells and surges, endless salt air and sea sprays, through long days and shorter ones, bright ones and darker ones, Cole had contemplated the miracle of their being on the sea and the price it had cost him. He wrote that even when the sea was serene, he knew it could at any moment turn into a furious storm. And beneath the surface, all manner of life struggled to stay alive, all of them like the earthly creatures above it, fighting to survive.

He told her that most of them walked a tightrope between a sense of adventure and the memory of others left behind, their pain breaking free there, over the sea. While some danced and sang, others prayed, and still others talked of their plans and futures among each other in subdued tones. He said no one pretended to feel good about the war zone they were traversing. And he wrote about missing her, his family, and home. He finished the letter with loving words, but she could detect how much the journey was changing him.

His second letter described another landing on an island that had come and gone. Of course he couldn't tell her where he was, and she wondered if they were back in New Guinea—in vague language he did convey a sense of the tropical. Since leaving land the last time, they'd seen some action. He said danger came from both above in the air and below in the black water. He confessed to having a severe case of homesickness.

Now that Janey had visited Cole's home, she could better understand that feeling.

Again, he ended the letter with words of endearment and promises to write more often.

In the third letter, he sounded wracked with sadness. Janey had to grasp the shirt over her chest when she read that the lure of the sea had given him the wrong impression, and he now knew a life on the water would never be his choice. In fact he wasn't sure he even wanted to live near it. He described poverty and the ravages of war on the islands, and low morale, fear, and seasickness on the ship.

In the saddest paragraph, he wrote:

All my life I've never been me. I knew what I wanted, but not who I was. An open sea is a lonely place, and it has made me re-examine what I wanted and what others have expected for me. Everything else got in the way back then, but here I've run up against myself.

And finally, in the last letter, Cole sounded more like himself, or at least the Cole she knew. Without giving any details, he gave her the impression he'd survived his first battle at sea. He sounded more confident and surer of himself again. Therefore, it shocked her when he finished by writing about the two of them and their future:

I should've told you about something when we were in Philadelphia, but now I have the courage to do it. There's a girl back home. We've been promised to each other since way back. I was young at the time, and when I left home and started traveling, I was cocky. I thought I could leave home behind and create a different life.

Now all I think about is what I had and how much I want to go back to it. I used to hate the idea of doing what was expected of me and pleasing my family, and doing my duty to my home and our land and friends. Now that's all I think of. I've had enough adventure. Now I just want to be safe and sound.

I'm sorry for having led you to believe otherwise. My feelings for you are real, and the weekend with you is a memory I'll always cherish, but when and if I get through this alive, I'm going to return to Tennessee and a girl named Marlene. I'm sorry, Janey. I wanted you to know so that you can be free again. You'll find the man of your dreams, and I hope you come upon him soon. You deserve the best.

****

Janey sat for a long time with his open letter in her lap, nothing moving but her mind. Cole wouldn't have come back to her anyway. She had chosen to believe him in every way, and she'd been wrong.

She wouldn't begin to try to understand what war did to a person, and she couldn't hate Cole. People didn't know how they'd change under extraordinary circumstances. No, she didn't blame him for changing his mind.

Much more shocking than his decision to choose Marlene was the fact that he was not planning to fulfill the dreams he'd told her about and that she still believed were genuine. The man she'd met on a bus wasn't scared of having big dreams and taking big risks to make them come true. Cole had been the last person she'd ever have expected to choose the safe path.

****

That night she helped in the diner, and during a break in the action, she and Tessa went out back, where Tessa opened a pack of Lucky Strikes and lit a cigarette.

"So when did you start smoking?" Janey asked.

"While you were gone. Want one?"

"Oh, hell," Janey said and balanced on her crutches as Tessa knocked a cigarette out of the pack and passed it over. "I tried it and wasn't a big fan, but why not try again?"

She lit up and coughed.

"It does take some getting used to," Tessa said sheepishly.

Janey looked at the cigarette and the curl of smoke coming out into the air. "I'm still trying to decide if I like them."

"It takes effort. I'm doing it, and it's getting easier every day. Obviously I need to look more sophisticated."

"You look like a nymph. Forget about it. That's never going to change." Janey tried taking a drag on the cigarette again. "I'm getting dizzy."

"Just be patient. Give it some time—it gets better. Keep puffing."

"Yes, ma'am."

After a few minutes of silence and complaining about some rude customers, Tessa stomped out her cigarette in the ground. It seemed she couldn't hold herself back any longer. "What's going on with you anyway? You look like you're a machine on slow speed."

Janey shrugged. Then gazed at her sister in a way that must have begged for a good listener and an open mind. In a low tone, she answered, "Some things happened back there. Some really…strange things."

"Such as?"

"Things I would've never expected."

"I'm in the dark here—you're going to have to say it. I can't read your mind."

"Of course. It's just that…I met a man, who happens to be Cole's cousin."

Tessa flung a hand into the air and shook her head,

then stared. "You met another man? Why do you always meet the men and not me? I can't even find one to latch onto and even try to make mine—there are none around here unless they're passing through. How did that happen?"

"I don't know how anything happened, but it was kind of wonderful there. I met an interesting family, a strange sheriff, and I got hit by a car." She paused and glanced down at her cast. "But you know all about that."

"Keep talking."

"You're so bossy."

"Keep on," Tessa said.

Janey shook her head and let memories flood in again. "I found a kindred spirit in a girl named Louz. I saw bears and had to orchestrate a cave rescue. I danced in the street on V-E Day and stayed out most of the night. I drank moonshine. I ate home cooking, Southern style, and drank sweet tea. I crossed a creek on crutches and trespassed on private property. And I might have fallen…"

"My, my. Do go on."

"…in love."

Tessa said, "And?"

Janey looked away into nothing, bringing his image forward in her mind. "He's not the most handsome man, but he's as funny as can be. He's not the most polished of men, but boy can he dance. He's not the best with words, but he sure can string some together that touched me."

She focused on her sister now. "He's so different, Tessa. He's a shepherd. Really a shepherd. He loves looking at stars at night. He drives a beat-up old truck instead of the family's Chrysler. He can talk endlessly or hold still. He can be shy, and he can be great fun. He's not worldly, but he's homesy. When I was with him…it was…"

"What?" Tessa demanded.

"Well, it felt wonderful, believe it or not. It felt right."

"But that *is* wonderful."

"I never thought an experience would change me so much. The change in me feels deep, And when I was there with him, life seemed to unfurl so naturally."

Tessa's eyes were huge. "When you talk about him, you look happy. You look radiant again. Do you have a photo?"

"No, I never thought about it."

"So here again, no photo. I have to conjure up an image in my mind. What does he look like?"

"He's handsome in a boyish way. Has a great smile. Warm, soft eyes. To me he's dreamy *and* earthy."

"And when did this happen?"

"My second day in Tennessee. On V-E Day, to be exact. That night was a dream, but circumstances threw us together for days after that. And I got to know him better each day."

"So what's the problem?"

"Isn't it obvious? His life is on a farm in Tennessee."

"Is it awful?"

"No, it's really very beautiful."

"So I must ask again: What's the problem?"

"Todd's a good man, too. And he's here where my life is. Near you and Mom and Dad."

Tessa harrumphed. "Well, let me tell you something. I know I'm the little sister here, and you'll probably never take my lowly advice, but if you've found what you want elsewhere, we're not going to do anything but wish you well and send you off with all our love and blessings. Mom and Dad, more than anything, just want you to be happy. And so do I."

Janey blinked hard as she stared at her sister. It seemed that Tessa had grown up overnight. She had made it through her awkward years—she would be fine without Janey's near-constant attention, and Janey believed her. Maybe more than anyone else, Tessa did want Janey to be happy.

Janey said, "I wish it was that simple."

"Do you still feel something for Todd?"

"Yes, and he offered me a nice life, too. I could probably make it right with him if I wanted to."

"Then I should tell you. He came by here and had dinner one night. By himself. He seemed to be fishing for information. About you."

After a long moment, Janey said, "Then I guess I need to go see him."

"So Todd or Mr. Tennessee. There's another obvious choice."

"To go forward on my own, you mean? Don't make any decision?"

"That's right, but is that what you want?"

That future flashed in front of her. She could take trips alone—she'd just done that. She could push farther away from the paired-up people. She could grab a meal at a food stand and eat it on the go on the nights when she didn't want to sit alone in a restaurant or eat by herself at home. She could put up wallpaper in her house. She could come home to Cheese and say, "You'll never guess what I did today... Exactly the same thing as yesterday!"

"No," she finally answered. "I never seriously sought love, but now that I've had it, I want it every day for the rest of my life. Doesn't everyone?"

"When you feel that longing, whose face do you see?"

It took only a split second for his image to form on the screen of her mind. It would always be a part of her. Luke would come with her, now, wherever she went. She was heartsick to think of his love, his longing for her.

But warm feelings toward Todd remained, too. It would be so much simpler if she could fall back in love with him and marry and continue her life here. It would be safer and less complicated. It would be the sensible way to go, the no-nonsense Janey way.

Chapter Twenty-Two

"Gotta Be This or That" - Benny Goodman, 1945
Philadelphia, Sunday, May 27, 1945

Janey had been to Todd's apartment only twice before. Located in an apartment building on Locust Street, it struck her as a stereotypical bachelor's apartment. Mostly bare except for a print on the wall above the divan, and a radio, and a coffee table with an empty vase on top. He had a small wooden breakfast table flanked by two chairs.

He did own a set of dishes and some cookware, but he'd once confessed they were a gift from his mother and he rarely used them. A bookcase held mostly classic American literature: *Moby Dick, The Scarlet Letter*, and *Huckleberry Finn*. On the kitchen counter, an empty coffee mug, some pens and pencils and whatnot.

It was a nice place but not opulent in the same way as he'd grown up. She'd always thought Todd was making some kind of statement with it. He didn't want to be seen as a rich and privileged son, heir to a lot of money.

She glanced around again as if seeing it with new eyes. She could live here with Todd and rent her house. Or he could move in with her. Nothing else would need much changing.

After she came in, Todd took her in his arms and

gave her a big hug. Pulling back she felt a lump in her throat. Together they had made a lot of great memories. And the things that had attracted her to Todd in the first place were still there. He was handsome, he was independent of his wealthy parents, he was intelligent and educated, and he could be very kind.

Although Sunday afternoon, he was wearing one of his black suit trousers and vest, white shirt underneath. It looked as though he'd just gotten a haircut. She returned the embrace, then let go and followed him to the kitchen. Nothing had changed, but he did have a pot of coffee on, and some pastries sat out on the table. For Todd, this meant he'd gone to a lot of trouble.

Todd moved about the kitchen with his determined and purposeful gait that hid the limp almost completely. "I was pleased to receive your note. I'd been hoping to hear from you. And I'm glad you prepared me for this." He nodded toward her cast and crutches.

"Yes, not what I'd expected at all," she said but would never say that none of it had turned out as she'd expected. "I've been back for a while but had to get settled in back at work. And see my doctor here, of course."

They sat across from each other at the table, an awkward silence between them. Janey said, "The cast comes off in about four weeks."

"What's the sock about?" he asked.

Janey had started covering the cast with one of her father's socks. She'd soiled the cast in Tennessee and all the moving around since then had made it even worse. It had been her mother's idea to cover it. "Almost immediately I got it dirty."

"How'd that happen?"

"Well...mostly from crossing a stream and then kind of dragging the crutches through on the ground to get through a barbed-wire fence."

He sat in silence and leaned back just a notch, but his face wasn't easily readable. "Obviously some things happened."

Janey nodded. "Some things happened."

Again, at least for the moment, he was asking in a casual manner, barely showing any emotion. "How was it?"

"The area is beautiful. People weren't as I'd imagined. Many things happened that I wouldn't have predicted."

"Such as...?"

Janey laughed once as more recent memories returned. "Just some of the most insane things. It did turn out to be a bit of an adventure. It's really too long, um, too much to tell you about in one sitting."

Finally his face showed something—he was letting down his guard. "In truth, I was being polite. I'm not sure I want to know the details. I've had all sorts of wild ideas walking around in my head ever since that day..."

"I'm really sorry for any grief I've caused you."

"And I regret my reaction. Looking back, I'm not very proud of my behavior. I should've been more understanding."

"I think you reacted the way most people would have. It was an awkward situation."

Now his face and eyes emitted a hesitant but hopeful sheen. "Did you get the answers you needed there?"

She had to look away. "That's what I'm still trying to figure out."

He rapped his knuckles lightly on the tabletop, a

classic Todd move. It seemed to help him pull his thoughts together. "Look, Janey. I know you think you know me well, and you do, to some degree. But I must confess to being a rather vain man. You may have figured this out already, but I want to be adored; I want someone who puts me on a pedestal and is thrilled to go through life at my side. I don't want to convince someone to marry me, I want someone who's convinced *she* wants to marry me."

"I do know that."

"So I'm not going to try to talk you into anything."

"I know that, too."

"I'm asking you not to accept my proposal if you have any doubts. Do me that favor, please. I don't want to go through life wondering if my wife settled for me but secretly carries a torch for someone else, dead or alive."

That was Todd's way of asking her to marry him again. The way they'd left it, he had retracted his proposal. But indeed, he must have regretted the things he'd said, and it sounded as if he still wanted to go through with it.

She said, "I understand, and you deserve no less."

"That said, I do think we could have a wonderful life together, Janey." His eyes softened, but he was still exercising caution. How could she blame him? "We're well matched in so many ways. We both have bright futures here, and we believe in the same things. I'll always put you on a pedestal, if you let me. And I won't ask you to quit your job and start having babies right away. We can make decisions like that together. You see, I love your mind as much as the rest of you." He checked himself and then laughed in a self-deprecating manner.

"I just told you I wouldn't try to talk you into anything, but now I'm doing just that."

Janey's heart went out to him. He probably thought she was still struggling to get over Cole, and she saw no need to tell him about Luke. She'd already given him enough to carry.

"By the way, my parents said to say hello. Dad also mentioned that he's just become a board member for the History Museum. They're looking for docents, and he'll recommend you."

The offer quieted her. Todd knew about her love of history and her dream of someday being involved with a museum. For someone who wasn't trying to talk her into anything, he sure was pulling out all the stops. "That's so nice. Please tell him thank you."

"When you're ready to talk about it, he'll pass on the name and number of a contact within the museum. He'll even make the introductions himself."

Janey wondered what had transpired between Todd and his parents since the day of his proposal. She'd met them on several occasions. Very cordial and not the least bit snobby. Did Todd tell them everything? Were they helping him get her back?

She said, "Such a nice thing to do."

"Anything for you," he said. "But only if..." He had to work up to asking, "Do you care for me, Janey?"

"Yes," she said without hesitation. There was a reason she'd spent a year going out with him and had almost become engaged. Her warm feelings for him were still there. Could she build on what they had before and make it grow?

He didn't need the details about Luke, but he deserved the truth about her feelings. "I just have to figure out if I'm ready and…if I care…*enough*."

She checked his reaction and hated the look of pain on his face that she'd caused.

"That's pretty tough to take."

"I know, and I'm sorry."

Finally he asked, "I'm not going to wait forever. When do you think you'll know?"

"Soon, I hope."

They sat through a protracted spell of silence.

"Well, I guess there's not much else to say, is there?"

She shook her head.

At the door, he grabbed her hand and brought it to his lips, then leaned over and kissed her on the mouth. His affection for her felt real. But what did she feel in return?

During the bus ride back to her neighborhood, she gazed at all the people on the streets, families in the park, and a group of older men sitting on a park bench smoking pipes. From a distance people seemed so carefree. How she longed for that feeling again. Had all of the older ones faced a tough decision similar to this? She knew her parents hadn't. They'd always been each other's one and only.

She searched and sorted through everything she saw through the window as though she might find a surprise answer there. Spirits had been lifted since V-E Day. The world had tilted in favor of the Allies, and everyone hoped for another victory.

She wanted that, too, as well as the way to a place of surety.

At home, she stared out her back window into the yard that was gathering the twilight. Then she went back to Cole's letters. She was struck, every time she read his last one, by his choice to go back home, still trying to understand it. In the face of all the fears and uncertainty of being in a war zone, Cole had decided against taking any large leaps, any big chances. He'd chosen the most secure path, the one that would've pleased the most people.

It made sense that his mind, driven by homesickness and loneliness, would go in that direction. But had he survived, would it have been the right one? In her heart, she believed the Cole she knew would not have made that choice. But how could anyone really know if the path they chose was the right one? Looking back, it would be impossible to know what would've come to pass if one had chosen the other way.

She opened her closet, pulled out a cardigan she'd last worn with Luke, and brought it to her face. Inhaling, she could detect just the slightest hint of him—something of the woods, it was, and it brought tears to her eyes. Then she picked up a framed photo, taken on her last birthday at the diner, of Todd and her with her parents and Tessa, all of them squeezed into a booth—she'd kept it on her bedside table ever since—and she examined the happy faces, the feeling of family and acceptance, home and continuity that she'd always thought she'd have to keep close.

But although Janey asked the moon at night, although she attempted to put her feelings down in a letter to herself, and although she prayed to the infinite universe for answers, she still lacked complete clarity. It was not going to simply come upon her.

It was up to her to decide. She had to choose.

In her heart, however, she knew which way to go

onward. But it still took her a long time to still her beating heart and quiet her mind. Finally, she pulled out a piece of stationery and a pen, knowing she had to do it now while she still had the courage. It took a lot of faith to make her do something sure to cause such pain.

And so, then and there, she began to write the most difficult words she'd ever put on paper.

Chapter Twenty-Three

"In the Blue of the Evening" - Tommy Dorsey/ Frank Sinatra, 1940
Philadelphia, Monday, May 28, 1945

She tossed with the sheets as though she were immersed in her own personal sea battle, as if she were a mighty ship going down. Drowning in a deeper awareness, alone at the bottom of the sea, like so many carriers and destroyers and battleships in the war zone.

In the morning, she put the letter in the post with shaking hands. Then she went to work and back to the best job she'd ever had, better than any she'd imagined. She had a beautiful desk and top-notch equipment in a large luxurious space and a good friend in her co-worker. She handled responsibility as though it had always been second nature to her.

After work, she went by her parents' diner and helped out, then ate her mother's famous chicken and dumplings with her garlicky mashed potatoes. They had time to eat together at a booth that night. Bertie and Reuben had managed to hire another cook and waitress, which had eased the load. Women who'd worked in factories were willing to work in a diner again. Janey could count on spending more time with them.

Plus, Tessa's semester was over, and she was taking a break from school for the summer. They could go shopping, see the movies, and meet for lunch on Saturdays.

When she returned to her house, a crazy yellow cat begged for attention.

Inside, she gazed around, flooded with warm feelings about what she'd accomplished here. Every day someone expressed surprise that she'd purchased her own house. Everything was set up just the way she liked it. She'd painted every wall in colors she'd chosen. She'd scrubbed and polished every plank of the wood floors. She'd taught herself how to put up wallpaper and window coverings.

In the kitchen, she'd already restocked her pantry and refrigerator with her favorite food and beverages. She'd revived her wilting plants on the kitchen windowsill that Tessa had forgotten to water and had brought them back to health.

Many nights, she found herself sitting in the stillness out on the back stoop after most of the lights in her neighborhood were out. She took stock of each little detail, cataloging it to memory. She remembered the planning and painting and decorating before she moved in, all of those months and years in the typing pool, her first promotion to Typing Pool Supervisor, then the promotion to Junior Executive Secretary, and finally to the top on Fifteen.

She knew this city. There wasn't one neighborhood she hadn't entered at least once. Then that glorious weekend with Cole, and all the good times with Todd here, how this city had always felt safe, warm, and hers to carry onward.

Overhead, the trees bent to the wind and scattered a skein of moonlight in all directions, pointing nowhere, never illuminating the way forward. Where was it all heading next? And what would happen to them all? She stared at the blue swaths on the moon's face, hoping for some celestial wisdom to rain down on her.

The burden of this choice was sure a heavy yoke. It didn't seem believable that she had arrived here. She would have to hurt one of them. For a long moment, the universe felt massive and unforgiving, and she felt no goodness in it.

But the night sky took her back to Tennessee. The stars had been much brighter there, and so too were some of her memories. Was Luke looking up at the sky tonight too? Without realizing it, she had been waiting to find him, and she doubted anything like it would happen again. Would he continue to wait?

Philadelphia, with her family, in her own house, and going to work to a wonderful job—well that was home, perhaps where she belonged. Where she knew what to expect. And a sense of *home* was a very good thing.

But was it enough?

Funny how she'd come back and nothing about it had changed. It was essentially the same, everything in its place. Only she had changed.

****

Summer came to Philadelphia. Women trimmed their rose bushes, lizards skittered across the pavement, and the fruit trees sported new green leaves on their branches. The streets overflowed with servicemen and children playing in parks and splashing themselves in fountains.

Cheese behaved strangely. He tore through rooms as if some invisible spirit chased him, then he stopped and looked around as if asking what all the fuss had been about. He clawed the furniture, and Janey had to remove him a few times, claws latched onto the upholstery as if for life. Maybe some inherent feline instinct had already told him that change was coming.

Janey desperately wanted to lure Cheese back, at least for the nights. He was so riled up, however, that he wouldn't curl up on the bed beside her.

"Come on, now," Janey cooed. "It'll all be okay." She stroked and scratched Cheese under his chin, which he loved. But still the cat wanted down. "Do you believe me when I say it'll be okay?"

Janey tried to hold him, but Cheese twisted his body the way only cats do, sprang from her grasp, and ran away.

When she lay alone in bed in the pitch-dark hours well after midnight—the cat still spurning her—and when she peered past her window, catching sight of a star that streaked across the black glaze of night and then vanished out of view, she knew her choice had been the best one.

She saw it all with one blink in time. A single life was small, a crashing wave, powerful for a moment, then gone. But at least she would know she hadn't slept through her lifetime—she had left home, done important work, and loved with every thread of her being.

And she'd learned that love needed no definitions or reasons, no restrictions or prescriptions. It wasn't scientific; it wasn't empirical. It didn't matter if one man was here and one man was there. She truly loved only one of them. In the end, it all came down to that.

Love.

Chapter Twenty-Four

"Just As Though You Were Here" - Tommy Dorsey
and his Orchestra/Frank Sinatra & The Pied Pipers, 1942
Philadelphia, Monday, May 28, 1945

That evening after work, she returned to Cole's letters, drawn in a way she couldn't describe. Beginning with the first one she'd ever received, she went through them again in chronological order. She read slowly, as if looking for something between the lines.

And yet his simple wording was enough. Again, she witnessed what a war had done to change a well-meaning person. During the Great War or World War I, as it was being called now, soldiers had suffered what was called shell shock, the after-effects of being so close to death and under attack while in the trenches.

Cole was already suffering something like that when he wrote these letters.

Janey let her hands lie on each page, the same pages he'd touched with his hands. Even then, she could feel him, his kind heart, his huge plans, the life he saw ahead. He'd taken to the sea along with a trunkload of dreams and ambition. He'd never meant to hurt anyone. He'd done the best he could do.

She'd once heard that those who were going to die knew it on a gut level. They knew what might be coming. But others said those who perish unexpectedly never saw it coming. Held within her highest hopes was the latter, that Cole hadn't seen it coming. And she had good reason to believe that was true. His final plan had been definite. He was going to come home to Marlene.

After she lay back on her pillow and closed her eyes, she let herself relive it all. That Friday when they'd met on the bus, that surprising first evening together. Then the best day of her life up to that point—Saturday—walking, talking, re-experiencing what they said to each other, then sitting across a dinner table, wrapped up in each other. And then Sunday, a perfect day of further exploration, seeing his dreams vicariously through his eyes, and then his impassioned and surprise proposal.

After he'd died, in her bed alone that night, all she could relive was the proposal and her refusal to get married on Monday morning, her choice to wait. How it had tormented her, back then. How she couldn't sleep.

On the night she learned of his death, as she was suffering, feeling as though she'd done him wrong, that she'd made a selfish decision, she'd felt a nudge. Not a dream, not something she'd imagined, but a nudge on her shoulder that touched her and moved her physically. Then she heard whispered words, "Stop it." In a male voice. Cole's voice.

She sat up in bed and turned on the light. The only explanation for the nudge was that Cheese had done it. He had finally returned to sleeping with her, and he lay curled up on the end of her bed. He peered up out of a deep sleep and blinked the way cats do when a light is suddenly turned on, then looked at her as if to ask, "What is it?"

This was not the way she'd ever imagined receiving a message from the afterlife; she thought it would be dramatic, full of poetic words, not a simple directive: "Stop it." Had it been real? She asked herself the question over and over and always came up with the same answer.

Once she'd heard that messages were often delivered soon after a person has died, while their spirit was still hovering quite close to the earth's surface, before it had taken full flight into the otherworld. And there it was: Cole had stayed near so he could insist she not go on punishing herself, so she could find peace.

And so she kept it to herself, this gift from Cole, never telling anyone.

With his letters still in her hands, she accepted in full the other gift Cole had unknowingly bestowed upon her. She wished to have a moment, just one moment alone with him, the two of them perhaps standing on a vast quiet plain with nothing else encroaching, so she could say, "Thank you."

Instead for one night, she took Cole with her to fall asleep beside her. She laid him down and wrapped her arms around him. Human to human, feeling his warmth and heart, she loved both his strengths and weaknesses, adored him just the way he was, then kissed him goodbye.

Nothing remained then, only love and the tiny corner of her heart that would always hold Cole.

Chapter Twenty-Five

"You Made Me Love You" - Harry James, 1941
Gatlinburg, Tennessee, Sunday, September 2, 1945

Janey mailed the letter to Todd the next morning. She hadn't been afraid of facing him in person; rather, she'd thought to spare him the agony of not only hearing of her decision in person but also having to hold himself together in front of her.

Todd wasn't a bad man, just not the right man.

It had taken some time to prepare for this journey. She not only decided to give a long notice to Walker Scott, she wanted to remain on the job until her replacement could be found and trained. It surprised her when Mr. Walker threw her a surprise party to celebrate her decision to move and start a new life elsewhere.

After her leg was out of the cast, she'd also begun working on her house, to get it ready to sell. Servicemen returning home needed housing, and she found she could make a tidy profit from her investment.

Tessa and her parents had taken Cheese for the time being until she could send for him. During her final dinner with her family, her parents were teary but ever so happy for her.

"If we ever take a vacation again," Bertie said, trying to hold back emotion, "we'll know where to go."

"You'll always have a place wherever I am."

"I hope this young man knows how lucky he is," Reuben said. "And if he ever doesn't, you know you can come back home to us."

Fighting tears herself now, Janey said, "I do know that, Daddy. And thank you. Thank you for understanding."

"You have to go where your heart leads you," Tessa piped in brightly. "And this…I know I've said it before, but this…*really* is the most romantic thing I've ever heard."

Janey smiled.

"Someday, when Mom and Dad aren't listening to our every *word*," Tessa said and glared at both parents, "you'll have to tell me *everything*."

"We're not stopping her," laughed Bertie.

"I'm getting out of here," said Reuben as he started to slide out of the booth. "Too much girl jibber-jabber for me."

Tessa said to Janey then, "You know I'm coming to visit as soon as possible."

"I'm counting on it," Janey replied.

And so she took the final lesson from Cole and brought it to life. Under duress, he'd chosen safety and predictability, and others over himself. Had Janey stayed and married Todd, she would've been doing the same thing. But she wasn't trapped in a war zone. She was free to let her heart choose.

****

The train pulled into the station in Knoxville, where a large crowd had gathered. Gas rationing had been lifted in the middle of August, so people were traveling in droves again. The train was packed with tourists, civilians, and servicemen returning from the European theater, and they'd recently heard on the news about a new and very powerful bomb that had been unleashed by the Allies on two Japanese cities, therefore anxious anticipation had been rippling across the country ever since. Most people felt the end was near in the Pacific, too. Everyone waited, poised for another celebration even bigger than the one before it, back in May.

She debarked into a crowd of people, all yelling and excited, some searching for others, people rushing into the arms of loved ones, and then she heard the shouts: "Japan surrendered. It's finally all over now!"

Around her people called out similarly, and the surrounding faces were jubilant, hugs were exhilarated, smiles were triumphant. Could it be? Could peace really reign over the world again?

Yes. She heard it over and over, and the smile it brought to her face was not only for the world but also for Luke and her. Another end-of-war celebration just like the one that had sparked their accidental date that turned out to be no accident after all. Instead, it offered a doorway to their destinies. This one even brighter, the day would from then on be known as V-J Day, and it was a very good sign.

Church bells pealed, and the sound of others celebrating was deafening, the scent of victory heady in the air. People were squeezed in, and she had to weave her way through, not even knowing which direction she should head. How would she find Luke in the midst of all this madness? Caught up in a sea of smiling faces moving together and against each other like part of the same swirling eddy, she lost all sense of direction.

Somehow she'd chosen the right way to turn, however, and just as it had happened on V-E Day, she ran right into him.

And his face—oh, my God! How she loved that face, that smile. It was all so certain in that moment. She had not taken the easy road but had embraced all she'd learned from herself and others. Unlike Cole, she had decided to take a risk. And like Todd, she wanted to be adored and loved fully, more than enough—even better than that. And there was only one place to find it.

She wanted to leap into Luke's arms and smother him with kisses, but she also couldn't rip her eyes away from his face so full of joy.

Standing right before her and looking at her in the only adoring way he could, he said, "I got a telegram saying a beautiful young woman might be getting off that train there."

Janey glanced around. "I don't see her."

"Oh, but I do," he said, eyes bright and smiling even more happily, if that were possible. "And I wonder why she might have come here."

"Well, funny you should ask, but I imagine it's really quite simple. You see, she's thinking about starting over, here."

At that moment, with their eyes locked, her heart allowed Luke all the way in. His expression became even more brilliant, and a big, sweet smile let her know that nothing really important had changed between them. He reached out gently, his hand touching hers.

This is where it begins again.

Only some lost time lay between them, a space they could cross. In May, so much had been about loss and secrets and betrayal, but all of that now lay behind them. Now nothing of the sort needed to be navigated. Now everything could center on the two of them, learning about each other, and falling even more deeply in love. Already, it was beginning.

Janey slowly slipped her hand in his, then gazed around, and peered back. "Excuse me," she whispered with only one small break in her voice, "but I'm not sure we've met."

He smiled. "I'm Luke Parker."

"I'm Janey Nichol."

Epilogue

"It Had to be You" - Helen Forrest and Dick Haymes, 1944

Gatlinburg, Wednesday, May 8, 1946

One year after that night, their house on the Parker/Huxley farm was under construction. They'd designed it in classic farmhouse style with a wide porch along the front and a nod to the current bungalow look of the day by including front-facing gables and a shingle roof. It would be painted dark green to blend with the natural surroundings, with cream-colored trim for definition.

The spot they'd chosen was far enough from the other houses to afford them privacy but still within a reasonable walk. They'd backed the house as close as possible to the woods behind it, where at this time of year redbuds and dogwoods bloomed color amid the endless green.

Wearing a work shirt, dungarees, and dusty boots, Janey took to the land every dawn just to feel first light on her face.

On this day, the roosters had already crowed, and birds were singing. The sun had crested the eastern ridge, sending rays of life-giving light that nourished man and animal, field and forest. Every day there were more bird's nests and cocoons where butterflies would emerge transformed. And ewes gave birth to lambs, their bleating sounds and beating hearts a sure sign that life was always renewing itself on this land.

Gazing toward the highlands, she saw Luke in the distance on horseback; white dots against the green meant he was already herding the sheep uphill for spring pasturing today. She watched him until he must have felt it, or he wanted to look down on the home site from on high. He turned around in the saddle, then reined Maisie around, removed his hat, and waved it high in the air.

Janey lifted her arm and waved, then left it in the air for a moment as though she might touch the heavens. Then, looking down at the simple gold band on her finger, she smiled. Under all those stars and swirls of galaxies, night time was no longer just for dreaming.

She glanced to the high country again, thinking about the land she'd purchased with her profits from the house in Philadelphia, the land that just happened to have the entrance to a cave system on it. What would she do with it? She didn't know, but it sure would be fun to figure it out.

Smoky Mountain rivers ran in her blood now. Its dense forests led her into dreamlands at night. Wildflowers mirrored her moods, and stones held her centered fast to solid earth. But the sky belonged to Luke, and the air floated love.

How much more could a heart hold?

A word about the author...

Ann Howard Creel was born in Austin, Texas and graduated from the University of Texas. She is the author of six children's books and six other historical novels. Currently living in a cabin in the Smoky Mountains, she writes full time, watches bears from her window, and of course reads other historical novels.

www.annhowardcreelauthor.com